PRAIS...
OF ...

P...

"Cozy readers will truly delight in the fact that this is the third in the series of these superfun books, and with each release the plots just keep getting better and better.... Strong characters and monumental surprises, this cozy is a definite keeper!" —*Suspense Magazine*

"Laura Alden has written another delightful mystery. The plotting is fast-paced.... Just wish I wouldn't have to wait so long to read the next in the series."
—*MyShelf.com*

"An engaging whodunit.... Fans will enjoy Laura Alden's complex murder mystery, thankfully without a recall in sight." —*Genre Go Round Reviews*

Foul Play at the PTA

"Well-crafted." —*Publishers Weekly*

"Beth Kennedy gives amateur sleuths a good name.... For those of us who appreciate good characters, it's just as satisfying as her first book." —*Lesa's Book Critiques*

continued . . .

Also Available from Laura Alden

CURSE of the PTA

Laura Alden

AN OBSIDIAN BOOK

OBSIDIAN
Published by the Penguin Group
Penguin Group (USA) Inc., 375 Hudson Street,
New York, New York 10014, USA

USA | Canada | UK | Ireland | Australia | New Zealand | India | South Africa | China

Penguin Books Ltd., Registered Offices: 80 Strand, London WC2R 0RL, England
For more information about the Penguin Group visit penguin.com.

First published by Obsidian, an imprint of New American Library,
a division of Penguin Group (USA) Inc.

First Printing, April 2013

ISBN 978-0-451-41506-6

Printed in the United States of America
10 9 8 7 6 5 4 3 2 1

For Jon.
Always.

Chapter 1

"**O**ld and boring," she said. "No doubt about it."

I looked up from my notes to see my best friend, Marina, staring at me with that it's-time-to-improve-Beth look on her face. "Forty-two isn't old," I said. "Forty-two is the new twenty-five."

"Stop making stuff up. And I notice you didn't say anything about not being boring."

"Boring is in the eye of the beholder." I went back to studying my notes. There were a lot of them. Tonight was the annual September organizational meeting of the Tarver Elementary PTA, and due to what must have been temporary insanity on my part, I'd volunteered to be the PTA's president.

I'd been secretary for two years, and you'd think I'd have soaked up knowledge aplenty about how a meeting is run, but I was realizing there was a lot to learn. Which shouldn't have been a surprise. Everyone else's job is always simple, and the previous PTA president had made running a meeting look as effortless as eating chocolate. I'd spent the last two weeks researching parliamentary procedure, reading up on management techniques, and wondering if I was up to the job.

Marina had made great fun of my self-assigned home-work, saying that it was just a PTA meeting, for crying out loud, but I wanted to be prepared. Really prepared. The PTA vice president, Claudia Wolff, would love to catch me making a mistake, the bigger mistake the better. Time spent making sure that wouldn't happen was time well spent.

"And anyway, I wasn't talking about you," Marina said from the too-small chair upon which she was sitting. The fifth-grade furniture was the biggest in the school, but it still wasn't exactly adult-sized.

"Oh?" I glanced at the classroom's wall clock. Ten minutes until the meeting began and the room was starting to fill up with parents and grandparents. Normally we had high school students in the gym to watch over the children, but the gym had spent the summer in a state of repair and the finish on the new floor wasn't quite ready for prime time. Instead, the kids and their keepers had been divided among two homes close to the school.

Which, thanks to the temporary suspension of my former husband's visitation schedule due to a Wednesday evening insurance seminar he was leading, meant my Jenna, twelve, was probably playing a shoot-'em-up video game. My Oliver, nine, was probably playing a quiet board game with some other quiet children. Jenna was of the opinion that since she was in middle school, she was old enough to stay home by herself, but she hadn't convinced me yet. Maybe when she was sixteen.

"No, I wasn't talking about you." Marina stood. "Not exactly."

"That's good," I said vaguely, sorting my stack of papers. Two more PTA board members came in and settled at the collapsible table the janitor had set up. Two down, one to go. Randy Jarvis, the treasurer, nodded at me. Claudia busied herself with a fluffle of movements that accomplished exactly nothing. She repositioned her chair. She cleared her throat. She moved her purse from her left side to her right. She fussed with her hair. I made sure my polite smile was on. This could be a very long year.

"It's your clothes." Marina plucked at my sleeve. "I was talking about your clothes. They're old and they're boring. You need to venture out of your rut, Beth."

"My rut is very comfortable, thanks." After all, there was nothing wrong with khaki poplin pants and button-up camp shirts. Average clothes that, I thought, went well with my average-ish height of five foot five and my completely average brown hair. And today I'd even slipped on a navy blue jacket. I thought I looked professional and businesslike, a style equally appropriate for tonight's meeting and for my career as owner of a children's bookstore.

"Clothes can be fun." Marina waved her arms. "Don't you want to have fun?"

"No, I don't. Not ever."

"Liar," Marina said comfortably, sitting back down, her red hair in disarray. "If that were true, you wouldn't have spent half of last summer playing disc golf."

"Exercise. For me and the children."

"Fun. It's all about fun. And those clothes are definitely not."

I crossed my eyes at her and looked at the clock. We had a missing board member, but it was time to start the meeting. "Good evening, ladies and gentlemen," I said. "Tonight's meeting of the Tarver Elementary School PTA will come to order."

"Um . . ." A slight, dark-haired woman, a PTA newcomer whose name I couldn't remember, stood up. "I don't know if this is the right time, but . . ." She walked to the front of the room and handed me an envelope. "It's from Nat. She says she's really sorry."

I took the envelope from her. Without opening it, I

knew what was inside. It didn't take any great leap to
guess that the empty board seat, reserved for the new
PTA secretary, Natalie Barnes, was going to stay empty
a little longer.

"What does it say?" Claudia asked, leaning over and
craning her neck in her attempt to read the letter.

"Just a second." I scanned the pages. Natalie's large
handwriting and her lengthy explanations filled up almost five sheets of paper.

Randy Jarvis, who'd been treasurer for as long as anyone could remember, grunted. "Bet she says she can't be
secretary."

I read the last page and handed the letter over to
Claudia. "You're right, Randy. She resigned." The scrawl-
ing pages had detailed how sorry she was, how much she
wished things were different, and how horrible she felt
about all this, but with the way things were, she was just
too busy to be secretary.

He nodded and opened the pack of corn chips he'd
brought from his downtown convenience store. "She got
gas from me the other day. Said she got a new job."

The PTA newcomer, who'd retreated to her seat as
soon as she'd given me the envelope, spoke up. "It's a
really good job, and with her husband on short hours, she
couldn't pass it up."

"No, of course not." It would have been nice to have
had a phone call from Natalie before the meeting, but
you couldn't have everything. "We still have a quorum,"
I said, "so we'll continue. But I'd like to add an item to
the agenda. New PTA secretary."

Feet shuffled around in the half-filled room. We had a
nice-sized group of about twenty, but you wouldn't have
known it from the flat silence. I saw a couple of people
half stand, then sit down. It was the fight-or-flight reaction starting to take effect, and who could blame them?

Volunteering to bake cookies was one thing; offering your services for an entire school year was quite another.

I could have stood up and made an impassioned speech about the many pleasures and rewards of being on the PTA board, but one accidental glance at Claudia would have made my words cling to the insides of my throat. Working with her this year was not going to be a pleasure or any sort of reward, unless I was being rewarded in a negative way.

What had I ever done to deserve Claudia? Sure, I'd skipped school once when I was a high school senior, but I'd been caught and had car privileges revoked for a month. I wasn't always as patient with my children as I could be, though, and my good intentions to have all three of us eat more fruit and vegetables were constantly being eroded by the smell of fresh-baked cookies just down the street from the bookstore, and—

Marina's overly loud throat clearing shook me out of my reverie. I blinked, briefly reflected that it was good to have friends who kept you from making an idiot of yourself in public, and went back to the agenda. We moved through approving the agenda, approved the minutes of the last meeting, and approved payment of the few invoices that had accrued over the summer.

The only old business item was my recap of last spring's senior story project. We'd paired Tarver Elementary students with residents of Sunny Rest Assisted Living. The end product was a softcover book of the life story of the residents as seen through the eyes of the children. Sales had done much better than expected by anyone—especially me—who'd come up with the idea in the first place. The fact that the Tarver PTA was making serious money and was receiving statewide attention was a fresh shock every time I thought about it. A nice shock, but still.

I finished with the latest sales figures. The pleased murmurs were music to my ears. There was nothing—nothing—that Claudia could say that would take this moment away from me.

"What does that mean in terms of money for the PTA?" one of the fathers in the audience asked.

I checked my notes to make sure I would be totally, absolutely correct when I publicly stated the number. I said it, and this time there weren't even any murmurs. Wide eyes and open mouths were the order of the day.

The part of me that was small-minded and petty desperately wanted to sneak a look at Claudia to see how she was reacting to the news. The noble and forgiving part of me knew that doing such a thing was beneath the person I wanted to be.

So I compromised; I snuck a tiny, fast look.

She looked just like the others. Eyes wide, mouth dropped open.

On the outside, I kept a polite smile on my face. On the inside, I was running around, shrieking with joy, thrusting my fists into the air. All last spring, Claudia had done nothing but question the whole story project. Everything from the concept to the choice of printer had been raked over the hot coals of her caustic commentary.

Sweet, sweet victory.

"We'll talk about the financial aspects of the story project in a minute," I said, nodding at a man sitting in the back row. "But first, we need a secretary." I looked across the audience. "Being PTA secretary is a thankless job that is never rewarded and brings you only criticism and more work than you imagined."

"Sign me up!" called a female voice from the back of the room. Carol Casassa waved wildly, grinning.

"She didn't mean that," said her husband, Nick, trying to pull her hand down. "Joke. It was a joke, honest."

Carol crossed her arms and pouted hugely.

So, yes, a joke. Too bad. Carol would have made an excellent secretary. I looked around the room, skating over Marina's upraised hand. She wanted to be secretary about as much as I wanted to gain back the fifteen pounds I'd so laboriously lost in the last six months. "Anyone else?"

Marina stood up, ignoring the way that I'd ignored her. "Can I nominate someone? Because if I can, I nominate Summer Lang."

All eyes skewed toward Summer.

The thirtyish woman had lived in Rynwood for only a couple of years, but the two of us had discovered that we had so much in common it was almost scary. Besides the straight brown hair and the tendency toward clumsiness when feeling uncomfortable, we shared a compulsion for list making that was not understood by most and made fun of by many, including my best friend, my offspring, and my employees.

Summer squirmed, looked at the floor, looked at her fingernails. "Um . . . well . . . I guess I—"

Claudia's voice soared out. "I nominate Tina Heller."

My eyes flew open wide and I felt the beginnings of panic stir around in my stomach.

"You want to do this, don't you, Tina?" Claudia said, prompting her bosom friend. "You can be secretary. I mean, it can't be that hard."

I kept my mouth closed. My mother had always told me that if you can't say anything nice, don't say anything at all. Forty years later, her admonition was finally taking effect.

"Oh." Tina, determinedly blond and always on a diet that for sure was going to help her lose weight this time, opened and closed her mouth a few times before anything else came out. "Sure. I guess I could. I mean, if you want me to."

I most certainly did not want her as secretary. "You accept the nomination?" I asked.

"Uh, yeah."

"Well, there you go." Claudia lounged back in her chair, smug as a bug in a rug. "We have a secretary."

Not so fast, missy. "There is another nomination on the floor."

Claudia sat upright, fast. "What do you mean? I nominated Tina, and she accepted. That's all we need, one nomination, and she's it. That's the way it works."

"Another nomination is on the floor," I repeated. "Summer, do you accept the nomination of secretary?"

Summer looked at me. Looked at the glowering Claudia. Looked at Randy, who was crunching through the last of his corn chips. Looked at Tina, who was biting her lips and texting madly. Looked back at me.

I hoped that she could magically see on my face the begging that was going on in my head.

Please run, Summer. Please please please, don't make me be president of a PTA board that I'll be arguing with for the next year over everything from meeting times to what color paper to use for the bake sale flyers. Please . . .

I held my breath.

"Okay," she said. "Sure, I accept."

The sharp pain in my chest eased to nothing. "Then we have two nominations." I tried to keep the elation out of my voice, but if Claudia's sour sideways glance meant anything, I hadn't done a very good job.

"But we can't have two nominations." Claudia tapped the table with her red-painted fingernail. "We always only have one. There can't be two."

"Why not?" I asked.

"Because . . ." Her glare sharpened to a point that ended in the middle of my forehead and started to drill deep into my skull. "Because that's the way we've always done it."

Of all the stupid reasons to do something, I'd always thought that was one of the stupidest. Easier, sure, and it was the way the world worked in a general sort of way, but I still thought it was stupid.

"That's the way we've always done it," she said again, "and there's no reason to change now. Tina accepted first, so she'll be secretary."

"Not necessarily." Reaching into the old diaper bag I used as a PTA briefcase, I reached for a manila folder and dropped it onto the table with a small plop. "Our bylaws state that in cases of multiple nominations, there will be a vote."

"Where? Let me see that." Claudia half stood and grabbed the folder. "Where does it say that? I don't see it anywhere."

"Page four," I murmured, earning a thumbs-up from Marina.

"Four? I don't see it. You're wrong about this. You must be."

I tucked my lips between my teeth, leaned over, and pointed out the pertinent paragraph.

"No, this only talks about . . . oh." Claudia slapped the folder shut. "Fine," she said. "We'll vote. Something like this, it has to be a board vote, right? I vote for Tina. Randy, how about you?"

Randy, who'd been busy collecting the last crumbs of his corn chips on the end of his thumb, grunted.

"There," Claudia said. "Randy votes for her, too. That's two votes and that's enough. Tina, you're the new PTA secretary. Come on up." Smiling, she pointed at the empty chair.

I dreamed a short dream of a distant and secluded

island populated only by Claudia. She'd be happy there, after a short period of adjustment. And even if she wasn't, I'd be comforted by my own happiness in knowing that she'd never attend another PTA meeting.

"Page five of the bylaws," I said, "states quite clearly that multiple nominations will be voted upon by the PTA membership."

"It can't." Claudia snatched at the bylaws and flipped through the pages. "It just can't."

"Page five," I said. "Robert's Rules of Order concurs. I can find the section number if you'd like."

Claudia didn't answer; she was too busy running her finger down the text on page five, muttering as she went. "Nominate . . . office of . . . multiple . . . PTA." Her finger stopped right where I knew it would.

After a moment, her chin went up. Grim-faced, she looked out at the people in the audience, one by one. "All right, then," she said. "We'll vote."

"By secret ballot," I said.

"Oh, absolutely," she said, smiling.

I watched her smile turn into more of a smirk and wondered what she was up to. Coercion by narrow-eyed glare? Telepathic mind control? Please. But Claudia looked far too confident for my comfort. What if . . . ? I shook my head and concentrated on the task at hand.

In short order, Claudia, Randy, and I rounded up paper, ripped the pieces into quarters, wrote down the names of both candidates on each one, folded each ballot in half, and passed one to each PTA member in the room.

There was a rustle while women fished through purses for pens, a few murmurings as the men present asked to borrow a pen from their wives; then the ballots were refolded and passed to the front, where they were deposited on the table in front of me.

I looked at the pile. It shouldn't have been a surprise that the ballots were given to me. I was president, after all, but somehow it I wasn't ready for this. Part of me still thought the presidency thing was a mistake of some kind. Erica Hale was president. She'd been PTA president for years. Surely she was going to walk in the room any second and motion me aside.

Only that wasn't going to happen. Erica had made it quite clear that she was done with the PTA. "I'll be in Italy from mid-August through October," she'd said. "You're on your own. And don't look like that. You'll do fine."

So. It was up to me to run this meeting and make sure it was run smoothly. I looked at the ballots and reached out to take the first one.

"You think you're the one who should count?" Claudia asked.

My hand froze.

"Don't the bylaws have something in them about counting votes?"

I revised my earlier fantasy involving Claudia and a distant island. It didn't have to be far away. A close one would do. And it didn't even have to be an island. It just had to be somewhere that Claudia was and I wasn't.

"We'll all count," I said. "You, me, and Randy; we'll each make a tally, then compare. A triple check."

She started to protest, but the audience was nodding in collective agreement. I felt an odd rush of pleasure. Maybe I could do this. Maybe I wouldn't want to crawl into the back of the closet when I got home.

Turning to a fresh sheet on my legal pad, I wrote the names of both nominees at the top and drew a vertical line down the middle of the page, dividing it in half. Tina on the left, Summer on the right.

Out in the audience, murmurs of conversation started

up and grew in volume. Marina was asking Carol and
Nick about their summer vacation to Nova Scotia, and
Summer was asking someone about an upcoming ski
swap. Good. Being eyeballed throughout this process
wouldn't have been good for my blood pressure.

An errant breeze made the ballots shift in their loose
pile. If Tina won, it'd be Claudia and Tina against Beth
the entire school year. Randy would swing between being a tying vote and a three-to-one vote in favor of whatever Claudia wanted to do, and since Randy wasn't big
on confrontation, there'd be three-to-one votes from
now until June.

Icky didn't begin to cover how I'd feel about that.
Okay, maybe Claudia and I didn't disagree on everything. We agreed on some things. Like . . . like . . .

I gave up the effort, took a shallow breath, and
reached for the first slip of paper.

A few short minutes later, I was steepling my fingers and
dreaming more island dreams, this time with me on the
island along with my children, our cat, our dog, and an
enormous pile of books. My pleasant reverie was interrupted when Claudia and Randy handed their tallies to
me. I unfolded their papers and looked at their totals.
Both agreed with mine. Exactly.

I signed all three tallies and had Claudia and Randy
also sign all three. Better to cross the T's with too long of
a cross and dot the I's with too big of a dot than to be
called up later for not doing things properly.

"Ladies and gentlemen," I said, and waited for the
chatting to die down.

I could have used the gavel, but something in me
balked at the idea. At the June meeting, the one in which
I'd been voted president, Erica had ceremoniously
handed me her gavel. "Use it wisely," she said, smiling,

"but not too well." Since I wasn't the gavel-banging type, I didn't want to use it at all. Before tonight's meeting started, I'd felt like a poseur pulling it out of the diaper bag and setting it on the table. Me as president was weird enough. Me wielding a gavel was ridiculous.

When everyone was facing front, I stood.

For a moment, I didn't say anything. All eyes were upon me, and surprisingly, I didn't feel uncomfortable. I didn't want to speak fast and sit down as quickly as I could, I didn't feel as if I were undergoing a sort of Marina-induced torture, and I had an odd confidence that I wasn't going to say anything deathly embarrassing in the next two minutes.

Wonders, truly, never cease.

"I'd like," I said, "to announce the name of the new secretary of Tarver Elementary's PTA."

Chapter 2

I looked at the nominees for PTA secretary. Tina and Summer had similar expressions on their faces: two parts apprehension and one part excitement. How could you not want to win, once you're running for an office? How could you not be nervous about the possibility of winning?

"And this year's secretary will be ..." Maybe it was Marina's presence that made me do it. Or maybe it was the teensy-weensy, almost nonexistent part of me that wanted to be in show business. For whatever reason, I took a dramatic pause and looked around the room, taking in the caught breaths and eager faces.

"This year's PTA secretary will be ... Summer Lang."

A smattering of light applause went around the room. Claudia drew a long line across the agenda item and didn't say anything. Randy nodded sideways at the chair next to him. "All yours," he said.

"Tonight, you mean?" Summer's straight brown hair seemed to straighten a bit more. "Like right now?"

I sensed that Claudia's mouth was about to open. "Yes," I said, speaking quickly so that Summer could be inaugurated without a snide comment. "Go ahead."

"Oh. Okay." Summer stood slowly, walked to the front of the room slowly, and sat down the same way. She looked at the audience. Blinked. Looked at the table. "Oh," she said. "I don't—"

But I was way ahead of her. "Here." I passed down my extra legal pad and a pen. The secretary's copy of the agenda was already in front of her. "Do your best to take notes." I gestured at the ancient tape recorder on the table, doing its creaky best to record everything we said. "If you miss something, this should help."

"Um. Good. Thanks, I mean." She uncapped the pen, drew a little squiggle, peered at the mark she'd made, and gave herself a small nod.

I tried not to beam like a proud parent. Summer would do fine. And I would never tell a soul what the vote count had been. Did anyone need to know that Tina had received all of two votes? No, they did not. Tina wasn't my favorite person by any means, but no one needed to be smacked with a defeat like that.

Then I started wondering who had cast those two votes.

The only certainty was Claudia. If Randy had truly grunted assent for Tina's nomination, wouldn't he have voted for her? And if he had, that meant Tina hadn't voted for herself. But if Tina *had* voted for herself, that meant Randy . . .

I shook my head. There was no point in thinking about it. Claudia's attempt to stack the PTA board had failed. Full stop. Time to move on.

"Okay, folks," I said. "If you'll look at your agendas, you'll see that the next item is PTA financial investments. The storybook project is generating enough money that we might want to consider investing a portion of it in something other than a savings account that makes us basically nothing in interest."

"What kind of investments?" Nick Casassa asked.

"Exactly what we need to find out," I said. "We have

a guest tonight who will give us a short course in investments for nonprofit organizations." I nodded to the man sitting in the back of the room who'd been wearing a bemused expression for the last fifteen minutes. "This is Dennis Halpern, a Madison-based financial consultant. Dennis recently opened an office here in Rynwood. He's also the author of a book on investing and was gracious enough to agree to speak to us. Dennis, thanks for sitting through the first part of our meeting. Welcome."

"Thank you, Beth." Dennis made his way forward to the teacher's desk. The four board members screeched our chairs around to face him.

He was sixtyish, average height, slope-shouldered, and the fat around his midsection was starting to droop over his belt. Unimpressive physical stature aside, he projected an air of intelligence and alertness.

I squinted at him, trying to figure out how he did that, and came to the conclusion that it was what his eyes were doing. He was paying attention not only to everyone, but to everything. His gaze flicked over the posters tacked up on the wall, taking in the map of the United States, an exploded diagram of the parts of a skyscraper, and pictures of Yellowstone National Park. I saw him take note of the flowers and books on the teacher's desk, the box in the back corner labeled LOST AND FOUND, and saw how he quickly scanned each face in the room.

An observant man, I thought, and was pleased that I'd been able to talk him into attending the meeting.

"So," he said. "I hear you folks have a lot of money."

Marina thrust her fist into the air. "We're rich! We're wealthy!"

"Comfortably well off, perhaps," Dennis said. "But not rich."

Randy moved his chair around a little farther, making the feet screech horribly. "Richer than a lot of PTAs."

"Which is why I'm here." Dennis leaned back against the desk. "Your president asked me to talk about possible investments."

"Is that legal?" Claudia asked. "I mean, can we even do that with PTA money?"

Dennis nodded. "Good question. My advice is to run options past your attorney. That way you can get a legal opinion before a decision is finalized."

I opened my mouth, then shut it. Erica. As a retired attorney, she'd always provided the PTA with legal counsel. Was she going to charge us for advice, now that she was off the PTA? If so, how much? And why hadn't I thought about this before? There was no way I was qualified to lead this group. I had no idea what I was doing and—

Stop that, I told myself. *Cut it out right now. You're president and people are depending on you. So . . . figure it out.*

"But that can wait," Dennis said easily, talking over my small crisis of confidence. "All I want to do tonight is present a few simple options."

"I like simple," Randy said.

Dennis laughed. "You're not alone. And that is certainly something to consider as we move along in this decision-making process."

"I have a question." Carol raised her hand. "What are we going to do with all that money? I mean, before we invest it somewhere, shouldn't we think about what we want to do?"

"Yeah," Claudia said. "It doesn't make sense to invest money if we're just going to take it out and spend it. We might have to pay penalties."

Why hadn't I seen this coming? If I could have turned back time, I would have gone back about ten minutes and told everyone that tonight was just for informational purposes, that educating ourselves about investments would be a good thing, that once we knew the possibilities, we could make a well-informed decision about what would be best for the PTA.

Tina's hand shot up. "My mom? She took money out of her 401(k) once and had to pay all sorts of penalties. If the PTA did that, it'd probably be a crime or something, wouldn't it? I mean, public money, right? You can't be doing that."

I wanted to bang my head against the table.

Dennis didn't flinch. The man, clearly, was a professional. "Helping you understand different investment vehicles is the reason I'm here."

"Vehicles?" Natalie's friend asked, frowning. "We're investing in cars?"

Yes, it was true. Inviting Dennis to speak had been one of my worst ideas ever. Worse than my idea of painting the family room lime green and way worse than the day I'd decided it would be a good idea to take Spot to the bookstore. Not quite as bad as the time I'd chosen to eat the slightly off-color chip dip in the back of the refrigerator, but it had to be close.

Claudia gave a wheezing cough.

"I think we should decide what we're going to do with the money," Tina said.

"Good idea," Claudia said quickly, and I got the sneaking suspicion that Tina had been primed to speak up on cue. "We should buy new soccer goals. And we have lots of money to pay for new playground equipment. I found this place online that has these really great slides. And we could even pay for some special-needs equipment."

"All worthy projects," Dennis said. "But if you'd like to have a sustainable base for—"

Summer raised her hand. "I think we should pay for a music teacher."

"We applied to the Tarver Foundation for that," Claudia said.

"And they still haven't made a decision. We have the money, why should we wait for them?"

"Because that's not something the PTA should pay for," Claudia snapped.

Summer put her chin up. "I'm guessing a whole bunch of people don't agree with you. And what's the PTA's mission, anyway? To promote the health, well-being, and educational successes of our kids through strong parent, family, and community involvement."

What Summer had said was one of PTA National's values, not the mission statement, but I was impressed, nonetheless.

"I don't see how buying soccer goals fits into that," Summer said, shaking her head. "I just don't."

"And I don't see how a music teacher fits into it," Claudia said.

"I do," Carol said.

Tina turned to look at her. "Well, I don't."

In one sudden surge, the room erupted with sound. Claudia was telling Summer that if she (Summer) didn't know how important soccer was to the health of children that her children must have no athletic ability at all. Summer was giving it right back to her, saying that anyone with an ounce of sense understood the importance of music and the arts to a child's development. Randy, stuck between them, was turning his head back and forth, trying to sneak in a short word every so often. His bursts of "It's—," "Both are—," and "Don't—" were completely ignored by the two women.

Out in the audience, Tina and Carol were going at it hammer and tongs over the merits of swim lessons for toddlers. Nick was volubly discussing designated hitters with a young father who'd never once said a word at a meeting. Red-faced and shouting, they were getting to their feet with clenched fists. Marina was alternating between telling the mother on her left that buying a drum set for her daughter would be an excellent idea and debating the father on her right about the best Green Bay Packer quarterback ever.

I looked at the melee in disbelief. All this, over a disagreement on how to spend money? What was wrong with these people? And it was going on much too long. Why wasn't Erica doing anything about it? She never let a meeting get out of hand like this, why wasn't she—

Oh. Right.

As Tina shrieked out, "There should be laws to keep people like you from even having kids," I wrapped my fingers around the wooden handle.

When Carol called back, "It's people like me that keep people like you from becoming a menace to society," I raised the gavel and swung.

Crack!

A few sets of eyes darted glances my way, but there was no decrease in the din.

Crack! Crack! Crack!

"Order!" I shouted. "That's enough, people! This is not the time or place for this kind of argument!"

The noise level went down several notches, then fell away to complete silence. I realized that I was standing up, one hand flat on the table, the other curled around the upraised gavel, leaning forward in a pose of intimidation. When that had happened, I had no idea.

"We have a guest," I said pointedly. "This is a sad way to introduce him to the Tarver PTA." I heard a few mumbles that might have been apologies, but I was too angry to pay attention. "And what kind of example are we setting for our children? Is this the way we want them to

"And I hate it when you get that polite look when I'm talking."

Fair enough. "What does Earth want with Beth?"

She looked left, then right, then leaned in close. "What did you do with the ballots?"

Over her shoulder, I saw Randy stump back into the room. Behind him came Carol and Nick, who were in a friendly argument about what was better, thin-crust or deep-dish pizza. Behind them more PTA members were starting to return. I glanced at the clock. A few more minutes. "For secretary?" I asked.

"No, the ballots for the 1852 presidential election." She looked at the ceiling. "How can someone so smart be so stupid? Of course the secretary ballots."

"They're in my bag."

"Well, tell me." She patted her hands on the table in a quiet imitation of a drumroll. "I'm dying to know."

"What part of secret ballot don't you understand?"

"What I understand is that you know more than I do, and I can't stand it."

"Summer won. And that reminds me." I reached into my bag and retrieved the ballots. Just out of her reach, I worked on tearing each one into tiny pieces.

"Aw, you're such a spoilsport."

She made a halfhearted attempt to snatch the ballots out of my hands, but I held them away and kept ripping and ripping until the bits of paper were small enough that it would have taken a team of CSI experts two full episodes to reassemble them.

"You are no fun." Marina slumped in her chair. "I hope this president thing isn't going to your head."

"So you're saying that if I'd still been secretary I would have handed over a pile of secret ballots?"

She heaved a theatrical sigh. "Your overly developed sense of right and wrong would have kept you from doing that, but you might have squeaked me a little information."

I snorted. "Again, what part of 'secret ballot' don't you get?"

"There's secret and then there's, you know, secret."

This explanation should be good. "How's that, exactly?"

"Sit and listen, my child, and you will learn. Look into my crystal ball. Look closely; look deep." She adjusted an invisible head scarf and cupped her hands around an imaginary crystal ball. "Listen well. There are three kinds of secrets."

"According to . . . ?" I tilted my head.

"Do you want to hear this or not? Three kinds." She held up her index finger. "One is the not-very-secret secret. What you're getting someone for their birthday or Christmas." Her middle finger went up. "Two is the mid-level secret. Secret enough that it should stay a secret to most people, but not so ultra-important that it can't be shared with certain responsible people." She half closed her eyes at me. "That's what this vote was. A level-two secret."

There was a certain logic to this. And maybe in a thousand years I'd tell her so. "Level three?" I asked.

"Ah, level three." She hitched a teensy bit closer, making our conversation a little more confidential, a little more . . . secret. "A level-three secret is the secretest kind of secret. It's the life-and-death kind of secret."

In spite of my natural inclination to disbelieve anything Marina said when she was in her new persona as a gypsy storyteller, I found myself leaning forward, pulled in by the spell she was casting.

"The kind of secret that you'd do anything to keep people from finding out." Her voice dropped to a whisper. "The kind that ruins marriages and ends careers. The kind that makes you leave a town forever. The kind that turns sons against mothers, sisters against sisters, and lifelong friends against each other. A secret that breeds violence and makes you long to wake up from the nightmare your life has become. But you can't," she said, drawing out the last word long and dark, "because you are already awake and there's nothing you can do. Nothing."

The skin at the base of my neck prickled. Marina's new persona was a little too effective for my taste. I'd rather have the Southern belle back. Or Greta Garbo. Or the Shakespearean actor who could never quite remember the lines. Even the cowgirl (who had never quite worked out, somehow) would have been preferable to this.

"And now"—she crossed her hands in front of her, making the crystal ball vanish—"now we return to the question of the secret ballot. Because now that we know it's not that much of a secret, I bet you won't have any problem telling me."

". . . No," I said, wondering what kind of secret it would take to make me leave Rynwood. To have a secret, you had to do something horrible, didn't you? I wasn't the best person in the world by a long shot, but I wasn't that bad. Of course, if Auntie May, the wheelchair-bound ninety-two-year-old terror of Rynwood found out that I hadn't cleaned out the freezer properly in three years, I might have to flee in the dark of night.

But a true level-three secret? I'd never done anything bad enough—or interesting enough—to warrant that kind of secrecy.

Had I?

"Beth?" Marina was looking at me uncertainly. "Are you okay? Because you're getting a funny look on your face. You know I was joking about all that secret stuff, right? I don't care if you tell me about the vote count. I mean, it'd be fun to know if Tina only got three votes, but—"

BANG!

The loud sound slammed into my eardrums, shocking everyone in the room to silence even as the echo bounced down the hallways.

Marina's face, normally ruddy with health and good cheer, turned instantly white. "Was that . . . ?"

"Yes," I whispered, not wanting it to be true, but knowing it was. The noise had been unmistakable.

It had been a gunshot.

Chapter 3

I was on my feet and running before the gunshot's echo died away. Marina's call of "Beth! Wait! You can't—" fell off my back as I passed a blur of PTA members half settled into their seats and then I was through the door.

Outside of the classroom, Tina stood stock-still, mouth open wide, staring down the hallway to the right.

I charged down the hard floor, my flat-soled shoes finding firm purchase, hearing a set of footsteps behind me. One glance over my shoulder and I saw Nick Casassa hot on my heels, a determined look on his face. We passed Mindy Wietzel, who was flat against the wall, fingers spread wide, eyes round.

Nick caught up to me and, in one simultaneous leap, we jumped over the short flight of stairs that separated the old section of the building from the new. Down here, the building split into two wings.

I pointed left and right. "Let's split up," I panted out.

"We stay together," Nick said in short breaths. "Safer."

I nodded. For no reason other than right-handedness, I pointed to the wing that went right.

We ran on. Behind us were footsteps and shouting; ahead was a dimly lit hallway. At its far end was a door that led to the playground. I saw a rectangle of darkness appear, then disappear, and my brain raced ahead of me.

The shooter was leaving through that door. He was getting away. We should run him down and catch him, we should—

Then I caught sight of a shoe.

It was a man's shoe, lying heel down and toe up, a position that meant a foot was still inside. The shoe was propping open a door.

I started to shout to Nick, but he was heading for the end of the hallway and putting on a burst of speed that left me far behind. I slowed from my flat-out run by putting my hand on the wall and went to the shoe. Sweating and breathing hard, I pushed open the door labeled TEACHERS' RESTROOM.

Inside, lying on the floor, very, very still, was Dennis Halpern.

I was pushed aside. "Give me room," said Lynn, a PTA mother who was, to her patients, Dr. Lynn Snider, a general-practice doctor who had spent two years working in the emergency room of Chicago's busiest hospital.

Lynn dropped to her knees, checked for a pulse, then put her hands on his chest and started pumping. "Call 911," she grunted.

Since I couldn't, because my cell was in my abandoned purse, I stepped out of the restroom and saw that half the PTA was trotting toward us, cell phones in hand. "Taken care of," I told Lynn.

She was pumping away with a steady rhythm that was breaking my heart. I sank to my knees across from her, on the other side of Dennis. "Is there anything I can do?"

"No," she said shortly, out of breath from her efforts. "Yes. Direct ambulance. EMTs."

I scrambled to my feet and grabbed the first person I could latch on to, who happened to be Tina. "Run out to the parking lot and wait for the ambulance. When they get here—"

"I'll bring them." She nodded and trotted off.

Nick reappeared, sweat dripping from his forehead. He shook his head. Whether he hadn't seen the shooter or hadn't been able to grab hold of him, it didn't really matter at this point.

"The rest of you," I said, "just stay back, okay? They'll need room."

"Who is it?" Summer asked. "Is it . . . ?"

"Dennis Halpern," I said heavily. "Our guest." My guest. The man I'd tried so hard to get to a PTA meeting. The man who—

Summer swayed, putting her hands out in front of her. "Is he . . . is he going to be all right? He is, right?"

I turned away without answering. There was no way I was qualified to answer her question. I wasn't a nurse or a doctor or an EMT or any kind of health professional.

But I knew. Even without seeing the despairing expression on Lynn's face, I knew.

Dennis was dead.

An eternity later, the EMTs slammed shut the back doors of the rescue vehicle. They climbed up into the front seats, and the driver started the engine. The boxy red truck rolled out of the parking lot and down the road, the lights and sirens that had heralded its arrival silent.

The crowd of onlookers—children too young to understand tragedy, women with crossed arms, men with their hands in their pockets—started to drift into the darkness as soon as the vehicle was out of sight.

Rynwood's chief of police, my friend Gus Eiseley, had arrived on the heels of the EMT crew. When he'd arrived, he'd asked everyone to stay until he'd talked to them, then looked around and asked, "Who was first to get to the victim?"

Before he'd even finished the sentence, I was raising my hand and pointing to myself and Nick. "Why am I not surprised?" he'd asked, and made a note.

I'd assumed the question was a rhetorical one and didn't even try to make up an answer. Yes, I'd ended up involved in a couple of other murder investigations . . . okay, three. No, four, depending on how you counted, but did that mean I was necessarily involved in any major crime in Rynwood? No, it did not. It was coincidence, that's all. I did not attract trouble.

Did I?

That uncomfortable thought stayed with me all through the rattling passages of the gurney, both the hurried inward one and the slow, almost stately, outward one.

Did I?

Now, with the ambulance gone and the sadness just starting, Gus turned to the PTA. "Ladies, gentlemen, I know you'd like nothing better than to go home to your families, but I need your help first."

Dusk was passing fast to darkness, but in the yellow glow cast by the parking lot lights I saw the heads nodding solemnly.

"Thank you," Gus said. "Officer Zimmerman and I will take your statements. We should have you out of here in no time. Beth and Nick, if you could wait until the end, I'd appreciate it." He ran a hand over his short-cropped gray hair.

Gus was one of those men whose age was hard to guess. Twenty years ago, when I'd first met him in the church choir, he hadn't looked much different than he did now. A little grayer, maybe, and perhaps a few more lines on his weathered face, but that was about it. Thanks to his wife, Winnie, I knew that he was fifty-two, but if he'd told you he was thirty-five, you'd think, okay, an old-looking thirty-five, but yeah, I'll believe thirty-five.

I quietly suggested that Gus talk to the ones with young children first, so they could get the kids home and in bed. "Good idea," he said. "They'll be antsy to get going, and I'll get better answers out of them this way. Thanks, Beth. I appreciate your input."

Effusive praise for a minor suggestion. I squinted at him. Very not like Gus. Maybe he'd taken a workshop on new techniques for working with citizens, and I was the guinea pig.

While we were milling around, waiting, Harry, the school janitor who doubled as daytime security guard, came in to lock up the school. He'd assumed our meeting was over, but one quick explanation and Harry moved to unlock more classrooms for the PTA parents to wait in.

"Sorry about this, Harry," I said.

"Nothing to be sorry about, Mrs. Kennedy." He unlocked the door to a fourth-grade classroom with a set of jingling keys. "Not your fault." He hung the keys on the belt that held up the navy blue slacks he always wore. Navy blue pants and light blue dress shirt were all he ever wore while working. The once or twice I'd seen him outside of school, it had taken me a moment to recognize him, in spite of his six feet of incredible thinness.

"No," I said, "I suppose it's not." But I wasn't absolutely sure that was true.

Carol waited with Nick and me as Gus and the much-too-young Officer Zimmerman interviewed the other parents. The three of us made up a very small and uncomfortable group. Gus had cautioned us against talking about the incident, saying he'd like to keep our impressions as clean as possible, so with that topic out of bounds, we talked about our children until Carol wondered out loud if Dennis had had any.

With that conversation stalled, we went on to talking

about the new downtown store, Made in the Midwest. But since I was the only one who'd met the owner or been inside the store, that didn't go anywhere, either.

A short sally by Nick for a discussion of the University of Wisconsin football team didn't get beyond, "What do you think of that freshman tailback the Badgers are starting?" We were reduced to discussing the weather when Gus stepped in. "Carol?" She picked up her purse, squeezed her husband's hand, and left with Gus.

Nick and I didn't even try to talk. We were staring at the air when Gus came in. "Nick?"

For a very long ten minutes I was left alone with the events of the last two hours. There wasn't much to be gained in going over and over it, but I couldn't seem to stop the continuous loop, couldn't turn it off, couldn't turn down the gunshot I kept hearing. Over and over and—

"How are you doing?" Gus dropped into the chair next to me. A full-sized chair, thanks to the kindness of Harry. He'd taken in the drawn looks and pale faces and lugged folding chairs out of some secret janitorial closet.

"Fine," I said, as brightly as I could.

"You're still a horrible liar," he said, rearranging papers on his clipboard.

"Maybe I'm such a good liar that you can't tell that I'm lying about lying."

He glanced at me, then went back to his paperwork. "That doesn't make sense."

I sighed. No, it didn't. "I'm tired, sad, angst-ridden, and depressed about the human condition."

A hint of a smile lightened his face. "That's more like it. You okay with staying a while longer? The kids are all set?"

"Marina took them to her house."

He nodded. "She can be an interfering chatterbox, but her heart is the size of an Oldsmobile."

As compliments go, that was as backhanded as any I'd ever heard. There wasn't a chance I'd pass it on to Marina without a hefty dose of editing. She still hadn't forgiven Gus for the way he'd treated me last spring, and I didn't want to make that situation any worse. "They haven't made Oldsmobiles in years," I said. "You need to get a new simile."

"It'll last me to retirement."

I sat up straight. "You're thinking about retiring?" Rynwood without Gus as police chief was as unthinkable as . . . as Rynwood without Auntie May. Knowing there was even a slim chance of Auntie May catching you in wrongdoing had kept the entire populace on the straight and narrow for three generations.

No one, but no one, wanted to hear the rattling cackle that preceded "Caught you, you little sneak" if you so much as forgot to hold the door open for the person behind you. And heaven forbid if you accidentally let a scrap of candy bar wrapper flutter onto the sidewalk. Yes, Auntie May was our conscience and our guide. Guide to what, I wasn't quite sure, but it was a certainty that we were better off with Auntie May than without her.

Well, a near certainty.

"Thinking about retirement," Gus said, "is a hundred miles from doing it. Besides, if I retired, Winnie would drag me to every garage sale between here and Milwaukee, and I'm not sure our marriage could handle it."

"Ha. You two are like one of those salt-and-pepper sets. You know, the kind that snuggle up against each other and look all wrong if they're by themselves."

"I'm not sure I'll tell Winnie that one." He clicked his pen. "And now we should get started so we can get you home. Let's walk through what happened."

I looked at my hands, fingers interlaced, thumbs pushing hard against each other. "I don't want to," I said in a low voice.

"Of course you don't." Gus's voice was patient. "No sane person would. But . . ." He left the sentence open, and I filled in the blanks all by myself.

But . . . it was my civic duty to tell Gus everything I could remember. I owed it to Dennis to describe everything I'd seen. Helping law enforcement set a good example for my children. Plus it was the right thing to do, and that was the truest and best reason of all.

"Okay." I watched my thumbs push against each other, their edges turning white. "This whole thing started when I heard that Rynwood was getting a new business downtown, a financial consultant."

"Dennis Halpern," Gus said.

I nodded. "I'd been thinking about getting Debra O'Conner from the bank to come talk to the PTA about investing, but she recommended Dennis. Said he knew more about investing than she ever would, plus he'd written a book. Summer Lang recommended him, too."

"It's not your fault he was murdered," Gus said. "Not unless you killed him, I mean."

I eked out a small smile. "No, I didn't kill him. But he was here because I invited him."

Gus flipped a page in his notebook and got busy with his pen. "If you want to continue to beat yourself up, go right ahead, but it's doubtful that he was killed randomly. If it wasn't random, it was either from circumstance or premeditated. Circumstance also seems unlikely, since that is usually the result of being in the wrong place at the wrong time, and it's hard to see how using the men's room in an almost entirely empty elementary school could be the wrong place."

"Or the wrong time?"

"Or the wrong time," he agreed. "That leaves a murder of premeditation, and that gets you off the hook."

I wasn't so sure that his explanation would hold up to the ugly light of reality, but since all he was doing was trying to make me feel better, I didn't start slicing great whacking holes in the analysis.

Instead, I went on to describe how Dennis had agreed to volunteer his time to help the PTA. "He grew up in Rynwood," I said, "did you know? Went here to elementary school." We might have been sitting in one of the rooms where Dennis had spent a school year. That desk there might have been where Dennis sat.

I sighed.

Stay away from that line of thinking, Beth. It'll just depress you, and what good will you be to anyone if you're sunk into a pit of despair?

Quotes from one of my top-ten favorite movies of all time, *The Princess Bride,* flashed through my head, and I began to feel a little less desolate. I told Gus about tonight's PTA meeting, about me calling for a break. How Marina and I hadn't left the room, so I didn't know who was where when. How people were coming back into the room when the gun went off. How Nick and I ran down the hall. How Nick chased what we assumed to be the gunman. How I found Dennis. How someone had called 911. And Gus had been there for the rest of it.

"Okay." He wrote and wrote, then finally stopped. "Now comes the hard part. Who was in the room with you and Marina when you heard the shot?"

"Nick and Carol Casassa," I said promptly. "And Randy Jarvis. Tina Heller wasn't in the room, but she was just outside the door. Um . . ." I closed my eyes, thinking, and gave him the name of two other PTA parents. "Those I'm sure about. Anyone else, I can't say."

"Keep your eyes closed," Gus said, "and see the room again, just before the gun went off, when you and Marina were arguing about what's secret and what's not."

"We weren't arguing," I said. "We were . . . talking."

"Think about the room just before the gun went off," he said. "You were at the table. Marina was on the other side of it. Randy Jarvis was sitting down. Nick and Carol were standing behind the back row of desks. Lynn Snider was talking to Rachel Helmstetter. Do you see anyone else?"

"Whitney Heer," I said, surprised. "I'd forgotten. Whitney and a friend of Natalie Barnes. I don't know her name, but I can get it."

Gus made a satisfied noise. "Good job."

I glowed a little. Getting praise from Gus was like getting a pat on the back from a much older brother. After our falling-out in the spring, I hadn't been sure our relationship would ever return to its former solid friendship. But after a few weeks of prickly choir practices, he'd asked, in an unusually diffident way, if I'd mind having breakfast with him at the Green Tractor.

I'd hesitated, but had eventually agreed. The meal had started off more awkward than a blind date between two freshly divorced people. We'd sat. Ordered. Sipped coffee (Gus) and tea (me). Studied a menu we both knew better than our social security numbers. It was Ruthie, owner of the Green Tractor, who'd made things right.

"Here." She'd shoved aside our napkins and silverware and slapped new paper place mats on top of the bright green ones we'd already had. Kid place mats, with line drawings for coloring in with crayons. A kitty-cat and puppy-dog place mat for me, a truck and car place mat for Gus. She'd dropped a handful of crayons on the booth's table. "If you two are going to act like children, I'm going to treat you that way." She stomped off, paused, then stomped back and surveyed us, hands on her hips. "And if I hear any fighting over the sky-blue crayon, you're both grounded for a month." She stomped off to the back of the restaurant.

I looked at the pile of crayons. "There's not even a sky-blue one in here," I muttered.

For some reason, that made Gus burst out laughing. Full-throat, belly-hurting laughter. Still laughing, he stood and went behind the counter. Came back with Ruthie's big bowl of crayons, fished out a sky-blue crayon and handed it to me. "No more fighting."

I'd smiled and taken the crayon. "No more," I agreed, because it was only fair that I take my share of the blame.

Now Gus tapped his pen to his notebook. "Any idea where Summer Lang was? No? How about Claudia Wolff?"

I shook my head. "I don't know. But neither one of them could have been the shooter. Both Nick and I saw that door shut, and Summer and Claudia were in the crowd that came from the other way just a little afterward. There was no way either one of them could have run around the building that fast."

Gus made a noncommittal noise. "Did you see anyone else in the building tonight?"

"No. But really, anyone could have walked in." Hope surged in me. "The building was unlocked, right? It didn't have to be someone at the meeting. It probably wasn't, right? Harry never locks the school down until the meeting is over, so anyone could have walked in. It's not like we have to show our ID to a security guard at the door, or anything, to get into a PTA meeting. It could have been anyone. And the killer ran off. Both Nick and I saw him run out the door at the end of the hallway. That's what Nick said, too, right?"

I was in babble mode. This happened when I was tired,

or embarrassed, or uncomfortable, or frightened. It was worst when I was a combination of all four. On I went.

"So, really, there's no need to look at us PTA members. You should probably see if Dennis had any enemies. Find out if he was divorced or was having an affair or . . . or cheered for the Minnesota Vikings instead of the Packers like he should. That can get people really riled up, you know. And you never know, maybe he'd cut someone off in traffic and—"

Gus flipped his notebook shut. "Beth," he said gently, "you know I won't be investigating this murder. The sheriff's office will be taking over. Their forensic team will be here first thing in the morning."

I sighed. "Sorry."

"Don't be. You've had a hard night." He smiled. "I wish I could have seen you banging that gavel. Did you really say you were going to whack everyone over the head with it if they didn't shut up?"

"What? Of course not! Who told you that?"

He chuckled, stood, and held out his hand to help me to my feet. "You look dead tired. Get your kids and go home. If you think of anything else that might help, let me know in the morning."

I picked up my purse. "Gus, do you . . ." I stopped. Not wanting to say it out loud, not wanting to make the words real.

"Go ahead," he said. "Ask. You won't sleep right until you do."

Sometimes it was a pain in the hind end to know the chief of police in your town. "Do you really think someone from the PTA killed Dennis?"

"It could have been," Gus said. "You know I can't tell any details, but yes, it could have been."

I worried the straps of my purse. Classic Gus, handing you the truth when you least wanted it.

"Then again," he said, "it might not have been. That's why we have what we in law enforcement call a murder investigation."

I continued to toy with the straps of my purse, twisting the faux leather around and around. "I don't want it to be anyone in the PTA," I said. "I really, really don't."

Gus slid his notebook into his pocket. "Go home. Get some sleep." He patted my shoulder on his way out of the room.

Slowly, I followed after him, carefully not looking in the direction of where . . . of the ongoing investigation. The hallways, silent now except for the distant voices of Gus and his officers, were a little creepy in their emptiness. Surely I'd been in the school at night by myself before, but I couldn't remember a single instance.

A voice came at me. "Mrs. Kennedy?"

I gasped and backed away fast, my purse to my chest, then saw who it was and relaxed "Harry. You startled me."

The janitor stepped halfway out of a doorway I'd never noticed before. Which was probably the exact effect someone had been after when they'd painted the door the same colors as the walls. "Sorry, ma'am. For scaring you, I mean. I just wanted to ask you something." When I nodded, he shuffled forward, large knobby hands at his sides. "Do they know who done it? Who killed that guy?"

If they did, they weren't saying. "No, I don't think so."

He nodded, as if that was the answer he'd been expecting. "Not like a TV show, is it?"

It never was. "They'll find him," I said. "Don't worry about that."

"Him?" He looked up. "So they know it was a guy and not a girl?"

"Oh. Well." Given my own disinclination for firearms,

I'd awarded my entire gender the same aversion. Which wasn't accurate by any means. Where I'd done most of my growing up, in northern lower Michigan, it wasn't at all uncommon for girls to go out hunting. And I knew a number of adult women who enjoyed target shooting. Knew a couple who had licenses to carry concealed handguns. Had heard of one who enjoyed going to gun shows. "I'm not sure, Harry. I suppose it could have been a woman."

"I don't like it," he said. "Why did he have to be killed in the school? It's going to bother the kids. When Mr. Helmstetter was killed, at least that was in the parking lot. Not in here. Not in the school." He looked left and right, seeing the hallways, but not seeing them.

The pain on his face was clear to see, and my slow-moving brain made a quick hard turn and started to see things from Harry's point of view.

Tarver Elementary was his responsibility. Its care and maintenance were his job and his pride. And as de facto security guard, the safety of its inhabitants was also his responsibility. This atrocity had happened on his watch, and the weight was sitting hard on his shoulders.

Poor Harry. None of this was his fault in any way, shape, or form, yet here he was, twisting himself into knots.

Harry reached out and rubbed an invisible speck of dirt off the wall. "Do they think it was someone in the PTA who done it?"

"I don't know." And I didn't. I didn't want to know the killer, didn't want to know someone who could fire a bullet straight into the heart of a human being, didn't want to have attended bake sales and worked father-daughter dances and sat through committee meetings with a murderer. "I hope not."

He nodded. "Have a good night, Mrs. Kennedy."

But . . . where had Claudia been? Not that she would have killed anyone, in spite of her evil temper, of course not, but why had Gus asked about her specifically? And Summer. Why had she been singled out?

I shook my head, doing my best to toss the ideas out of my skull. No. No one from the PTA had killed Dennis. The idea was too silly to consider.

Ridiculous.

Beyond ridiculous.

But all the way home, while I picked up the kids, while I got them to bed, and after I got myself into bed and covered myself with a big purring black George cat, I wondered.

Was the idea silly?

Was it?

Chapter 4

The morning after the murder of Dennis Halpern, I sat down at the breakfast table with the kids.

This was such an unusual occurrence that both children stopped reading the backs of their cereal boxes and looked at me. I wasn't too concerned about Jenna since she was in middle school, but Oliver's classroom was right down the hall from where ... from the murder scene.

"Are you eating breakfast with us?" Oliver pushed his box of Froot Loops my way.

"She won't want to eat that sugary stuff." Jenna gave her box of Cheerios a shove. "Here, Mom. You like these, don't you?"

"Thanks, but I have an apple and a banana in my purse."

"Are you sure that's enough breakfast?" Oliver frowned. "My teacher says breakfast is the most important meal of the day."

Oliver's fourth-grade teacher, Mrs. Sullivan, was a frequent customer at my children's bookstore, and I'd been pleased as punch when we got the letter announcing that Oliver would be in her classroom. With more than twenty years in teaching, she knew how to keep kids focused, yet her natural good humor made it easy for the kids to have fun.

"Mrs. Sullivan is exactly right," I said. "But people your age"—I reached left and right and tapped them both on the nose—"and people my age have different nutritional needs." As in, they burned off food like little power plants burning coal, but in me food transformed instantly to thigh dimples. I'd worked hard to lose weight the last few months, and I wasn't going to let Froot Loops be the thing that led me back to the dark side. Chocolate, maybe. My friend Alice's cookies, possibly. But breakfast cereal? Not a chance.

"Is that why you don't eat toast and jam in the morning?" Jenna slathered a knifeful of the strawberry variety on a thick slice.

"Yup." Her eating habits would change too, someday, but I didn't tell her that. And maybe I'd be wrong. Jenna, my hockey goalie–playing daughter, was as athletic as kids came. Who knew? Maybe she'd grow up to be one of those women who stayed toned and fit their entire lives.

"You're doing it again," Jenna said.

"What's that?" I asked, smiling, my head mostly full of an adult Jenna who'd just won the Chicago marathon.

She exchanged a look with Oliver. "She's imagining what her grandchildren will be like."

Last month I'd made the tactical error of answering Jenna truthfully when she'd asked me what I was thinking about. I'd been daydreaming about spoiling the next generation of Kennedys by gifting them with wonderful children's books every week. The book of the week club, for Beth Kennedy's grandchildren only. My daughter had been appalled.

I'm not sure if it was the thought of getting married and having babies that troubled her or the shadowy concept that I could possibly want more children in my life. Either way, the expression on her face had been priceless. I'd hugged her hard and told her it was just a silly daydream and not to worry about it. Her concern had subsided, especially after she'd told Oliver. My son's re-action had been sheer hilarity, which made everything easier.

Now Oliver bounced in his seat. "Fat babies in diapers with spit-up all down their chins."

Jenna grinned. "Babies crying so loud, it hurts your ears."

"Babies with goofy smiles." Oliver tried one on.

"Cute," I said, rolling my eyes. He was, but that kind of behavior didn't need to be encouraged. "Finish your breakfast, please. And I have something to tell you."

Both of them stopped, their spoons halfway to their mouths.

"Last time you had something to tell us at breakfast," Jenna said, "was when Grandma Emmerling had to go to the hospital."

"And the time before that was when Mr. Helmstetter was killed," Oliver said.

Hmm. Every once in a while, I should sit down with my children at breakfast and give them some good news. I tried to imagine what might be newsworthy enough to rate a breakfast-table announcement but came up dry. One more item to add to the list of things I needed to work on.

"Something happened last night at the PTA meeting," I said.

"Something bad?" Oliver asked, milk dripping off the side of his spoon.

I nodded. "Very bad. I'd invited a man to talk to us and he . . . he's dead."

"Like a heart attack or something?" Jenna asked.

"Not exactly." I pushed away the image of Dr. Lynn kneeling over Dennis, bright red blood splotching his shirt and spreading over her hands. "I'm afraid he was killed."

"Whacked over the head dead?" Oliver's face was maybe a touch pale, but his eyes sparked with interest.

"Strangled?" Jenna asked.

"Maybe he was poisoned." Oliver looked at his spoonful of cereal and wolfed it down, grinning as a drop of milk ran out the corner of his mouth.

"Or maybe he was stabbed to death."

I looked from my beautiful young daughter to my endearingly cute son. Their ghoulish interest was natural, I supposed. They didn't know Dennis, and they had no idea how much sorrow would ensue from the events of last night.

"Chief Eiseley will catch the bad guy, won't he?" Oliver asked. "Like before?"

Jenna snorted. "He only came in the end. Mom did most of the work." She looked at me, excitement giving her face a lively glow. "Who did it, do you know? Have you fingered him yet?"

Fingered him? Where had she picked up that term? And her excitement was a little troubling. A man was dead, after all.

"Yeah, Mom." Oliver bounced in his seat. "Did you finger him? Are you going to be in the newspapers again?"

"When you go to school today," I told him, "there will be yellow strips of plastic taping off the men's restroom down the hall from your room. You know what that means, right?"

"Sure. It means a crime was committed there."

Ah, television. "It means you're not to go in there. And if there are policemen or policewomen working, you're not to bother them. They have a job to do, and they won't have time to answer your questions."

Suddenly, I had a vision of the forensics team, heads

down, working through evidence while being peppered
with questions from a hundred small children. "What's
that for?" "What you doing?" "Have you ever killed any-
body?" "Have you caught the guy who did it?" "Do you
carry a gun? Can I see it?"

Those poor people. I battened down my smile and
focused on Oliver. "Stay out of their way, okay? They
need to do their jobs. Leave them alone and they'll be
able to catch the bad guy faster."

Oliver looked at me "Won't you be—"

There was a slight shuffle under the table. Jenna had
kicked her brother, but it must have been a message-
delivered-message-received kind of kick, because he
didn't yelp. I studied my children, trying to get inside
their heads.

"Chief Eiseley," I finally said, "is handing over the
murder investigation to the county sheriff's office. There
is no reason for me to have anything to do with this."

Jenna kept her face still and nodded. Oliver, after
watching his sister, did the same thing.

"I'm glad you two understand," I said. "Finish up. We
leave for school in five minutes."

I stood and went into the study to get my purse and
briefcase, pleased they'd understood so quickly that I
wouldn't be involved with this investigation, congratulat-
ing myself on the maturity of my children.

Then I heard their giggles.

After I dropped Oliver off at Tarver and Jenna at the
middle school, I drove through the mid-September
morning to my bookstore, the Children's Bookshelf.
Downtown Rynwood had remained remarkably pros-
perous through the last few years of economic hardship,
a fact I'd puzzled over until my store manager, Lois, had
laughed and pointed out the front window.

"Look at this place," she said. "It's like Mayberry out there. Downtown has everything you need. A diner, a grill, a fancy restaurant. Shoe store, department store, pharmacy, bank, insurance agency, flower shop, newspaper. We even have a grocery store. How many downtowns still have one of those?"

She was right. Rynwood had managed to maintain the core businesses that make a downtown stable. But that didn't answer the question of *why* it had stayed stable.

Sometimes I thought it was the distance between the buildings. Wide enough to allow angle parking on both sides of the street but still close enough that it was easy to chat with someone on the opposite sidewalk.

Or sometimes I thought the stability was due to the town's comfortable architecture. It was a happy mixture: two- and three-story brick buildings combined with a few wooden clapboard buildings, combined with a couple of oddments like Randy Jarvis's corner gas station and convenience store covered with smooth blue fiberglass siding that had faded to an unusual purple color. They were all connected by brick paver sidewalks and wide flower boxes, and it somehow made one big happy downtown.

Then again, sometimes I thought it was because of the store owners. We all lived in Rynwood, and that alone can make a huge difference to the success of a business. Plus we were a diverse group, male and female, old and young, outlandish and staid. That, too, was probably a factor.

But most often I tried not to think about it at all. As Marina had told me ad infinitum, think too much and you forget to have fun. And the corollary, think too much and you'll find something to worry about. If I was worrying, I wasn't having fun. If I wasn't having fun, my children were less likely to have fun, and I wanted them to grow up knowing that you could be a grown-up and still go outside to play, that being an adult wasn't all working and paying bills. That life was there to be enjoyed.

I'd come to that not-so-profound conclusion on my last birthday. Better late than never, Marina had said, rolling her eyes. I'd stuck my tongue out at her, which always made her laugh, and promptly blown out all the candles on my birthday cake in one blow.

Now, though, the magic of downtown Rynwood seemed to have dimmed. Sure, the sky was blue and the sun was bright and the birds were singing, but the shining happiness I'd been wallowing in the last few months had lost its luster.

I parked in the alley behind the store, as per usual, and unlocked the back door. My normal morning chores of list making and tea brewing held no appeal. Odd, for me. I decided what I needed was a talk with Flossie.

After relocking the back door, I slipped out the front and walked across and down the street. Flossie Unter- mayer, a former professional ballet dancer who had trav- eled all over the world with a Chicago-based troupe, had grown up in Rynwood, stocking shelves and running the register at her parents' grocery store. When she'd retired from dancing, she'd come back to Rynwood to take over the family business, leaving the world of dance behind forever.

I'd often wondered if there was a story behind that abrupt move, but it had happened almost two decades before I'd moved to Rynwood, and I'd never felt com- fortable asking. And there was another thing. Though she spent a lot of time with a certain Mr. Brinkley, she'd never married. Flossie, now eightyish and more limber than I'd ever been, was a wise and wonderful person, but there was something about her that didn't invite ques- tions into her past.

Sure, I could have asked Lois, who was a lifelong Rynwoodite, but that would have felt disloyal. No, either I'd buck up and ask Flossie myself, or I'd just never know.

I pushed open the glass front door of Rynwood grocery—no new-fangled automatic entry doors here—and went in search of Flossie.

A young man in his late twenties was cleaning the register checkout belts. "Morning, Patrick."

"Hey, Mrs. Kennedy. What's up?" Patrick, Flossie's great-nephew and heir apparent to the store, smiled at me. "Did you pick up some of that hamburger yet? It's only on sale through the end of the week."

"I'll try and remember to buy some before I head home today. Is your aunt around?"

He pointed his chin toward the rear of the store. "She's out back, doing the garbage."

I laughed. "Haven't been able to take that chore away from her yet?"

"Stubborn old woman," he said. "I keep saying that I'm here to make her life easier, and she keeps saying that if I make life too easy for her, she'll turn into a rocking-chair-sitting, baby-bootie-knitting old woman who just takes up space on the planet and might as well be put out on an ice floe to die."

"Does she even know how to knit?"

He shook his head. "She couldn't sew on a button if her life depended on it."

Smiling, I walked through the baking supplies aisle, cut between the meat case and the dairy case, stepped off the cheery white-and-green linoleum tile and onto the plain concrete that delineated the storage area, and pushed open the back door.

Flossie was not, as one might have expected, heaving piles of cardboard into the recycling bin or tossing black garbage bags into the Dumpster. Instead, she was sitting on top of the low retaining wall separating the store from the insurance agency next door, face up to the blue sky, smiling.

I shut the door and walked over to sit next to her.

She didn't look at me, just kept her gaze on the new day.

For a long moment, we sat together in silence. Enjoying the cool morning, enjoying the companionship, enjoying life.

The moment stretched long and deep. It wasn't until a muffler-challenged car tore through the alley that we began to talk.

"It's mornings like this," Flossie said, "that make me glad I'm still alive and kicking."

I looked at her fondly. "You say that every morning. When it's ten below with a thirty-mile-an-hour wind, you say that. When it's gray and dreary and dripping rain for ten days straight, you say that. When it's pushing eighty degrees at eight a.m., that's what you say."

"And true every time." She nodded, her short, silvery curls bobbing. "Mornings are made for appreciation, don't you think?"

In my house, mornings were made for rushing around like a nutcase, frantically trying to make sure the kids were ready for school, that the dog had been out, and that both my socks were of the same general color.

But I knew what she meant. And if the calm that radiated from her was the result of appreciating morning, maybe I needed to take my store's garbage out in the morning instead of doing it at night.

"So." Flossie turned to look at me directly. "I hear you tried to be a hero last night."

"What? Oh, no. I'm not the hero type."

She chuckled. "I heard you and Nick Casassa tried to

chase down a gang with automatic weapons and hand grenades."

And by tonight, the story would have grown even more ridiculous. "Not exactly." I told her what happened, then asked, "Did you know Dennis?"

"Knew of him. He was much younger than me. He had an older sister who dated my babiest brother for a time, but I was gone by then."

Gone to Chicago, returning only after her career was over. But Flossie had never sounded regretful about those lost days, so why should I think she was? Then, for one brief second, the politeness that kept me from diving too deeply into her personal life blinked out. "Do you miss it?" I asked. "The dancing, I mean?"

She kept her gaze on the sky and didn't say anything.

Politeness surged back, and I felt heat stain my face. "Sorry. I shouldn't have asked. Forget I said anything."

"I wasn't ignoring your question," she said calmly. "I was just trying to decide how to answer."

Oh. Well. That was different. I kept my mouth shut and waited.

"In all the years I've been back home, no one has ever asked me if I missed dancing."

Any other time or place and I would have said, "Really? You're kidding." But sitting here, catching some of the peace that enveloped Flossie, I stayed silent and gave her time to find words.

"Maybe an analogy would be best," she said at last. "As I recall, you swam competitively when you were young."

"All the way through high school." Years of training, of competition, and of hair that smelled like chlorine.

"And when you weren't on a team any longer, did you miss it?"

I thought about the luxury of sleeping in instead of getting up in the winter dark for morning practices. I thought about the excitement that had coursed through me when I stepped up onto the starting block. The hugs and cheers and tears of teammates. The long bus rides to other schools. The long meets.

"Some of it I missed a lot. Some I didn't."

"Do you still?" Flossie asked.

". . . No." Which was surprising, because for years I'd assumed I did. "No, I don't." I thought about it some more. "What I miss most, I guess, is . . ." But what did I miss? Something, certainly.

Flossie filled in the gap. "What you miss is being young," she said. "Your swimming was a part of your youth, and you miss the energy and the optimism and the sense that the world was out there waiting for you."

I looked at her. "And that's how you feel about dancing?"

"If I thought only about the dancing, I'd miss it every minute of every day. But it's never just the dancing. The rivalries, the fussing with the costumes and the costumers, the inability to ever, ever eat what I wanted . . . no. That I do not miss at all."

"You're happy." I said it as fact, not as a question, and she turned to me with a wide, brilliant smile.

"Beth, dear, you have no idea how happy I am."

"Do you think I have any chance of being like you when I'm your age?"

She laughed and put one arm around me for a quick hug. "Every chance in the world."

Thus reassured, I walked back to the store with a light heart. Everything would work out. Jenna and Oliver would grow up to lifelong happiness, I'd grow into Flossie's wisdom, the store would continue to support me into my old age, and Rynwood would continue to be Rynwood.

As I opened the front door, I was considering how long I'd stay in the large pseudo-Victorian house my former husband, Richard, and I had purchased when Oliver was born. No need to stay there by myself after the kids went on their own ways. But where would I move? There were some lovely small bungalows a few blocks from downtown. I could walk to work from there and—

"Well, if it isn't the Green Lantern." My manager stood in front of me, hands on her hips.

Today, the sixty-two-year-old Lois was wearing butter-yellow cropped pants, white sandals, and a fluorescent-green shirt. Both of her wrists were crowded with rubber bracelets. Her necklace might or might not have been pieces of colored macaroni strung on a thread, but her dangling earrings were definitely marbles.

I ignored the jewelry and gestured at the sandals. "White, after Labor Day? Are you sure you want to flout fashion dictates so flagrantly?"

She snapped a bright purple rubber band against her wrist. "Did I miss the memo on using words that start with F today? And I'm not exactly worried about the fashion police. They're too busy following Kelly Osbourne around."

"Who?"

"Stop trying to change the subject. What I want to know is why you were trying to run down a killer with nothing but your bare hands."

Ah. That explained the Green Lantern comment. Sort of. "At the time, I didn't know there had been a murder."

"Had you or had you not heard a gunshot?"

"Well, sure, but—"

"And did you or did you not run pell-mell straight toward the sound of said gunshot?"

"Yes, but—"

She rocked back on her heels and crossed her arms. "I rest my case."

I raised my hand. "May I present my final argument?"

"You may."

I made a 'come along with me' motion, and we walked to the back of the store. As I started the morning routine of tea selection, water heating, and mug choosing, I told Lois what happened the previous night. "The county sheriff's office is probably in charge of the case already." I handed Lois a mug that said KEEP CALM, EAT COOKIES and picked up my own, one Jenna had bought me years ago. Why she thought I'd like a mug featuring a yellow smiley face that sported a pair of sunglasses, I didn't know, but I treasured the cheap ceramic as if it were china made by Royal Doulton.

When I came to the end of the tale, Lois was looking at me oddly. "What?" I asked.

"The basic question is still on the table. Why on earth did you run *toward* a gunshot? Most people would hit the ground, freeze in place, or run in the opposite direction. Not you." She blew on her tea, making tiny brown ripples, and raised her eyebrows. "Why?"

"It wasn't just me. Nick did, too."

She made an impatient gesture, as if what I said wasn't important. And it probably wasn't. "You weren't thinking about your own safety. You weren't thinking about what might happen if you got in the way of bullet number two—and don't tell me there wasn't a second bullet, because you had no way of knowing there wouldn't be one—you just ran straight toward what was likely to be extreme danger. Why?"

The full import of what I'd done finally sank into my tiny little brain. "I . . . I . . ."

What had I been thinking? Or more, why *hadn't* I

been thinking? How could I have done such a thing? I should have thought about what might happen. I should have thought about the danger. I should have considered what might have happened to me and the consequences for my children. I should have . . .

Lois *tsk*ed at me and shoved a chair behind my knees. "Sit, you silly child. You hadn't really thought it out, had you? And now you're shaking. Let me take that mug before you drop it. That's a good girl. Now, take a deep breath. And another. There. Feel better?"

I nodded. The dark spots that had been shadowing the edges of my vision faded to gray and then dissolved completely.

"Okay, then," Lois said. "It's time for promises. Hold up your hand. Let me get . . ." She cast about for the nearest book. "Here. Put your left hand on this copy of *Tuesdays at the Castle*. Right hand up and repeat after me: I do solemnly swear that I will never again run straight toward what might be certain death."

I pulled my hands away. "That doesn't make sense. You can't qualify a term like certain death."

Lois hooked her index finger under her chin. "How about 'I swear I will never again run straight toward the sound of gunshots'?"

It sounded like a very good idea. "I want to, but . . ."

She sighed. "But you don't want to make a promise you can't keep. Well, we'll just have to hope you won't run into any more gunshots. I mean, really, how likely is that in a town this size?"

Next time I talked to my physicist brother, Tim, I'd have to ask if he could run the statistics for me. Or not. Because if I told him, I'd have to explain why I wanted to know, and he would inevitably tell his son, my beloved seventeen-year-old nephew, Max, and Max would tell his Grandma Emmerling, also known as my mother, and after her recent back surgery, I didn't want Mom to worry about me.

Or scold me, whichever came first.

The bells tied to the front door jingled. "Hello?" Alan, owner of the antique mall, wandered back. "Ah, there you are, Beth. I wondered if you'd be in today after last night's excitement." He hefted a small white bag. "Alice sent over some of her oatmeal-raisin cookies. She considers them medicinal," he said, winking. "Maybe she's wrong about that, but do we want to take the chance?"

Alan and Alice, both retired schoolteachers, had opened the antique mall a few years ago so that Alan could pursue his hobby of collecting antiques without having to purchase a ten-thousand-square-foot house and so that Alice could reap some financial benefits from making the best cookies in the world.

Lois dove into the bag and started handing out the morsels of goodness. Alan patted his stomach. "No, thanks. I've already had my quota today." As the two of us munched, Alan asked, "Lois, did you know the gentleman who was killed?"

I blinked at them. Of course. Dennis had attended Tarver Elementary, and Lois had lived in Rynwood all her life. Lois was bound to have known him.

"Nope," Lois said, spattering a few cookie crumbs on the sleeve of my shirt. "His family moved to Madison about the time he would have started junior high. He was a year or two behind me, and I was much too cool to hang out with the younger kids."

I brushed the crumbs off my shirt. "You were cool?"

She grinned. "Can't fool you, can I? Of course I wasn't. I didn't get cool like I am now until recently."

Though I wasn't sure that anyone who wore what she'd worn last week—a shirt with flowers the size of teapots and pants with horizontal stripes—could be considered part of the kingdom of cool, I let the comment slide. "Was Dennis?"

"Was he what? Cool?" She shrugged. "Hard to tell in someone who's only ten years old."

She was probably right. Although coolness is inherent and not something that can be learned, it usually doesn't emerge until adolescence. At least as far as I could tell. Coolness was something I only observed from afar. I'd had a brief brush with the concept when I'd dated the handsome and rich Evan Garrett, but I'd ended that relationship in May and hadn't come within spitting distance of cool since.

The front door jingled again. "Hello? Is anyone in here? Oh, there you guys are."

Whitney Heer, a young woman I'd met last spring, walked back to join us. She was pregnant, halfway through her second trimester with her first baby, and she'd begun to haunt the bookstore with happy frequency. I'd first guided Whitney toward the shelf of new-mother books. Once done with those, she'd worked through the Sandra Boynton board books and was moving on to the classic Winnie-the-Pooh releases. It had been a natural move to ask her to join the PTA. Maybe she wouldn't have a child in Tarver for a few years, but why wait until the last minute?

Whitney was wearing a loose, flowing, cotton plaid dress that looked as comfortable as pajamas. "Morning, ladies. And gentleman." She grinned at Alan. "Are you here for the same reason I'm here?"

"Yes, but I had an excuse." He pointed his elbow at the white bag. "I brought some of Alice's cookies."

"Seriously?" Her blue eyes flared wide, then went back to normal. "I mean, how nice of you to bring cookies to Beth and Lois."

I'd assumed they were also for my part-time help,

Sara, when she arrived, but I took pity on the pregnant girl. "Here," I said, holding out the bag. "We've had ours already. Right?" Lois's mouth was opening, and I bumped her ribs with my elbow.

"Oh. Right," she said. "Eat up."

Whitney held her hands behind her back. "Oh, no, I couldn't."

"Yes, you can," I said. "I know what being pregnant can be like." I jiggled the bag, making the cookies rattle against each other. "Oatmeal raisin. You know you want them. They're calling your name."

"Whitney!" Lois squeaked. "We're yours!"

With a quick whip of her arm, Whitney snatched the bag out of my hand. "I couldn't eat this morning, and now I'm starving and—" Her next words were lost amidst a monstrous bite of cookie.

I looked at Alan. "So what's the reason you and Whitney are here?"

Lois did an eye roll. "Yes, folks, she really is that clueless."

Alan chuckled. Whitney's giggles sent crumbs flying in all directions. She slapped her hand over her mouth. "Sorry," she mumbled, and made a huge swallow. "Sorry," she said out loud. "It's just that, well, you were right there and all. I was in the other room most of the time."

Light dawned. They wanted a blow-by-blow account of the whole business, the gunshot, the running, the fear, the ambulance, the body bag, the whole sad tragedy. "You want to hear about what happened last night," I said flatly.

My distaste must have been obvious, because her face went quiet, a speck of raisin on her lip. "No, it's not like that. It's more . . . well, I'm worried." She laced her hands over her mostly flat belly. "For the little bug, you know? Travis is worried that Rynwood isn't safe. After what happened last spring, you know, and now this, well . . . it doesn't look good."

Alan murmured an agreement.

"I understand your husband's concern," I said, "but I'm sure the police will find the killer soon."

"The Rynwood police?" she said doubtfully. "Chief Eiseley is, like, the nicest guy ever, but how many murders has he ever had to solve?"

More than you'd think, I almost said. "The investigation is being turned over to the Dane County Sheriff's Office."

"Oh. Well, that's good," she said. "Say, I heard you and Nick Casassa almost had the guy. Did you work with one of those sketch artists?"

So much for the being worried thing. I started to say something annoyingly weenie, something along the lines of not being able to talk about an active investigation, when the front door jingled again.

Rachel Helmstetter, mother of Blake and Mia, widow of Sam, walked in, spotted our small group and came back to join us. "Morning, everyone. Have I missed anything?"

She grinned, and almost against my will, I smiled back. Rachel had come a long way in the last year. After her husband had been killed, she'd taken the helm of his mobile shredding business. She was transforming it from a nice little venture for two partners and their two trucks into a business that had the potential to expand into Madison and out to Milwaukee

And she was making it look easy. It wasn't, of course. During the lunches we had every so often, she'd confess her doubts and fears. I'd encourage her to stifle the doubts and tramp on the fears and we'd both return to work refreshed. Every so often, I'd chuckle at the idea that fear-laden and worry-filled Beth Kennedy was helping Rachel.

Then again, who knew better how to work through fears than someone who was used to being afraid?

"I was just asking Beth about a sketch artist," Whitney said.

"Really?" Rachel asked. "Didn't the guy have a ski mask on? That's what I heard, anyway."

"Sorry I'm late." Sara rushed in the back door. "It won't happen again, I'm really sorry."

I looked at my watch. "You're all of three minutes late. Don't worry about it."

The front bells jingled again, and Glenn Kettunen, owner of the local insurance company, came in and headed straight toward us with the accuracy of a target missile. On his heels was PTA mother Isabel Olsen, and behind her was PTA mom and bank vice president Debra O'Conner.

Alan was asking Rachel something, Lois was talking to Sara, Whitney was turning and calling to Isabel, and Glenn was looking jovial, which was always an indicator that he had time to spare.

The noise was reaching the level you found inside one of those slick city-style bistros with hard floors and brick walls and tin ceilings, the kind of restaurant I stayed away from whenever possible.

I looked from one friend to another. All talking, all waving their hands, all seeming to be having the time of their lives. I made my thumb and middle finger into a circle, put it in my mouth, and blew.

The resulting earsplitting whistle had the desired effect. Silence.

"Thank you," I said. "Now. While in many ways I understand your curiosity about last night, I do not appreciate how a man's murder seems to have become entertainment." Everyone had the grace to look ashamed. Everyone except Glenn.

"Oh, come on, Beth," he boomed out in his bigger-than-life voice. "Have a heart. We know it's a tragedy. But you can't blame us for wanting to get the story straight. You were there, and we weren't."

I sighed. "Okay. But don't you dare transmogrify what I tell you to something more exciting." I gave Glenn the same look I gave my children when they were about to tell me "Yes, Mom, my homework is all done." "I know where you live, and I will hunt you down if you change one single word." I scanned the small crowd. "And that goes for the rest of you, too."

Heads nodded, so I forged ahead and related the events of the previous night. As I spoke, I tried to see the scene in black and white, trying to keep away from the vivid red I so didn't want to see. It worked. Mostly.

"And that's all I know," I finished. "Gus said the sheriff's office is taking over, so from this point on, I won't know any more than what we'll read in the papers."

"You don't really think it was someone in the PTA, do you?" Rachel looked at me, worry showing in the twist of her mouth. "Who do you think did it? I'll need to tell the kids something."

"Yeah." Glenn's bald pate shone in the halogen lights. He'd lost the majority of his hair before he was thirty and had started shaving his entire head soon after. Now in his midforties, he claimed to have no idea if he still had any hair. "You've caught more killers than Gus has. Who do you think did it?"

No way was I going to tell this group that I'd spent half the night going over and over the meeting in my head, trying to remember anything and everything. If I mentioned a single name—not that I had a name in my head; of course I didn't—half the town would have that person tried and convicted before lunchtime.

"I'm not thinking about it at all," I said firmly.

Glenn started laughing. "Tell that to someone who might believe you."

I turned to Sara. "I'm not thinking about it at all."

She shook her head. "Sorry, Mrs. Kennedy. Your ears are going all pink."

Foiled again by my body's stupid reactions. "Fine. I may be thinking about it, but I don't know anything and I'm not going to guess. The fine people from the sheriff's office will find the killer soon. That's what they do."

Debra looked at me, but didn't say anything. I knew what she was thinking, though, or close enough. How soon was soon? How long would we have to walk down the street knowing there was a killer roaming free?

I crossed my arms, cupping my elbows with the opposite hands.

Soon. It would be soon.

The nonemployees in the room straggled away, and soon just the three of us were left. I turned to Sara to ask if she wanted a cup of tea, but she preempted my question.

"I know you were just being nice about me being late." Blond and blue-eyed, tall and thin, intelligent and bookish, Sara had been all bones and angles when she'd first come to work for me three years ago. Now she was finally getting curvy, and, although she didn't yet know it, she was going to be a drop-dead-gorgeous woman.

"I'm really, really sorry," she was saying, "and I promise it won't happen again and I'll shut up now because you probably don't want to hear about how late I was up last night working on my pee chem lab."

Lois frowned. "I thought I told you to stop peeing on your chemistry project."

"I told you before." Sara pulled her hair out of its rubber band, shook it loose, and ponytailed it back up again.

"It's a physical chemistry class. And there's nothing funny about it."

Lois and I exchanged a glance. Sara had sounded downright snippy. Which was completely unlike the college senior.

When Sara turned to the sink and flipped through the basket of tea bag selections, Lois pointed at me. I pointed at her. She shook her head vigorously. We both put our right hands into fists and slapped them against our palms three times. On the fourth slap, I laid down my two splayed fingers. Scissors. Lois kept her hand as a fist. Rock. Rock grinds scissors.

Rats.

Grinning, Lois pushed me toward the young woman. "Pretend it's a training session," she whispered, "for when Jenna gets older."

Social, athletic Jenna had about as much in common with the studious and scientifically minded Sara as I had with Marie Curie, but I knew what she meant. I stood beside Sara, watching her go through the tea bags over and over.

"Sara," I asked. "Is something bothering you?"

"I'm fine," she said quickly. "Just fine."

A possibility occurred to me. Sara wasn't from Rynwood. She was from ten-mile-distant Madison, but maybe she had relatives here in town. "Did you know Dennis Halpern? The man who was killed last night?"

She picked up a tea bag—lemon zinger—and said, "No. I've never heard of him before." Her eyes went wide, and I noticed for the first time the red bloodshot streaks. "Mrs. Kennedy, were you related to him? Oh, wow, I'm so sorry. I never thought, and here everyone was wanting to know about last night and all the time you're—"

"No, I'm not related." I shook my head. "Not as far as I know, anyway."

This earned me a small smile, but it disappeared much too quickly. I watched her long, slender fingers as she dunked her tea bag in the hot water. Pianist's fingers, my grandmother would have said. Surgeon's fingers, my grandfather would have said, and in Sara's case, my grandfather would have been dead-on because Sara was aiming for medical school and orthopedic surgery.

I watched Sara dunk the tea bag far beyond normal dunking requirements and wished I knew what was bothering her. If she didn't want to tell, there was no reason she should. But I could make sure she had every opportunity to change her mind.

It wasn't until late in the afternoon, not long before the store closed, that I had another chance to talk to Sara. The day had been full of curiosity seekers in search of details about the night before (with an occasional outburst from friends who felt the need to scold me for trying to be a hero), and I was starting to look at my watch a little too often. Tomorrow would be an easier day, and it couldn't come too soon. Everyone I knew in town had either stopped by or called—even my former nearly significant other, Evan—so with any luck, the next day things would be back to normal.

I was smiling at the thought while I sat at my computer in my tiny office at the back of the store. A normal day tomorrow. How very nice that would be. I could start thinking about the Halloween orders and—

Suddenly, my mom senses went *twang!*

I'd heard something. I was sure of it. Something like . . . yes. There it was again.

I pushed back my chair and stood. Went to the door and looked around the corner.

There, standing next to the early chapter books, was Sara. But it was a Sara I'd never seen before. The normally chipper and perky young woman had laid her arms on the end of the shelving and put her head down. Her shoulders were shuddering with sobs, and her quiet sniffs were enough to make me want to cry.

I went to her side. "Sara," I said softly. "What's wrong?"

"Nuh-nuh-nothing."

Had I been this dramatic when I was her age? Sadly, I was sure I had been. "Sara, please tell me what's bothering you." I hesitated, then put my arm around her shoulders and gave her a hug. "Please let me help. I want to, you know."

"But ... don't ... you see?" she huffed out between her tears. "That's the problem!"

I didn't see. Not at all. But it didn't do to point out logic to someone in emotional distress. And if men could learn that simple fact, marriages all over the world would improve.

"If you want," I said, "come into my office. We can sit down and talk about whatever it is that's troubling you."

She drew in a long breath and stepped back. "Um, thanks, but I'm fine." She rubbed her face and her hands came away wet with tears. "Really, I'm fine." To prove it, she smiled wide, a grimace that didn't carry an ounce of happiness. "I'm just tired; that's all."

"Tired," I said. "You're sure about that?"

Her shoulders came back up. She looked at me straight on. "Honest, Mrs. Kennedy. I really am just tired. I'll catch up on sleep this weekend."

I nodded and let her get back to work, watching the top of her blond head bob between the shelves as she went to help a customer. She'd sounded like she was telling the truth. But was she? I watched her greet the woman, saw her manufactured smile, and wondered.

The next morning was Friday, the day I'd recently decided was perfect for delivering books to the local schools. For years I'd made it a point to personally drop off books that teachers had special ordered. It cost me two hours of time almost every week, but it generated a tremendous amount of loyalty, and that was beyond price.

Plus it gave me an opportunity to peek in on my son. Not Jenna, though, not now that she was in middle school. She'd made me promise with a triple cross-my-heart-and-hope-to-die-stick-a-needle-in-my-eye that I wouldn't come anywhere near any of her classrooms.

"I will die," she said. "Just die. Middle school is different, Mom."

She was right, but in spite of my promise, I'd found it difficult almost beyond bearing to walk in and out of the middle school without seeing her. So close to my daughter, yet so far. But Oliver would be at Tarver for two more years, so I had two more years of happy kid-peeking.

I plopped the box of books on the counter of the front office. "Good morning, Lindsay. How are you this fine day?"

Lindsay, six feet tall and skinny as a runway model, was as competent a school secretary as you could imagine. Teachers, parents, and the rest of the school staff continued to be amazed that she'd choose to work at the school instead of finding a higher-paying job at some fancy office in Madison. We all wanted her to stay forever, and since we couldn't do anything about the size of her paycheck, the parents had banded together and made a quiet schedule for presenting her with gifts of chocolate, cookies, and muffins.

"Getting fat," she said, thumping her bony hips. "Put on almost a pound since school started."

I looked at her.

"Gotta nip that stuff in the bud, you know." She grinned. "Want a chocolate-chip scone? Mrs. Eberhard gave me a plateful."

"Did I hear you say scones?" A round-faced woman stood in the doorway that led to the back offices. "Chocolate chip?" She spoke with the soft-edged tones of someone from the South. Charleston, South Carolina, to be specific.

"Morning, Millie." I smiled at the school psychologist. "I'll split one with you."

"Oh, my dear." She shook her head sorrowfully. "I like you very much, but scones are not to be split and shared."

"Especially Mrs. Eberhard's," Lindsay said. "Here." She held out a plate, aiming it alternately at me, then at Millie. "Scone, anyone?"

Since it would have been rude not to take what was offered, I took the smallest one. Which was still probably three hundred calories too big, but it was Friday, after all. I'd make sure to work it off playing with the kids tomorrow. Absolutely. For sure.

We ate the first two bites in reverent silence, giving Mrs. Eberhard's scones the attention they deserved. "How's it going with the new vice principal?" After lengthy deliberations, the school board had hired Stephanie Pesch in July. All I knew about her was that she had come highly recommended and that she was young.

"She's a very nice young lady," Millie said. "I think she'll do well."

"Good thing she's wasn't hired by the high school," Lindsay said, laughing. "She's a hottie."

I smiled, then asked the dreaded question. "Have the kids been affected much by Dennis Halpern's death?"

Lindsay squinched her face. "Staff and faculty more than the kids, I think. Kids are bloodthirsty little buggers."

"It's not quite real," Millie said. "To them, Mr. Halpern's murder is more like a television show that's being filmed right here at the school. They didn't see what you did, Beth."

No, they hadn't, and for that I was profoundly grateful.

"Oh, wow, I forgot." Lindsay's eyes went wide. "It must have been . . . awful."

I'd started to clench the muscles at the back of my neck, anticipating more questions, preparing for more curiosity, steeling myself to being dragged back to that night and having to tell the story all over again. But Lindsay was looking at me with sympathy, and Millie's large brown eyes were full of nothing but kindness.

"Yes," I said. "It was awful."

The room was quiet as we finished eating the scones. Millie dusted off her hands. "Well, back to work. Tests to analyze and all that. Lindsay, thank you. Beth, if you need to talk—or even if you don't need to—you know my door's always open."

I watched her go. "She's a nice lady."

"Yup." Lindsay nodded. "Say, if you want—" The electronic beeping of the phone cut across her sentence. "Oh, drat." She made a face as she picked up the phone. "Good morning. Tarver Elementary."

I waited a moment, but when she said, "Sure, I can do that for you. Just let me pull up that program, okay?" I waved good-bye and headed down the hallway to find my Oliver.

He was where he should be, inside his fourth grade classroom. From what I could tell of his concentrated look and hunched posture, the class was practicing writing. Mrs. Sullivan was a big believer in teaching cursive handwriting. No matter how loudly the students protested that they didn't need to learn cursive, why should they when everything was done on the computer, she ignored them with a bland smile and handed out worksheets.

Oliver had been in tears over the "The quick brown fox jumps over the lazy dog" homework. "I can't make a *Q*," he'd wailed. "It keeps turning into a *G*. I'm never going to get this right. I'm going to get an F on this homework, and I'm going to fail fourth grade and never get to go to college."

The tears coursing down his face had made my own eyes prickle even as I was trying not to laugh. "Sweetheart, look," I'd said, pointing at the handout. "Read what it says at the top of the page."

He'd sniffed. "Um, it says . . . you will not be graded on this homework. It says it's for ref . . . refer . . . reference purposes only."

"That's right. Do you know what that means?"

"Um, there's a reference section in the library. My homework is going to be in the library?" He'd sat up straight, mouth opening in horror.

"No. A reference is something you can look up." Sort of. "Mrs. Sullivan is going to keep your homework"—I tapped the tearstained piece of paper—"and at the end of the year, you'll write this sentence again."

"And you think I'll be better then?"

I squeezed his shoulder. "You'll be lots better."

He looked at his homework, and I could almost see the direction of his nine-year-old brain. "So I don't have to do a really good job on this?"

"You should do the best job you can," I said firmly. "You should always do your best."

"But if . . ." His voice faded off when he saw my face. He sighed. "But it's hard to always be trying so hard."

I'd kissed the top of his head. "Once you get in the habit, it's not so bad."

Now, as I watched the tip of his tongue sticking out the side of his mouth as he practiced his writing, I hoped my words had sniggled deep down inside him. If I could teach my children that you should always do your best and if I could show them that nothing mattered more than having a kind heart, then I could count my parenting as successful. Of course, it would be nice if they'd end up with a solid sense of humor and a slightly above-average dose of ambition. And if—

"Hey, Beth."

I turned. "Hey, yourself, Pete. What are you doing . . . ?" Then I made the obvious connection. "Oh. Right."

Pete Peterson owned and operated Cleaner Than Pete, a company that cleaned up things no one in their right mind wanted to touch with an eleven-foot pole. He'd started with sewers that had backed up into people's houses, expanded to tidying up vandalism, and then branched out into crime-scene cleanup.

We'd met two years ago while he was cleaning a murder scene, and last year, after his sister had moved to Rynwood with her young daughter, we'd started running into each other more often.

Pete was one of those friendly guys who didn't have a worry in the world. His typical stance was a round-shouldered comfortable slouch, hands in pockets, smile on his face. Medium height, balding, and permanently cheerful, Pete smiled easily and laughed often.

"One of these days they're going to figure out a way to keep water from being so heavy." He set the full bucket of soapy water he was carrying on the floor and flexed his hand. "Are we on for golf tomorrow?"

"The kids are already working on their strategies." Last May, Pete had volunteered to teach Jenna and Oliver how to play disc golf. The four of us had spent many a Saturday afternoon hurling plastic discs at various objects from various distances. His niece, Alison, and his sister, Wendy, occasionally joined us, and the ensuing hilarity was the stuff of which memories are made.

Pete mimicked a throw with a wrist twist at the end. "Jenna been working on that new move?"

"Every day." With Jenna, doing her best was not a problem—at least when it came to sports-related activities. Her hockey coach had endorsed the disc golf, saying that it would help her hand-eye coordination. Since she was starting to dream dreams of Olympic teams, anything that might improve her goalie skills was added to her list of things to do.

"And how about you?" Pete's smile went down a notch, from happy-go-lucky to things-could-be-worse. "It sounds like you probably had a rough couple of days. You okay?"

"Sure," I said. "It's just . . ."

Pete waited, something that few people knew how to do. Most people—myself included—would try to supply you with the words, but sometimes all you needed was a few seconds to figure out what you were really feeling and another few seconds to translate those feelings into a semblance of a sentence.

"Well, there are two things, really," I said at last. Pete nodded, so I went on. "First is that Dennis was killed.

That's hard enough. Then that he was killed at a PTA meeting that I invited him to, so I feel sort of responsible." I rubbed my eyes. "And I ran right toward what could have been deadly danger without once thinking of my children, and we didn't even catch the guy, and we couldn't save Dennis from dying, and now the whole town's talking about me and . . . and that's a lot more than two things, isn't it?" I laughed, but it came out so shaky and pathetic that I stopped as fast as I could.

"None of it is your fault," Pete said. "You know that, right? I mean, it seems pretty clear that Halpern's death was premeditated, so having him killed at your PTA meeting doesn't mean a thing. And you can't help your reactions. Maybe you ran toward danger, but it was with the intent of helping. How can you fault yourself for that? And as for everyone talking about it?" He smiled. "I think they're all proud of you."

Proud of me? As if. But it was nice of him to try and make me feel better. "In my head, I know none of it is my fault. It's here that I'm having troubles." I tapped my chest, and then I finally heard what he'd said. "You think that whoever killed Dennis planned it ahead of time?"

"Sure. If the killer was a nutcase who wanted to kill a whole bunch of people, coming into an elementary school at night is a pretty dumb place to do it."

My mind skated over and far away from the idea of mass death at Tarver. "Do you really think it wasn't a random killing? You're not just saying that to make me feel better?"

"I'm about as good a liar as you are." He grinned. "Your ears turn red, right? I stutter."

I laughed, and this time it was a real one. "I'll remember that."

"Ah, I should have kept my mouth shut. Now you

know all my secrets." Pete picked up the bucket. "So the next question is, who killed Halpern? Any ideas?"

I gave him an answer that was cast-in-stone correct. "I have no clue. And finding the killer is a job for the police. For the sheriff. I'm staying out of this completely."

"Sounds good," he said easily. "See you tomorrow, then?"

We set a time to meet in the park—barring rain—and he went back to his labors. But as I watched him walk toward the restroom where Dennis had lain, I found myself staring at the door at the end of the hallway, the door through which the killer had escaped.

And I wondered.

Chapter 5

The weekend passed happily enough. Friday night we made pizza and played a video game Jenna had been given for her birthday. Saturday morning was spent on chores, homework, and hockey practice. Saturday afternoon was disc golf, and the evening was a chicken casserole and a nice long walk with the three of us and Spot, our solid brown dog. Sunday morning we went to church, where I sang in the choir, and the rest of the day was spent reading and watching a movie.

Monday morning I parked in the alley and looked up from locking my car to see Lou Spezza being towed along by two energetic dogs. Mutts, by the look of them, with a healthy dose of golden retriever and maybe a smattering of husky. "Morning," Lou called. "Happy Monday to you." He stopped at the bottom of the stairs that led to his above-store apartment and, after a short choking moment, the dogs also stopped.

"And to you." I smiled at him. Lou's new store, Made in the Midwest, had filled in the only empty downtown storefront, and everyone from the chamber of commerce on down was giddy that we had one hundred percent occupancy. "I didn't know you had dogs." I walked behind the two stores that separated us and crouched in front of the canines.

"Didn't until Saturday." He stooped and patted the head of one dog, then the other. "Meet Castor and Pollux."

I held out my hand, knuckles up, and had it promptly licked by two long tongues. "That's a good boy. Yes, you're a good boy, too."

"They are, aren't they?" Lou beamed, his dark mustache curving up on both ends. He caressed the dogs again, his muscles rippling under the thick black hair that covered his arms.

Lou was fiftyish and strong enough to move extremely heavy boxes by himself, and that was all I knew about him. I'd never seen any sign of a wife, and the one time I'd asked, he'd looked so sad that I'd changed the subject immediately.

His happy face dimmed. "Say, you're a friend of that Summer Lang, aren't you?"

"Yes. Why?" His face went grim, and I started to get a twisty feeling about what he was going to say next.

Lou glanced left and right, then behind him. He moved in a little closer. "They're saying she might be the one who killed that man, that Dennis Halpern."

"That's nuts," I said, loud enough to have the bricks walls bounce my words back to me. "Summer wouldn't kill anyone. Why on earth would she?"

"They're saying she had a fight with him right before the PTA meeting."

The mysterious "they" was on the loose again, and they were starting to irritate me, right down to the bone. "Where did you hear this?" If Summer and Dennis had argued, it was news to me.

"Just now, at the convenience store. I went out to get a newspaper and I was behind two women who were talking about it."

"Who?"

But he shook his head. "Sorry. I don't know their names. But I'd say younger than you by a few years. And from the sounds of it, I think they're in your PTA."

I'd been petting Castor (or was it Pollux?), and my hand stopped mid-pet. "What makes you say that?"

"Oh, ah." He pulled at one end of his mustache. "Well, as I remember, and I'm getting up there in age, so don't quote me on any of this, mind you. As I recall, they were commenting on the, ah, on the fact of your presidency."

I looked at him, but he was concentrating on picking loose dog hairs off his shirt. There was a ninety-nine-percent chance that I knew who the two women had been, and there was a one-hundred-percent chance that they'd been bad-mouthing me.

"Thanks, Lou." I gave the dogs one more pat each, stood, and headed for Randy Jarvis's convenience store.

From halfway across the store's parking lot, I could see that a gaggle of people were gathered around the coffee station. Randy was standing behind the counter, silent as usual, taking in the action with the calm complacency that was his habitual attitude toward almost everything.

Come to think of it, I'd never seen him get upset about anything. Not when a gang of teenagers robbed him, not when an elderly man drove into one of his brand-new gas pumps, and not even when a monstrous cloudburst of a rainstorm flooded his store. Ankle-deep in thick, brown water, Randy hadn't stumped around in anger or broken down in sobs at the wreck of his store. He'd glanced around, then phlegmatically gone to work cleaning up the mess.

There was something to be said for such an approach, but I wasn't sure we got to choose the basic way that we approached life. I was a list maker. Randy was a plodder. Marina was a court jester. As I pushed open the glass door of Randy's Quick Mart, I looked at the faces and added a few more. Denise, my hairstylist, was a talker. CeeCee Daniels, PTA member, was a follower. Kirk Olsen was a doer, but only after someone had told him what to do. Which made his recent career switch to stockbroking a puzzle Marina hadn't yet grown tired of trying to solve. Violet Demps was a thinker. And Glenn Kettunen was . . .

"I'm shocked, shocked to hear this," he said.

Glenn was an actor.

"Shocked about what?" I asked.

The entire group turned as one unit to face me.

"Well," Glenn said heartily. "If it isn't our friendly neighborhood bookstore owner. What brings you out so early on a Monday morning?"

I gave him a look. "What are we so shocked about?" I scanned the faces. "Anyone?" Not one of them met my gaze. "Randy?" I asked over my shoulder. "Were Claudia and Tina in here earlier?"

CeeCee gasped. "How did you know?" she asked in her high, little-girl voice.

Ever since she'd been a happy collaborator in the picketing of my store, I'd found it hard to be anything more than polite to CeeCee. And even politeness was difficult some days. This was one of those days.

I ignored her question and turned to Randy. "What were they saying about Summer?"

Randy sipped at a cup of coffee. "That she'd been fighting with Dennis before the meeting the other night."

"An argument?"

"Yeah." Randy nodded and laid his fleshy arms on the counter. Which must have been hard to do, considering the size of his stomach, but maybe his counter had been specially designed. "Claudia said that's how things get started, is with fights." He looked at me sorrowfully.

"She's right, you know. And they say Summer has a mean temper."

A pox on Claudia. And whoever "they" might be. "Did you hear the argument?" I asked.

Randy shrugged. "Just what Claudia said."

I whipped around and faced the others. "Did any of you hear Summer and Dennis Halpern arguing?"

Kirk spoke up. "I saw Summer looking plenty mad right before the meeting started."

"But you didn't hear or see her talking to Dennis."

"Well, no, but . . ."

I waited. When he didn't go on, I prompted him. "But what?"

He shuffled his feet. "Nothing."

What he was thinking and not saying was probably along the lines of: But Claudia said Summer's your hand-picked PTA secretary and you won't believe anything bad about her, that you won't see the truth if it's about to bite you on the nose."

"Repeating what Claudia said about Summer is, at best, sheer gossip." I said this loudly and clearly. "At worst, you could be interfering in a police investigation. If you have solid information, talk to Gus. If you don't, maybe you should consider keeping quiet."

I fixed each and every one of them with a hard mom look, the one that says "pay attention to what I said or you'll be sorry."

But even as I walked away, I was regretting my outburst. My mom powers didn't have any hold over adults.

Instead of helping, what I'd done might have made things even worse for Summer.

"You said that out loud?" Marina stared at me. She was in the act of handing me a skirt with a slit up to there and a knit shirt with a deep V-neck down to here, and I welcomed the pause in the action. Marina's latest improve-Beth scheme was a makeover of my wardrobe, and it was starting by way of her asking if I wanted any of her old stuff she was getting ready to donate. "You said that in front of real live people? Seriously?"

"I'm afraid so."

"Afraid?" She shook the clothes. "Take these. Go into the bathroom and try them on. What are you afraid of, exactly?"

I tossed the skirt over my arm and held the shirt up against me. "In these clothes, I'd be afraid of hypothermia."

"Just put them on. You were defending Summer. What's wrong with that?"

"Because I'm sure it came across as me being"—being what? I thought back to what I'd said and tried to hear the words from the point of view of a listener—"being snotty."

"Oh, fiddle-faddle. It was the truth." Marina pointed at my shoes. "And those have to go. How can anyone get mad at you for telling the truth?"

I looked at her.

"Okay, okay." She grinned. "Maybe there's lots of reasons."

The bottom of the V-neck was landing somewhere in the land south of my bra and north of my belly button. I pulled it higher. "What I'm afraid of is that my outburst will hurt Summer."

Marina reached out and rearranged the shirt so the V was an inch lower. "Do you really think any of them will tattle to Gus about Summer fighting with Dennis just because you called them gossips?"

I laid the clothes over the back of one of Marina's kitchen chairs. The only possible way I'd ever wear that skirt or that blouse was on top of a pair of overalls. "I suppose not, but I sounded like a mom. Scolding adults never does much good."

"What, you think kids pay any attention when they're being yelled at?" Marina asked.

"Sure. Until they start school. Then not a chance."

"Speaking of chances...," she said, fingering the clothing I'd rejected.

"Not a single solitary one."

"You'd look like a goddess in this." She put the skirt up against her waist.

"I'd feel like an idiot. And where would I wear something like this? If I'm ever invited to a wedding in Las Vegas, I'll call and ask to borrow it."

She sighed. "I wore it when the Devoted Husband and I went dancing, back in the day."

I eyed the skirt's waistband. It might have reached halfway around her, but probably not. "What day was that?"

"The one right before we got married." She twirled and the deep red skirt flared out.

A vision of Marina's engineer husband dancing the night away was not something I wanted to come sneaking into my dreams on little cat feet. "Anyway," I said, "I shouldn't have said anything to that group. It'll just get back to Claudia, and it'll be harder than ever to work with her."

"But Gus probably knows about Summer already, don't you think?" Marina reached into the bag she'd dragged down from her attic and pulled out another ensemble. This one included an iridescent pair of pants that looked like something from a harem and a blouse that looked suspiciously see-through. "About Summer and Dennis fighting, I mean."

I thought back to the night of the murder. Of how long Nick and I had sat in that room. Thought about the carefully worded questions Gus had asked. "You're right," I said. "He probably does know."

"Of course I'm right." She brandished the clothes at me until I took them. "Someday you'll quit arguing with me about every little thing and start agreeing with me right off the bat. It'll save us mountains of time."

"What, and miss all this fun?"

I started to put the new clothes on top of the others, but she *tut-tut*ted. "Now, now. No rejecting without at least giving them a chance."

I held out the pants, then laid them on the chair. Held the top up to myself, then laid it on the chair. "Of course you're right? Are you saying you're never wrong?"

"Moi?" She dug back into the bag. "Since you're rejecting the glorious outfit I wore to a New Year's Eve party the year we got married, I'll go straight to the dress you're guaranteed to fall in love with at first sight. And speaking of right and wrong, what's wrong with Oliver?"

I looked down the hall to the family room, where Zach, Marina's youngest, was playing Wii bowling with Jenna and Oliver. The sounds of electronic pins tumbling down were drowned out by young cheers.

"Nothing's wrong with Oliver," I said.

Marina halted, her arm thrust deep into the bag. "You haven't noticed anything?"

"No. He's fine. Or was this morning. Do you think he's coming down with a cold?" I turned and made a move for the living room—Mom to the rescue!—but Marina called me back.

"It's not like that," she said. "It's more like . . . like he's worried about something."

My mothering cells went from a full-red alarm alert to a soft orange status. "I'll bet it's because his classroom is right down the hall from where Dennis was killed. He was upset after Agnes died. Maybe this is bringing back the memory." Two years ago, the principal of Tarver Elementary had been murdered. In her home, not at the school, but her death had troubled then seven year-old Oliver deeply.

But Marina was shaking her head. "No, I don't think that's it. He and Zach were trying to one-up each other on who had talked to the forensics team the most." She pulled a garment half out of the bag, glanced at it, glanced at me, then pushed it back down. "Oliver won, by the way, because Pete Peterson said hello to him."

Good old Pete. "What makes you think something's wrong?"

"He didn't want an after-school snack today."

"No snack?" That didn't make sense. Oliver always claimed that he was starving to death when he was done with school.

"Nope. Tried apples, bananas, and pears. Tried potato chips, cookies, and brownies. Nothing." She held out a glittery silver sheath.

I took the dress and put it on the seat of the chair. I was afraid that if I draped anything else over the back that it would tip over in one of those slow-motion topples. I'd lunge forward to save the clothes from hitting the floor, Marina would do the same, our heads would thunk together with a sickening noise, and we'd both fall to the ground, unconscious, while our children went on with their virtual bowling game, oblivious to our injuries.

Far better to put the dress on the chair's seat. "Other than the snacking—"

Marina interrupted. "The nonsnacking, you mean."

I looked at her. She'd spent almost fifty years in the land of hyperbole and exaggeration; now she was going to start living a life of accuracy? "Okay, the nonsnacking. Other than that, have you noticed anything wrong?"

"Not unless you think his dedication to trying to beat his sister in Super Mario is cause for concern."

When Oliver started getting up at three in the morning to sharpen his video game skills, I'd start worrying. Until then, it wasn't exactly high on my worry list. The nonsnacking thing, on the other hand, was a very bad sign.

"I'll talk to him," I said. "He's probably going through some kick on . . . on . . ." There had to be something appropriate to fill in the blank, but nothing was popping into life. ". . . On a gluten-free diet." Which didn't make any sense at all. "Who knows what lurks in the minds of nine-year-old boys?"

"Probably nothing we really want to know about." Marina made a face.

But I did want to know. I wanted to know what my children were thinking from the minute they woke up in the morning to the second they went to sleep. It couldn't happen, of course. I didn't even know what *I* thought about all day long. And if I did know what was going on in the heads of my offspring, I'd probably be alternately proud and horrified with a heavy emphasis on horrified.

Which led to another complication. If I did know what they were thinking, would I have to punish them for their thoughts? That didn't seem fair. Then again, actions spring from thoughts and—

"Speaking of things lurking in minds," Marina said. "What's in yours?"

"Nothing," I said. Nothing worth repeating, anyway.

"Please, my deah," she said, suddenly in Southern-belle mode. "Ah do declare that you are a worse liar now than evah." She shook her head sadly. "You didn't even say a word and those little eahs of yours started turning pink."

I touched my earlobes. "They are not."

"Just the teensiest bit." She held her thumb and forefinger a fraction of an inch apart. "And if you don't believe me, go look in the mirror. No need? I didn't think so. Now, tell Aunt Marina what's troubling you."

"What makes you think something's wrong?"

"Please. Oliver isn't snacking, and you've been sitting in my kitchen for half an hour and haven't once looked at the clock."

"You're calling me a clock watcher?"

"When you have to get home and start dinner for your kids, you are."

"That's not clock watching; that's taking care of my children."

"Tomato, tomahto." She flipped her hand back and forth. "Does anyone actually say tomahto? Never mind. What I really want to know is if there's something you want to talk about."

Then she sat back in her chair and waited.

It was moments like this that reminded me why Marina Neff had been my best friend for two decades. On any given day she could try the patience of a canonized saint. Her children, both Zach and the older ones who'd already left the nest, had learned to tolerate her by ignoring eighty percent of what she said. Her DH rarely heard anything anyone said, so that worked out. Then there was me, and I'd long ago learned to look past the over-the-top antics and listen to the kind heart underneath. Some days it was harder than others. Today, not so much.

I sighed. "Would you believe me if I said I wasn't sleeping well because I've been troubled about the devaluation of the dollar?"

"Nope."

I studied my dull reflection in the oak tabletop and thought about what I didn't want to think about.

"It's Dennis, isn't it?" Marina asked.

Using my index finger as a paintbrush, I traced an outline of my head.

"Please don't tell me you're feeling guilty about his death."

"Okay, I won't."

Her shoulders rose and fell as a small sigh gusted out of her. "And how many times will I have to tell you it's not your fault before you start believing me?"

"You'll have to get in line behind Gus and Pete," I muttered.

"Two smart guys. You should listen to them."

I drew my outline again. It didn't look any better the second time. "I'm the one who asked Dennis to come to the meeting. He didn't want to, but I called him and called him and he finally agreed."

"Not your fault."

"And now Summer is being pilloried by the entire town." My words cracked, and guilt came pouring out. "If there's a fly in her house, Summer traps it in her hands and takes it outside. There's no possible way she could have killed a human being. So she had a fight with Dennis, what of it? She knew him from somewhere before; that's all. She was the one who gave me his name in the first place, so she must have thought he was okay. It's a small town, they could be neighbors, for all I know, and arguing about . . . about tree trimming."

"It's not your fault."

"I try and think that. Over and over. And just when it's starting to work, I suddenly get this feeling that if it weren't for me, Dennis would still be alive."

Marina reached across the table and held my hand quiet. "Beth, listen to me. None of this is your fault."

I looked straight into her understanding eyes. "How can it not be?"

She patted my hand. "Because it isn't, okay? And

you'd better not doubt me. I'm a mom, and moms know these things."

"Does it work when you're not my mother?"

She ignored that. "There's one way to get you off this guilt trip, you know."

"What's that?"

"Find the killer."

"Oh, no. Not that again. There's no way I'm going to—"

She plowed right over my objections. "We'll start tomorrow, right after lunch. Wear black." One final hand pat; then she stood. "Zach?" she called. "Turn off that TV. It's almost time for dinner."

I opened my mouth, then shut it again. There was the odd chance that she was right. I thought of all the wondering I'd done the last few days. Wondering about Claudia and Summer and wondering about the door at the end of the hallway and about Dennis and about all the whys and whens and what-ifs.

It was time to stop wondering. And time to start thinking.

Chapter 6

There are a lot of things in this world that I don't much care for. When I was a child, I thought growing up would mean never having to do anything I didn't want to. How kids get that idea, I do not know, but we all did and they all do. Of course, if we knew at age seven that every day of our lives would be filled with doing things we'd really rather not, none of us would choose to grow up at all.

"Doesn't sound like a bad idea," I said.

"What's that?" Marina asked. She was just ahead of me as we walked into the Rose Room. The noise level was that odd muted loudness peculiar to funeral homes and really bad parties.

"Wearing black is a bad idea," I said, picking an imaginary dog hair off my black pants, "when you have pets."

She slid me a glance. "Your cat is black and your dog is brown. If you're picking off white hairs, they're your own and not a household mammal's. So what, pray tell, is a bad idea?"

I didn't answer. Didn't have to. Marina knew how I felt about funerals, and since visitations at funeral homes were an extension of the funeral experience, I hated them, too. A character flaw, without a doubt, but it was thick and deep and no matter how many times I went through the visitation/funeral sequence, I hadn't learned to embrace it. Any of it.

"Oh, come on." Marina hooked her arm through mine and nodded at our surroundings. "Lovely room, soft music, fresh-cut flowers. What's not to like?"

It was a lovely room. The Scovill Funeral Home was in what had originally been the residence of a family who'd made their late 1800's fortune in Wisconsin lumber. When the lumber boom had ended, the family moved away to find greener entrepreneurial pastures.

The Scovill family had owned it for almost fifty years, and they'd done a tremendous job of restoring, renovating, and maintaining the Victorian-era building. There were polished oak doors and polished oak trim. Beveled glass in the windows, period wallpaper everywhere. Plaster medallions decorated the ceiling, and the carpet was so thick it almost needed mowing.

But no matter what the decor, no matter what the music, and no matter how nice the flowers were arranged, I couldn't get my thoughts away from the sad fact that the place existed because people died.

I hated funerals and I hated funeral homes. Every time I said so, Marina told me I should quit being so afraid of death. She was probably right, but how does one go about doing that? It's not like you can try it once and see how you like it.

"Look at that." Marina bumped my rib cage. "The box is closed. That should make you happy, yes?"

Absolutely yes. To me, open caskets were the worst part of it all. That particular quirk was probably due to an unfortunate incident in my youth while at the visitation for a friend's grandmother. Somehow I'd managed to trip on a flat carpet and fallen forward against the casket. The resulting thump had dislodged Grandma just enough to give me shrieking nightmares for weeks.

"Still does," I said, eyeing the casket. It was hard to see through the mass of people, but I could make out the long, dark oblong at the front of the room.

"What?" Marina asked. "Speak up. It's a little loud in here."

We inched deeper into the room. Here, the acoustics were such that we could hear the conversations of the people immediately adjacent to us, but beyond that we could hear only murmurs.

I didn't want to hear anyone else's conversation. Marina, however, was listening to the couple next to us as they quietly but fiercely argued about where to go for their upcoming anniversary. I knew them vaguely from church, and since I could tell Marina was about to offer a suggestion (or else point out that they wouldn't be having many more anniversaries if they didn't stop fighting), I said, "Looks like half of Rynwood is here. Between the two of us, is there anyone we don't know?"

Marina made a quick scan of the faces. "There's a whole group over there I don't know. And I'm not sure who's standing next to Mack Vogel."

I craned my head around to see who was standing next to our stocky, white-haired school superintendent. "That's Mack's sister. She and her husband live in Virginia."

"Hmm." Marina was still scanning the room, but her gaze had changed from that of recognition to one of speculation. "Do you realize who's here?"

"Lots of people." Actually, it was one of the biggest turnouts I'd ever seen at a visitation. I'd heard Dennis had had a number of ex-wives and a large assortment of children and stepchildren. Maybe a lot of the people here were family. Or maybe in the years Dennis had lived in Rynwood he'd made a lot of friends. Or maybe his parents had known a lot of people. Auntie May was holding court up near the front of the room. If I remembered, I'd ask her. Or not. If I asked, she would tell me, and the sitter I'd hired for the evening had to be home by ten.

"Exactly."

"Exactly what?" Having a conversation with Marina could be like trying to run while bouncing a ball on cracked concrete. Sometimes you and the ball were moving in the same direction, sometimes the ball took a hard turn while you kept going straight.

"I bet the odds are good," she said. "More than good. I bet they're up above ninety percent."

"What, that these shoes are going to permanently deform my toes before the end of the night?"

"That there's, like, a ninety-five-percent chance that the killer is in this room." She closed one eye and nodded slowly. "This very room."

I looked around. Saw friends and acquaintances. Fellow business owners and PTA parents. Church members and residents of Sunny Rest. Saw a room full of people with whom I shared the streets and sidewalks. Most of them I liked, many of them I liked very much. Sure, there were a few I didn't like, but I didn't want any of them to be a murderer. Not even the ones I would be happy to see move to another continent.

It was a selfish wish, of course. I didn't want to know someone who could kill. I didn't want to know a murderer, I didn't want to know that I'd sold a book to someone who could end a person's life.

Marina bumped my shoulder. "Now, there's a good candidate for a killer if there ever was one."

"Mack?" I asked doubtfully. It wasn't unheard of for him to turn red and blustery at school board meetings, but that was due to his inability to suffer fools for more than their prescribed five minutes of speaking time. But Mack, kill someone? I didn't see it. He was more the lawsuit type than the type to take the law into his own hands.

"Don't be silly. Mack Vogel wouldn't get his hands dirty. No, I mean her." She jerked her chin at a fiftyish woman with blond hair that stayed blond courtesy of regular visits to the hair salon. She was standing with a woman about her own age, another blonde, only her hair color was courtesy of nature. Or so I'd heard.

"Marcia?" I asked.

"Of course Marcia. See those beady little eyes? See how she's looking at you? If looks could kill, you'd be roasting over a spit and half-done by now."

Lovely image. But I knew why Marcia Trommler hated me. Just under a year ago, I'd fired her. It had been an easy decision to justify: She'd come in late, she'd leave early, she'd called in often to say she couldn't make it into work because of her grandson's swimming lessons, and so on. I'd never been fired, but it must be a horrible feeling. So it was easy to understand why she hated me. I didn't like it, but I understood.

I watched her now as she chatted with Melody Kreutzer. Melody worked at Glenn Kettunen's insurance agency, doing I didn't know exactly what. Glenn always said she was worth her weight in gold, but that could have meant she wrote up more life insurance policies than anyone in the region or that she had knack for ordering out lunch and bringing it back still piping-hot.

Marcia kept darting little glances in my direction, Melody kept adjusting her numerous and ubiquitous bracelets. The two actions seemed almost to be choreographed. Marcia glared at me, Melody fiddled with a bracelet. They talked, Marcia glared, Melody fiddled. It needed only a catchy jingle and they could have been a public-service announcement for signs of obsessive-compulsive behavior.

"If she was the killing type," I said, "she would have killed me last year."

Marina nodded. "Good point. She's the kind that will lash out in anger. Makes you wonder if she has a license to carry."

"To . . . carry?"

Marina rolled her eyes. "License to carry a concealed handgun."

"Oh, right. I knew that."

"Of course you did. Just like I know who wrote *Billy Budd.*"

"Herman Melville," I said. "And why did that come up?"

"Saw it on the DH's Netflix queue list. I was pretty sure it was a book first, though."

I should have known.

"How about him?" Marina surreptitiously pointed to Lou Spezza. Surreptitiously for Marina, anyway. I could tell because she kept her index finger below the level of her shoulder.

"His store's only been open for a month," I said. "Far as I can tell, he didn't even know Dennis."

"Then why is he here?"

When she saw that I didn't have an answer, she gave a small crow of triumph. "One point for the good guys."

"I thought we were on the same team."

"Of course we are. But that doesn't mean I can't enjoy scoring points off you every once in a while."

"Some friend you are. Now, give me one good reason why Lou would kill Dennis."

"I have lots." She waved her hands around. "Lots. Like . . . like Dennis was parking behind Lou's store without permission."

"That's a reason to kill someone?"

"Haven't you ever heard of road rage?"

"In an alley?"

"Road rage can happen anywhere," she said darkly. "Besides, he looks like a killer, don't you think? Those hairy arms?" She shuddered. "Imagine that arm wrapped around your neck, choking the life out of you." She hacked out a breath. "And that big black mustache is a dead give-away. No innocent person has a mustache like that."

I looked at her. "If a mustache is an indication of murderous intent, the police would have arrested Joe Sabatini days ago."

She sighed, and for good reason: I was right. Last summer, Joe Sabatini, owner of Sabatini's, the town's premier pizza place, had grown the bushiest mustache I'd ever seen. It was the result of a lost bet over the Stanley Cup play-offs, and he'd morosely said he'd have to wear it until the next year's play-offs.

Marina furrowed her brow and studied the crowd, which by now had swelled even larger. "Are you going to shoot down all my theories?"

"Only the ones that don't make sense."

Her gaze lasered in on someone, but there were too many people in the room for me to figure out the identity of her latest target. "Why do you make things so difficult?"

"Why do you ignore the facts?"

"Facts, schmacts. I don't need logic to tell me *that* woman would run down anyone who got in her way." She flung out her arm and pointed her index finger straight ahead.

I moved to her side so I could follow the line. "Alice? You must be joking. She's more likely to feed someone to death than to shoot them."

"Of course not Alice." She shook her finger. *"Her!"*

The crowd moved and shifted, and suddenly a line of sight opened and I saw exactly who Marina meant. And she was right. That woman would run over anyone who got in her way. But since the running over-ing would be done with a wheelchair, and since the occupant of the wheelchair weighed less than a hundred pounds, you couldn't exactly claim murderous intent even if all four wheels ran over a fallen torso.

There was only one problem. "Give me one good reason why Auntie May would kill Dennis Halpern."

"At age five, he rode his tricycle over her petunia bed and she's harbored a grudge ever since."

I considered the theory. It wasn't bad. Matter of fact, it was pretty good. There was only one problem. "Whoever shot Dennis ran away. On two feet."

We both studied the diminutive form. Auntie May hadn't been out of her purple wheelchair since she broke her hip years ago and moved to Sunny Rest where she could terrorize the residents, the staff, and visitors without having to set foot outside.

"Well, bugger boo." Marina made a clicking noise with her tongue. "Another perfectly good theory down the tubes."

I glanced over at her. "You don't really think Auntie May killed him, do you?"

"Of course not." She looked affronted. "And I don't think Lou or Marcia did it, either."

"Do you have any honest-to-goodness, take-it-to-the-judge suspects?"

"Can I count my standard theory?" Her eyebrows rose in same way Spot's did when he saw anyone come within five feet of his leash.

"The one that says Claudia did it?" I asked.

"It's my favorite," she said, clasping her hands together under her chin. "Wouldn't it be lovely to know that she was stuck in some prison somewhere and that she wouldn't be seen in Rynwood for years upon years? Come on, admit it."

The idea did have a certain attraction. However . . . "Why would Claudia kill Dennis?"

"Because she can't stand the idea of you as PTA president."

"Then why didn't she kill me?"

"Because she wants to make the run up to your death a slow and agonizing wait."

I eyed her. "That doesn't make any sense."

"Why does it have to? Does murder always make sense? I bet most times it doesn't. And if Claudia is involved, I'm sure it doesn't."

Or at least that's what I think she said. I was only half listening because in our shuffle forward toward what I always thought of as a receiving line, we'd wound up standing behind a man I knew only by sight. He lived in Rynwood and worked at a high-powered law firm in Madison, but since he didn't shop downtown, didn't attend my church, and since his children were grown, our paths had never crossed.

I only knew who he was due to seeing him occasionally at the country club, back in the days when I was dating Evan. The man was wearing a dark blue suit, white shirt, striped tie, and polished shoes and was talking to another fiftyish man dressed almost identically. They resembled each other physically, too, with their squared shoulders and how their heads set and how their hands moved. Brothers, maybe? Although their resemblance was more in the way they carried themselves than in the shape of their faces or bodies.

"Beth, are you in there?" Marina asked.

I put my finger to my lips and tipped my head at the pair in front of us.

"No, it's been a while since I saw him," Evan's friend was saying.

His companion said, "We had a drink together last summer. I was coming out of court and he was passing by. It was nice to catch up."

Two attorneys. No wonder they looked alike. They'd probably gone to the same law school.

I gave myself a mental shake. Bad Beth, for thinking such a thing. There were plenty of lawyers out there who were kind and considerate people who wanted only to help others. They were out there somewhere. I was sure of it.

"Wish I'd made the time," Evan's friend said. He sounded regretful, as people do. "He called me a few weeks back."

"Dennis did?" A gap opened ahead of them, and the companion moved one purposeful step forward. Evan's friend did, too, making it an almost simultaneous move.

"He wanted to make an appointment. I had him talk to my secretary, and we were set to meet next week. He said it wasn't a rush. He wanted to make a small change in his will."

The companion made a "huh" noise. "That reminds me. My daughter and her husband are having a baby. I should make some changes in my own will."

Their talk quickly went into attorney-speak. Marina clutched at me. "Did you hear that?" she whispered fiercely. "Did you hear?"

"Makes you wonder, doesn't it?" I mused. A small change to one person could be a big change to someone else. To some people, a bequest of, say, five thousand dollars, would be an insult. To others, it would be the difference between having a full stomach and going hungry. Was everything relative? Was there, anywhere, a universal truth? Was there any single belief that all humankind shared and—

"I bet that's why Dennis was killed." Marina's face was alive with speculation. "He was going to cut someone out of his will, and that person killed him before the papers got drawn up."

Trust Marina to make a situation as melodramatic as possible. "He said a small change, remember?"

She shrugged. "Who's to say what's small and what isn't?"

As that was exactly what I'd been thinking, I couldn't disagree with her. On the other hand . . . "Maybe instead of cutting, he was going to add someone to his will." A new grandchild, maybe. Or maybe he wanted to increase what he'd like to donate to his alma mater, wherever that might be. Or maybe—

"Maybe he had a mistress and wanted to leave her a bunch of money."

Back to the soap opera. "Dennis was sixty years old. What would he be doing with a mistress?"

"Don't be such a naïf, Beth."

Naïf? What new TV show had she been watching?

"Men are men at any age," she went on. "Get a couple of willing participants and who's to say what goes on behind closed doors?"

I was suddenly glad that doors did, in fact, close. There were a lot of things I didn't want to see. Or even speculate about. And, speaking of which, it wasn't exactly appropriate of us to be talking about Dennis and his imaginary mistress at his visitation, of all places. "We really shouldn't be—"

"Oh, no." Marina's eyes went round. "What if his mistress was"—she leaned close to whisper in my ear— "Summer? He wanted to break it off but she didn't, and she got angry and—"

"No," I said loudly. Loudly enough that the lawyers in front of us turned to look. I gave them an apologetic smile.

They glanced at each other, and though I didn't see the mutual eye roll, it was inherent in the lift of their eyebrows. They turned back around and I glared at Marina.

"No way did Summer kill Dennis," I said quietly. "No way was she his mistress. That's just stupid, and you know it. Summer and her husband are happily married, and you're just making up stories to satisfy your bizarre need to make things as exciting as possible. Summer is our friend, and you will stop this right now."

"But maybe—"

"No." I crossed my arms. "Quit with the wacked-out theories. If you want to help, you have to think like a sensible person."

She sighed. "But that's hard. And not nearly as much fun."

"This isn't about you having fun; it's about Dennis." I nodded toward the front of the room, where the long rectangular box lay in rest. "And about his family. They're the ones who deserve to know what really happened."

Then I thought about what I'd just said. Yes, they deserved to know what happened, but did it really matter? When the police tracked down the killer and sent him away forever, Dennis would be just as dead. Would knowing that the murderer was in prison help them heal any faster? Would the knowledge of justice being done ease the pain?

I didn't know. And, with any luck, I'd never have to learn the answer.

"Okay," Marina said. "No more fun. We're going to think. And if we're thinking that Dennis changing the will had something to do with his death, we need to find out who's in the will."

A shift in the line thinned the mass of people in front of us, and suddenly we saw the entire Halpern family standing in a line. A long line. A really, really long line.

"Wow," Marina breathed. "I had no idea Dennis had such a big family."

I took a quick head count. Even assuming each of his children had married and was accompanied by a spouse, that still resulted in eight children. "I'm sure some are stepchildren."

"And every one a suspect," she said with satisfaction. "One of them is bound to be the killer, don't you think, protecting her or his inheritance? And even better, we don't know any of them. No emotions involved. It will be all clinical and detached."

One of the women in line turned. The moment I saw her face, Marina's latest theory went out the window. "Back to the drawing board," I said, nodding at the woman and the man next to her.

"Is that Staci Yost?" She peered at the woman. "And her husband . . . What's his name . . . ? No, don't tell me." She snapped her fingers. "Ryan. I had no idea that Dennis was Staci's father. Or I suppose Ryan could be a stepson. Or Staci could be a stepdaughter, come to think of it."

The permutations of an amalgamated family's structure were extensive and more complicated than I wanted to think about at this point. "Shhh," I cautioned, because we were at the start of the line.

"I'm so sorry for your loss," I murmured to a fortyish man. "Dennis was a fine man. He will be missed."

"Thank you for coming," he said. "My dad would have been pleased to know how many people cared for him."

He released my hand and turned to Marina. I went on to the next person in line. We exchanged similar comments and I went on to the next grieving family member.

"So sorry for your loss. . . . My sympathies to your family. . . ." And then I was shaking Staci's hand. She was one of the younger mothers in the PTA at not yet thirty, and she'd impressed me with her constant willingness to pitch in to do the hard work. "It's for the kids," she'd always say, shrugging off my compliments. "I don't mind a little work if it's the kids who benefit."

I squeezed her hand and tried to give her a hug around the shoulders with my free arm. "Staci, I'm so sorry. I had no idea you were related to Dennis. If there's anything I can do, let me know."

Her body stood straight and tall against my light embrace. "You're already done enough, thanks so very much."

The brittle words startled me. "I'm . . . very sorry."

"Oh, sure you are." She jerked her hand out of my grasp. "If it wasn't for you, my dad would still be alive. My kids would still have their grandpoppa."

Her fierceness struck at me hard. I hadn't once considered that the grandchildren had lost a grandparent. How could I have been so thoughtless? I knew full well what it was like for children to be without a grandfather. Why hadn't I thought this through? "I . . ." But what could I say?

"Staci," Ryan murmured.

"What?" She twisted the question into a piercing accusation. "Beth's the one who asked Dad to go to that stupid PTA meeting in the first place."

Her husband put his hand on her shoulder. "This isn't the time or place."

"I think it's exactly the time and the perfect place." She flung out her arm and pointed at the gleaming casket. "There's my dad. He was killed at her meeting. How can it not be her fault that he's dead?"

The room had fallen silent. There was no noise, only a hushed quiet that held a terrible tension.

"I'm so sorry," I said, stumbling over the tears that were filling my throat.

Then I fled.

Chapter 7

After I dropped the kids off at school the next morning, I parked the car behind the store and went straight to the police station, not passing go, definitely not collecting two hundred dollars, and not even pausing at the store to check e-mail.

My family had eventually learned that the best place to e-mail me was through the store's e-mail, and my morning mailbox was often crowded with single-sentence imperatives from my mother ("Start teaching Jenna how to cook"), questions from my sister Kathy ("When was the last time you called Mom?"), bad jokes from my sister Darlene (Question: Why did checkout lines start asking, "Paper or Plastic?" Answer: Because baggers can't be choosers), and questions from my seventeen-year-old nephew, Max.

Max was the only child of my physicist brother, Tim, and his molecular biologist ex-wife. When they'd divorced a few years back, they'd renovated their house southwest of Chicago into a duplex, pleasing the three major parties involved. It puzzled everyone else, but it made the shared custody arrangement easy on Max, and that was the most important thing.

The big problem these days was how Max was going to tell his science-fixated parents that his current career plans didn't include any sort of science. His e-mails were full of plaintive queries such as: "Mom and Dad make *jokes* about liberal arts colleges. They're never going to let me go to one," or "Dad thinks reading fiction is a waste of time. He's going to hit the ceiling when I tell him I want to teach high school English."

Our back-and-forth e-mailing on the topic was getting a little more frantic now that Max was a high school senior. "Mom and Dad want me to take a tour of college campuses. But they're all tech schools. What am I going to do?" My calm replies were having less and less effect, and a long and unpleasant phone call with my brother was starting to become an inevitability.

I sighed as I scuffed down the sidewalk. Tim wouldn't understand why Max had been talking to me instead of him. Tim wouldn't understand how Max could possibly turn his back on his inherent mathematical abilities. Tim would think that Max was being shortsighted and not seeing things clearly. Talking to Tim about something he didn't understand was an extremely frustrating exercise. He didn't understand that he didn't understand, and that made a true discussion impossible.

Poor Max. How he'd turned out to be such a good kid with a father like that, I didn't know. I'd had a hard enough time having Tim as a brother, but at least my dad had listened to me when I'd needed to talk. Though Dad had died far too young, he'd lived long enough to help shepherd the four of us kids through school.

I pushed open the door to the police station, my mind full of family.

"Good morning, Mrs. Kennedy." Officer Sean Zimmerman, handsome and impossibly young, smiled at me from his desk behind the high counter. "How are you today?"

And just like that, his easy grin pulled away the thin

gray curtain that was coloring my morning. Why dwell on the problems between Tim and Max? Max would eventually stand up to his dad. If not, I'd go down there and smack their heads together myself.

"Peachy," I said, smiling back at him.

"Chief Eiseley said to send you in." Sean nodded toward the short hallway. "And just so you know, he came in with a bag of Alice's cookies."

I thanked him and headed in the direction of his nod. The hallway's hard flooring was showing its age: dull and worn in the middle, vaguely bright on the outsides; no amount of buffing would bring back the original seventies-era blue-green. Which might not be a bad thing, really.

I knocked on the jamb of Gus's open office door and peeked in.

"Hey, Beth. Come on in." He stood and came around the desk. "Let me get these papers off the chair. There you go. Sit right down." He held out the chair and helped me settle in. "Coffee? Water? Gotta to have something to wash these cookies down. Water? No problem." He handed me a bottle and a plate of two cookies. "There's more of everything."

As he went back around to sit in his squeaky-wheeled chair, I set the plate on the edge of his desk. The solicitous attention was disconcerting. A few short months ago, the two of us had had a falling-out of proportions massive enough to make me think I'd never be invited to set foot in this office again. Yet here I was, and here Gus was trying to make up for his earlier treatment of me. It was all very strange.

"So." Gus pushed the plate of cookies at me. "When you called last night, you said you wanted to talk to me about something you overheard at Dennis Halpern's visitation."

"The county's taken over the investigation?"

Gus pulled a cookie out of the white bag sitting on his desk. "That happened the next day. A new guy, Barlow, is heading it up."

"What happened to Sharon Wheeler?"

Deputy Wheeler and I had met a few times. We'd had a rocky start, but had come around to having ... well, you couldn't call it a working relationship, but we'd gotten to the point where she at least appeared to take me seriously.

"Maternity leave. Barlow seems okay, but he's not from here. He's from Oregon. Or was it Washington?" Gus pointed a peanut butter cookie in a westerly direction. "Somewhere out there."

"I'm sure he's perfectly qualified to run a murder investigation."

Gus grinned. "That sounded pretty prim and proper. He'll do fine, I'm sure. So. What do you have for me?"

I told him what Marina and I had overhead about Dennis wanting to change his will.

During the telling, he nodded, ate his cookie, took notes, and made a series of interested noises.

"Interesting," he said when I'd finished. "I'll pass this on to the county folks."

"I'm not sure how much it will help." The bottle of water in my hand was lukewarm, but it was wet, so I took a swallow. "Without knowing how Dennis wanted to change his will, it's not very useful."

"Don't know about that." Gus made another note. "If Dennis had mentioned changing the will to any of his family, it might have triggered something, even if no one knew for sure what the change was. Good work, Beth."

The praise made my head swell a little, but his next sentence deflated it down to pinhead size.

"I hear there was quite a scene at Scovill's yesterday."

"Oh." I looked at my shoes, something I'd recently sworn off doing, as it was hardly ever a good idea for a single mother of two youngish children who owned her own business to look at her scuffed and worn footwear. Demoralizing at best, downright depressing at worst. I kept the dark thoughts at bay by thinking of the nice new back-to-school shoes I'd bought for Jenna and Oliver. Yes, that was much better. "How did you hear about that?" I asked.

He half smiled, half didn't, and didn't answer my question. "Don't take what Staci said to heart. She's young and she's grieving. You were a handy target, that's all."

How nice for me. "And here I thought I'd left my bull's-eye shirt at home last night."

Gus laughed. "I can think of other people I'd rather see wearing one." I looked at him speculatively, but he just smiled.

On my way out, I sketched Sean a wave. He was on the phone, taking down the address of a vacationing homeowner ("Yes, ma'am, we'll keep an eye on your place when you're gone. All part of the service here in Rynwood.") and gave me a distracted nod.

I was distracted myself, to tell the truth. For all I'd been able to joke with Gus about Staci's accusations, I'd spent a good share of last night staring at the bedroom ceiling. Even when I had, at last, fallen asleep, my dreams had been shadowed by the specter of Auntie May haranguing me in front of the entire student body of my high school. She went on and on about feeding the kids more vegetables, and then the dream morphed into me on a unicycle, riding around in Tarver's parking lot.

"I've never even been on a unicycle," I muttered at the sidewalk. "And I don't really want to."

"Excuse me?"

I looked up to see a man standing directly in front of

me. "Oh, um . . ." His dark hair was turning white in a salt-and-peppery way, so I guessed his age to be fiftyish, but the worn expression on his face added a decade. "Sorry. Just talking to myself." I smiled, hoping to lighten his obviously sad mood. No luck. "Nice day, isn't it?"

He glanced at the blue sky dotted with lamblike clouds. "I hadn't noticed."

A female voice came from behind me. "How could you?"

While it wasn't quite a shout, it was louder than plain scolding. I turned around and saw a blond woman patting a Rottweiler's head, her many bracelets jingling. "Leaving this poor thing in the sun without water could have killed him," Melody Kreutzer said. "How could you do that to this wonderful dog?"

The three oversized teenaged boys shuffled their feet. "I dunno," said the biggest one. "I guess we weren't thinking. Old Rover here's okay, isn't he? I mean, he is, right?"

His two buddies made mumbling noises that weren't quite words. They were smaller in size, but each one of the three easily topped a bulky six feet. Melody was about my size, but their sheer mass made her look like a pixie.

"It's a crime to mistreat an animal," Melody said, staring at them hard. "If he dies, all three of you could go to jail."

I wasn't sure she was right, but the boys seemed convinced. "We're really sorry, Mrs. Kreutzer. It won't happen again," the biggest one said. "Right, guys?"

"Right," they chorused. "Never."

"Well." Melody crossed her arms and tapped her fingernails against her biceps. "This one time, I'll let you go. But if I see this happening again, I'm going straight to Chief Eiseley."

The boys skittered off down the sidewalk. I turned to share a smile with Mr. Sad, but he was gone. I moved down the sidewalk to Melody and waved hello. "Good for you. I bet that dog is the best-treated pup in town for the next six months."

Melody pushed her hair back. "Maybe I was a little hard on them, but seeing an animal mistreated just makes me so mad."

Mad enough to tackle a trio that had been in and out of juvenile court for the last half dozen years. I didn't know much about Rynwood crime, but even I knew about the Harvey brothers.

"Tackling those three was pretty brave," I said.

"Oh, I don't know. Brave would be being afraid and going ahead and doing what you're afraid of. I was too mad to be afraid." She smiled. "And I'm going to be afraid of Glenn if I don't get a bag of Alice's Amazingly Awesomes before they're all gone."

I watched her go, wondering what it would be like to be completely unafraid. Melody seemed to be managing it, and she'd had children. Well, one. He was grown and had moved to Oregon years ago. Still, she was a mother and must have suffered those motherly fears.

I stood quiet and tried hard as I could to not be afraid of anything. Tried to be unconcerned about my children's upcoming teen years. Tried to assume that their future career choices and spouses would be the perfect matches. Tried to think that I'd find a new spouse for myself after the kids were grown. Tried to see my old age surrounded by loving grandchildren and giggling great-grandchildren.

For one brief, shining second, I almost had it. A moment without worry or apprehension. A moment without anxiety. Without fear.

Almost, but not quite. Because in that near-moment,

I realized that the only possible way that I wouldn't worry about my children was if I were dead.

And then I was back to feeling guilty about Dennis.

My thoughts dark and dreary, I walked to the store, my shoes tapping the sidewalk cheerily. "Stupid shoes," I told them.

Luckily, they didn't answer.

I was in my office, alternating between reconciling the accounts and slogging through a pile of returns, when Marina bounced in, bringing with her the scent of fresh air and sunshine.

"I'm kidless until school's out," she said. "It's time for lunch, and don't say you don't have time because your staff has cleared your schedule for the next hour."

"Maybe my staff doesn't remember that I vowed not to leave this chair until I balanced the checking account."

"That's the stupidest vow I ever heard." She reached for the back of my chair and spun me away from the desk. "Obviously, I was born so I could rescue you from it. Here's your purse." She opened the bottom desk drawer where I kept the oversized handbag, pulled it out, and put it on my lap.

"And we're not going to the Green Tractor, either," she said. "You'll have one of those horribly healthy salads, with maybe a side order of cottage cheese if you're ready for a walk on the wild side. Not today." She poked at my upper arm. "You need a little more flesh on those bones if you're ever going to attract a man, and I know just the place for that."

Ten minutes later, we were seated in a booth at the Grill. Technically Fred's Eclectic Collections and Food from the Grill, the restaurant was packed from stem to stern with the oddball collections Fred had amassed over the years: toasters, musical instruments, sports equipment, gas station paraphernalia, airplane parts; Fred's stuff was hung from the ceiling, mounted on walls, and spraddled across high shelves.

The women in town held private debates on whether or not anything on those shelves was ever dusted, but to my knowledge no one had dared climb on a chair to take a look. Some things were better left unknown.

Marina pointed at her paper place mat while our waitress looked on. "I want one of those." The place mats doubled as menus, and there was room left over for a legend about the beginnings of Fred's first collection. "Hamburger with cheese and a large order of fries."

The waitress looked at me. I read and reread the menu. During the months I was trying so hard to lose weight, I'd managed to stay away from the Grill, where the menu was hamburgers, hot dogs, brats, and French fries. The only variation beyond that was the size. Medium, large, and obnoxious.

"Hamburger," I said. "No cheese, and a medium fry."

"Drinks?"

"Ice water for both of us." I cut off Marina's protest. "That's it, thanks."

Marina pouted. "How is it you can take the fun out of being bad?"

"How is it that you want to ruin your health, rot your teeth, and shorten your life span?"

"Well, if you put it that way." She put her elbows on the plastic laminate table and cupped her chin in her hands. "So. Tell me everything Gus said."

I furrowed my brow. "Well, let me think a minute. First he said 'Hey, Beth. Come on in.' Then he said, 'Let me get these papers off the chair.' Then he said—"

Marina uncupped her chin and made a T with her hands. "Time out. Let me rephrase that. Tell me everything Gus said that I actually care about. And I know you're just getting back at me for dragging you out to lunch, so yadda yadda yah."

I grinned at her. We'd been friends for a very long time. By the time our ice water arrived, I'd given her a quick summary. By the time our food showed up, I'd given her all the details, including the fact that Gus had already known what had happened at the funeral home last night.

Marina drizzled ketchup over her fries while I sprinkled malt vinegar on mine. She picked up her first fry. "I love you," she told it, then popped it in her mouth. "Is there anything better than Fred's fries? Truly not possible, so don't try to argue." She ate another, practically swooning, then refocused on our conversation.

"So," she said. "Gus will pass on what we learned to the county cops. Which leaves us with two conversational points to cover before your overactive sense of duty pulls you back to your store. One." She held up her index finger. "Last night."

I really didn't want to talk about Staci's accusations, but I knew Marina wasn't going to let me do that.

She pointed a fry at her eyes. "Not red." She pointed the fry at mine. "Red. You didn't sleep for beans, did you? Which means you're taking Staci's ravings to heart."

The salt shaker called to me. A little extra salt wouldn't hurt, this one time. "I can't help feeling that she's right. Everyone else is telling me it's not my fault, but what if they're wrong and Staci's the one who's right?"

Marina bit deep into her burger, rolled her eyes with gustatory pleasure, chewed, and swallowed. "Then you'd better help find the killer."

"Isn't that why we have police?"

"Sure, but you know how understaffed they are. And they don't have the strengths you have. Play to them, sweets. Play to them."

I tried to think of any abilities I might have that would help the police catch whoever had killed Dennis and came up dry. "I used to think I was good at alphabetizing, but Yvonne's half again as fast."

"Sometimes you are such a putz. Say, and this is the number two thing—have you found out what's bugging Oliver?"

I hadn't, and not for lack of trying. "He claims he's fine."

She looked at me over the top of her burger. "Yesterday after school he said he'd rather stay inside than go out and play."

I stared at her. "He said that?"

"Afraid so. The other kids went out in the backyard. He stayed inside and watched reruns of *Phineas and Ferb*."

The hamburger in my hands, which thirty seconds ago had been the most appealing food I'd ever seen, smelled, or touched, suddenly didn't interest me at all. I put it down and pushed it away from me.

"I'll talk to him tonight," I said.

Marina nodded slowly, then started talking about a new lasagna recipe.

I tried to pay attention, but most of me wasn't listening. Because there was something wrong with my son, and he wasn't talking to me.

Chapter 8

That night I sat in the same Tarver classroom I'd sat in a week ago. So much was the same, yet so much was different. The map of the United States, the skyscraper diagram, and the pictures of Yellowstone were still there. The teacher's desk had the same silk flowers in the same vase, the same books were on the shelves. Even the contents of the lost-and-found box didn't look any different.

Yet nothing was the same. Dennis Halpern was dead, irrevocably and irretrievably gone forever. My instinct was that the blame for that was mine, and I'd have to find a way to live with the responsibility. There was nothing I could do for his family to make up for their loss, but maybe, after a while, I could do . . . something.

And there were a couple of other things that were different. I scanned the classroom, counting heads. About fifteen things, really, and they were missing.

"Where is everybody?" I asked Claudia.

She glanced up from her perusal of a playground equipment catalog, looked around, and shrugged. "Running late, I guess."

A glance at my watch told me I should start the meeting. A look at the clock on the wall told me I could wait a couple of minutes. And since we were at the school, using the school clock was the *de rigueur* time.

I made a show of studying the meeting's agenda, but my mind wasn't on forming new committees or on the date for the father-daughter dance. No, what was topmost in my head was Oliver.

I'd picked up the kids a little early so I could get some dinner into them before heading to the PTA meeting. On the drive home, Jenna had plugged herself into her iPod and started bobbing away in the backseat to music only she could hear. A perfect time for a heart-to-heart with my son.

He was staring out the car window, tapping the glass every time we passed a tree. There are lots of trees in Rynwood.

"Ollster?" I asked. "Mrs. Neff said you didn't go outside to play after school the last couple of days. Are you feeling okay?" I knew he was fine, of course. He was showing none of his typical signs of illness. No sniffling, no tugging at his ears, and not even the slightest hint of a cough. But asking was a good way to open the conversation.

"I'm good."

He spoke without turning away from the window. I could see most of the left side of his face, but it was hard to read much from less than half a face.

I almost asked him why he didn't go outside, but decided on a different approach. "I thought you really liked to play in Mrs. Neff's backyard."

"Yeah. I do." *Tap-tap. Tap.*

Not a very successful approach. Time for another shot. "Are you having troubles with any of the other daycare kids?"

"What do you mean?"

Good one, Beth. Ask the kid an open-ended question and he sends you one in return. "Like, maybe you had a fight with Nathan. Or maybe you and Zach are arguing about who gets to go up in the tree house first."

"Oh." *Tap-tap*. "No. We're good."

He was good; they were good; everything was good. Only, clearly, everything wasn't.

I'd reached out and laid my hand on the back of his neck. "Sweetheart, if something's bothering you, please talk to me about it. I'm your mom and I'll always understand. Okay, Ollster? You can always talk to me about anything."

Tap. ". . . Okay." *Tap-tap-tap*.

Tap-tap. "Beth?" Claudia was rapping her pen against the tabletop. "It's past time."

I looked up, then out. Five after and there were only a few people out in the seats. Marina, Tina, Whitney, and Nick and Carol Casassa. Strange.

"Before we start the meeting," I said, "I'd like to have a moment of silence in honor of Dennis Halpern. The meeting will begin when I tap the gavel." I bowed my head and felt the others around me do the same. My worries and concerns fell away as I ached for the Halpern family and sorrowed for a life cut short.

Dennis, I am so sorry. So very, very sorry.

When I heard the rustlings of movement, I lifted my head and banged the gavel lightly. "This meeting of the Tarver Elementary PTA will come to order." Summer took roll. "Are there any additions to the agenda?" I asked, and was ready to slide right into a motion to approve when Claudia said, "I'd like to add 'Resignation of Secretary Lang' to the agenda."

There was a large gasp. I didn't know if it came from me, from Summer, or from one of the five people in the audience. I stared at Claudia, but she kept her gaze on the table in front of her. So be it. "Summer, please add that item to the agenda. And, if the board doesn't object, I would like to move that to the top of New Business."

In short order, the minutes of the last meeting were

approved and the old business was taken care of. All was done with quiet voices; all was done while the elephant in the room was growing larger and larger.

"New business item A," I said. "Resignation of Secretary Lang." Suddenly I wished for glasses that I could peer over. "Claudia, do you have something to say?"

"Well, I just want to say that with the current situation, Summer should resign. Maybe she can't be an effective secretary with all this going on, is all I mean."

Claudia was talking without once looking at Summer. The word "coward" popped into my head and wouldn't go away. There was nothing in the PTA bylaws that covered a situation like this—how could there be? We had policy about the number of unexcused absences from meetings, we had policy about votes from which we had to abstain. But who would draft a policy that included suspicion of murder?

"Why exactly," I said carefully, "do you think Summer is unable to fulfill her duties?"

"Um . . ." Claudia tapped her pen, looked out at Tina, bit her lips. "She . . . might be . . . well . . ."

I wanted to launch into a tirade about being innocent until proven guilty. To rant about the evils of gossip and innuendo, not to mention the dangers of slander. Instead I said, "Since there doesn't seem to be any valid reason for the resignation of our secretary, I recommend that the board take no action. Next item on the agenda is the date of the father-daughter dance."

And just like that, I squashed Claudia's preemptive strike against Summer. Maybe I really could do this presidency thing. It was nice to be able to do something right. On the other hand, if I was doing okay as president, why were most of our regular meeting attendees AWOL?

Setting the date for the father-daughter event took roughly three seconds. Now officially known as the Sam

Helmstetter Scholarship Fund Dance, it was always held the second Saturday in November. Until the storybook had been published, the dance had been the PTA's most successful fund-raiser, and it was still important for our finances.

"Okay," I said, checking the dance off my agenda. A small ache sounded somewhere inside me. Last year, Evan had taken over when Jenna's father had been out of town for a job interview. Evan had worn a tux and made her feel like Cinderella.

I drew a second check on top of the first one. This year Richard would be in town to take his daughter to the dance, so there'd be no reason for . . . for anyone else to be involved. Which was good and right and as it should be.

Yes. Just as it should be.

"Next," I said, "is the allocation of storybook funds." With my handy-dandy mom-created peripheral vision, I saw Claudia start to puff up with breath. Before she could form a word, I leapt into the forming fray.

"I'd like to propose the formation of two committees. A week ago, a preliminary discussion fell quickly into an argument. In front of a guest." I sent a hard look to my fellow board members, then to the audience. Most people had the grace to look embarrassed; some, such as the person next to me (not that I was naming names), looked stubborn. Fine.

"That," I said, "was not the finest hour for our PTA. To prevent another similar and similarly useless discussion, I'd like to form two ad hoc committees. Two, because there seem to be two drastically different points of view on how to allocate the money. And ad hoc, because once the decision is made, there is no reason to continue the committees."

Heads nodded. Even Claudia's.

"Then I'd like to entertain a motion to form an ad hoc committee with Claudia Wolff as its chair and another with Summer Lang as chair. Claudia's committee will be charged with studying sports-related expenditures. Summer's committee will be charged with studying fine arts expenditures."

Randy grunted, then said, "So moved."

"I'll second," Claudia said quickly.

"Discussion?" I asked.

"Who else is going to be on the committee?" Summer asked.

Claudia made a rude noise in the back of her throat. "Whoever you can get to be on it. Good luck with finding anyone. Tina, you're on mine, right? And how about you?" She skewered Whitney with a glare.

Whitney blinked. "Me? Oh. Well . . . I . . ."

"Good." Claudia nodded. "Give me your e-mail address so I can let you know about meetings."

"I'll work on sports funding," Nick said.

His wife crossed her arms. "And I'll work on your committee, Summer," she said. "Be glad to."

"Okay, good." Summer looked at me. "Anyone else?"

I tried to, but didn't quite, stifle a sigh. If there was one thing I didn't need, it was another thing to do. But since this whole two-committee thing was my idea . . . "If you want help, sure."

Marina waved her hand. "Me too!"

I looked at her. She beamed at me, and I got the sneaking suspicion that her motives weren't as pure as the driven snow.

"Good," I said. "We have two full committees. Now we need a vote. Those in favor of the motion, say aye." There were four "ayes" of differing shapes and sizes. "Those opposed, say nay." And silence. "Thank you. I'd like the committee chairs to work toward getting a solid proposal to this board by the November meeting. I'd like to see a short-term plan and a long-term plan, in addition to different possibilities for varying amounts of money."

Claudia and Summer nodded happily, and I adjourned the meeting. Immediately, Claudia and Tina went into a huddle. Whitney got up to stand nearby and was ignored. Nick handed Claudia a piece of paper. "Here's my e-mail. Let me know when you want to have a meeting." He headed out, his wife at his heels, an expression of tense fury on her face.

Marina watched them walk out of the room. "Apples and oranges have nothing on those two," she said. "How is it they stayed married so long?"

"They both like Peter Sellers movies," I said, waving good-bye to Summer. "Do you think it's because of forming committees that hardly anyone was here tonight? Maybe I should stop e-mailing the agenda around before the meeting."

"Um . . ." Marina coughed, started to say something, then stopped.

Claudia and Tina laughed, glanced at me, then looked at each other and laughed again.

A tinny rendition of the "Chicken Dance" sounded. I looked at the few people in the room, trying to guess whose cell phone was ringing. Claudia reached into her purse. Bingo.

"Or maybe," I said, shoving my papers into my bag, "maybe it's me. I'm doing such a horrible job as president that no one wants to be on the PTA. And the whole town knows that Staci thinks it's my fault her dad is dead. Maybe everybody thinks that. Maybe—"

"I'm really sorry," Marina said. "It was just a joke."

I stopped, midshove. There was no possible way that Staci had been joking. Absolutely zero chance. "What are you talking about? What was—?" I stopped. "Is your face turning pink?"

A faint tinge of blush was creeping up the sides of her neck, spreading across her cheeks, and up onto her forehead. There were two possibilities. Either she was having a hot flash or she was embarrassed.

But Marina was embarrassment-proof. I'd never once seen her blush—not when she'd lost her bathing suit top at a crowded beach, not when she'd burped loudly during a conversational lull at the most expensive restaurant on this side of Madison, and not when she'd tripped and fallen flat in front of a set of gymnasium bleachers packed with basketball-watching townspeople.

"It was a joke," she repeated.

"Have you been posting on your blog again?"

A couple of years ago, Marina had started up a blog she'd titled WisconSINs, posting the comings and goings of Rynwoodites. She'd had fun with it, but the number of her postings had fallen off after a few months. Save for an occasional resurgence when something really juicy happened, the blog was essentially silent these days.

She shook her head. "I promised the DH I'd stop that. He's all uptight these days about data mining and privacy and stuff."

Seemed like a reasonable concern to me. "What was a joke?"

Her shoulders hunched forward. "Please don't be mad at me."

Uh-oh. Jenna had been the last person to use that phrase with me. She'd been trying to mitigate my reaction to finding out that when she'd been in the driveway, practicing hockey stick handling skills, she'd accidentally sent a puck through the back window of the car.

I crossed my arms. "You can't make a promise about an emotion. They just happen."

She put her hands to her cheeks. "How about promising you won't yell at me? I hate it when you yell at me."

"How about telling me what you're talking about?"

Her chest went up and down as she heaved out a sigh. "Well, this morning, when I was taking the day-care kids to the park, I ran into Dorrie. Did you know she's taken up tai chi? She was on break from the Green Tractor and—"

"What was a joke?" I asked.

Marina sighed. "Dorrie was asking about, you know, last week's meeting and Dennis and all that, and I said, joking like—honest, it was a joke." She stopped and looked at me. "I said—"

Claudia snorted and looked up from her phone. "She said there must be a curse on this PTA. I just got this text from CeeCee. She said she'd heard about the curse from Isabel Olsen, who'd heard it from Mindy Wietzel, who'd heard it from Lynn Snider, who'd heard it from Auntie May, and where she heard it from, who knows, but now that Auntie May knows, everybody in town does." She glared at Marina. "You just killed any chance of making this PTA into something special. Who's going to buy our books now? Who's going to come to the dance?"

"I was joking," Marina said weakly.

"Of course you were," I said. "Who would believe in a curse? That's ridiculous."

Claudia swept her hand around, gesturing at the empty seats. "I'd say more than one person believes."

Though I didn't for one second believe in a curse on the PTA, I could see that Dennis's murder might make people a little leery about attending meetings. I said as much to Marina as we walked to her house. The kids, who'd been in the gym being watched over by a high schooler, were ahead of us. Each of them had chosen a pebble from the school parking lot and were now kicking them home.

"You really think so?" Marina was walking with her head down. No spring in her step, no lilt in her voice, no sparkle of mischief.

"Sure. Curses are just superstition. Who really believes in them these days?"

She started to say something, but I interrupted her. "And don't start giving me examples. There's no such thing as curses or hexes or ghosts." At least I didn't think so.

"So it's because Dennis was killed that people didn't show up tonight?"

"Absolutely. They're a little jumpy, that's all. Things will get back to normal before we know it."

"So you're not mad at me?"

Her voice was small. Her whole attitude of shame and self-doubt was so uncharacteristic that I started to wonder if she was getting sick. "Not a bit."

"Claudia sure seemed mad."

"And you've cared about her feelings since when?"

Her laugh sounded startled, as if I'd surprised her into doing something she hadn't expected to do. "I should care about them, I suppose. If I were a truly good person. Like you."

Oh, please. "If I were truly good, I wouldn't be wishing that Claudia would move to a different school district."

"Hey, here's an idea." She hopped over a crack in the sidewalk. "Let's gather up information on other school systems and send them to her anonymously." She started to talk about a magnet school she'd read about in Oregon. "It'd be perfect for her middle son, you know, Tyler. Or is Taylor the middle one? Taynor's the oldest. I think."

She went on to espouse the virtues of experimental

education for other people's children. I nodded, smiling, listening as much to her tone of voice as to her words. She might worry about her self-created and nonexistent curse tomorrow, but for now she was happy.

After I'd tucked the kids into bed, I went downstairs to the study to jot down some notes about the next PTA meeting. Or, more specifically, how to make sure attendance at the next meeting returned to normal.

I sat in front of the computer and found a notepad. Underneath an Oliver doodle of Spot—at least that's what I thought it was—I started writing. "E-mail Debra O'Connor." A bank vice president would be a credible person to spread the word that the so-called curse was one of Marina's jokes. "Talk to Flossie." Another ideal noncurse believer. "Talk to Ruthie." If the owner of the most popular diner in town couldn't convince people that curses didn't exist, no one could.

There were other people who might be influential, but I'd start with those three and see what happened. With any luck, this would all blow over in a week or two.

I sat back. Was believing in luck in the same category as believing in a curse?

"Different," I said out loud, startling George. The black cat had come in to sit on my lap, and my voice had woken him out of his sound sleep. "Sorry, guy."

It took a few pets, but he settled back down into a purr. "Now what do I do?" I asked him. He didn't answer. I'd intended on doing a few chores before getting into bed with a library copy of the latest Sarah Addison Allen book, but now there was a cat on my lap.

Well, there was always e-mail to read.

I skimmed the thirty or so e-mails in my inbox. Deleted most of them, read a few, answered a couple. Scrunched my face at the ones from people who wanted to hear all about the incident at the funeral home.

"Not going to happen," I murmured, and deleted those, too.

I sat there, thinking about PTAs and Dennis and death and finances and, on impulse, went to his company's website.

There was a nicely worded notice about the death of the company's founder, a commitment to carry on, and a photo montage featuring Dennis at varying ages. I endured that for a few pictures, then clicked to another page. This one discussed the different ways in which Halpern and Company could help your financial portfolio. The next page—and its associated subpages—went on at length about the different financial vehicles available to their customers.

My eyes went glassy somewhere in the middle of a description of asset-backed securities ("a type of debt security collateralized by specific assets"), and I moved on to a page titled "Investing 101," which turned out to be a lecture series Dennis had put together. The entire series had been videotaped and was available online.

"What You Always Wanted to Know About Investing But Were Afraid to Ask," was lecture number one. "Good title," I told George. "Don't you think?" He didn't answer, but his purring did seem to grow a little louder.

My index finger hovered over the mouse. Did I really want to do this? No. Was I being a coward if I didn't? Yes. Was there anything wrong with being a coward? I hesitated. George stood to rearrange himself, bumping my elbow in the process, making my finger touch the mouse hard enough to start the video.

"Good evening," Dennis said. The camera focused on his smiling, affable face, panned out to a roomful of people, then came back to Dennis. "Tonight," he said, "I'm going to answer all your questions." He put on a thoughtful look. "No, let me be more specific. Tonight I'm going to answer your finance-oriented questions. The easy ones. We'll do the hard ones some other time. I stayed up late to watch the football game and I'm not up to anything too difficult."

For a minute, maybe two, I watched as Dennis alternately charmed and informed his audience. In that video he was still living, still breathing, still laughing and talking and thinking and assuming he had years left to him.

Then I shut off the computer, picked up the sleeping cat, and went up to bed.

The next day was Sara's day at the store. Thursday was an odd day for her to have free, I'd thought when she'd told me her schedule, but what did I know about course schedules for science majors? My major at Northwestern had been journalism, and j-school majors rarely ventured into the realm of chemistry and physics and biology. Psychology, maybe, but that was different.

Lois, Yvonne, and I were at the front counter discussing the fall event schedule when Sara rushed in, red-faced and out of breath. "See? I told you." She grinned at us.

Yvonne, since she'd had the day off last time Sara worked, looked puzzled. I looked at Lois. Lois looked at me. Today Lois was appearing downright staid and almost stolid in a below-the-knee black skirt and white blouse. The only hint of personality showing was in her pendant necklace. A bright red miniature high-top basketball sneaker. She'd started to whisper about leopard-print underwear, but I'd cut her off at the description of the narrowness of the thong.

"Told us what?" I asked Sara.

"That I wouldn't be late ever again."

Ah. Right. I glanced at my watch. "You're actually ten

minutes early, which completely absolves you of your two earlier minutes of lateness."

"It was three," she said. "I don't want to take advantage, or anything."

And yet you so often heard that today's youth had no work ethic.

Lois sniffed loudly. "Kids today. When I was your age, you wouldn't have caught me coming into work early. Ever."

I pushed a box of tissues at her. "You don't come into work early now."

"Old habits die hard." She pushed the box back. "And here's Sara coming in long before she needs to. I tell you, she's well on the way to establishing a habit of a lifetime. Nip this in the bud, child. Nip it in the bud, otherwise you're dooming yourself to a life of sweat and labor and toil."

Sara giggled. "But I don't mind working hard. Really I don't."

"Hard work feels good," Yvonne said. "You sleep better if you've put in an honest day's work."

And she should know. Yvonne had spent a number of years in prison for a crime she didn't commit. Freed now for more than a year, she was still grateful for the low-paying, benefit-less job I'd been happy to give her. Her depth of knowledge regarding picture books was, as far as we could tell, bottomless, and her ability to match customer to book was almost frightening in its accuracy. I liked her very much and hoped she'd never leave.

Lois shook her head, sighing. "You three make me want to run off and play hooky."

I pointed in the direction of the workroom. "Before or after you unpack the new graphic novel releases?"

Her face lit up. "They're here?" She scrabbled in a drawer for the box cutter and practically ran to the back of the store.

There was a short pause while we watched the supposedly work-allergic Lois whoop with excitement as she sliced open the boxes. "Here's the new Matt Phelan. And Vera Brosgol's latest. And Nate Powell. And you did order that one about the Louvre! This is just gorgeous . . ."

Yvonne and Sara and I smiled at each other. Then the bells on the front door jingled, and the day's business began in earnest.

The morning passed quickly. A steady stream of customers combined with the regular ringing of the phone kept us all busy until noon. I sent Sara, who was looking a trifle pale, off to lunch first. "I brought mine," she said. "Is it okay if I eat in the workroom?"

"Of course it is. And take a full hour. Read that new Elise Broach book. Start the new Rick Riordan. Take a nap. Just don't come back for an hour."

"You know, for a mean old slave-driving boss, you're not so bad."

I shooed her off. "I don't want to see you for sixty straight minutes," I called after her.

Halfway into her prescribed hour, I poked my head into the workroom. Sara was sitting in a metal folding chair that I knew for a fact to be remarkably uncomfortable, head down and hand moving. Her hand held a mechanical pencil, and I was pretty sure she was working on her chemistry lab, but since the papers scattered across the table were scribbled with numbers and equations, she could have been calculating the mass of the earth, for all I knew.

I watched her for a moment. Did her parents know

how hard this child worked? Were they proud of her? Did they rush to hug her when she came home for vacations? I hoped so; I sincerely hoped so.

Halfway through the afternoon, there was a lull in customers and phone calls. Lois zoomed back to the graphic novels and Yvonne opened the software documentation no one had yet read. I looked around. There she was, sitting on the floor in front of the early readers, alphabetizing. Those books seemed to unalphabetize themselves as soon as you turned your back.

I called to her. "Sara, why don't you take a break? It's a beautiful afternoon. Go for a walk." As in, get outside before you fade away from lack of vitamin D. As in, get some exercise because sitting over books is sapping your muscle tone and giving your shoulders a pronounced curve that isn't permanent yet, but might be if you continue like this much longer.

"Oh, can I?" She put her hands on the floor and pushed herself to her feet. "That'd be awesome, Mrs. K. I'll be back in fifteen minutes. I promise." She bounded like a two-legged blond gazelle to the workroom.

So, not a walk, but another bout of studying.

I went to my office and sat down. Fingered a stack of catalogs. Flipped through a stack of invoices. Picked up a roll of postage stamps. Tightened it, then released it, listening to the whispery flutter as it uncoiled.

If Sara were my daughter, how would I feel? Would I be doing anything differently?

Tightened. Released. Tightened. Released.

Truly, there was only one thing to do. I stood and went to the workroom. Sara had a monstrously thick textbook flopped open in front of her, and her hand was busy writing notes into a spiral notebook. Her eyes were going back and forth faster than seemed possible for total reading comprehension, and she was muttering as she read.

"Inhibitors of mRNA synthesis. Yeah, I remember. And if an adenoma shows a bigger release of aldosterone out of the adrenal gland, you can expect . . ." She frowned. "You can expect . . ."

I knocked on the doorjamb.

"Oh, wow, I'm sorry." Sara jumped to her feet. "Is my break over? I'm really sorry. I'll get back to work right away."

I unfolded a chair and sat down across the table from her. "Sit a minute."

"Sorry about the mess." She piled up her books and papers and pencils and started shoving them into her backpack. "I really am."

"Sara." Gently, I pulled the backpack away from her. "Sit. Please."

"Um." She looked longingly at the bag and sat down slowly. "You're mad at me, aren't you?"

"Why on earth would I be mad?" A new thought popped into my head. "No, I take that back. I am a little angry." Her head dropped. All I could see of her face was the unlined, pale skin of her forehead. This was going to be a difficult conversation, and I had no idea where to start. "What is an adenoma, anyway?"

"It's when you get a tumor of a gland. You know, like the pituitary gland?"

One more thing I didn't want to know anything about. You only knew about diseases like that if you were intimately involved with them. Ergo, I didn't want to know.

"Are you studying for a test?" I asked.

"Kind of." She pushed at her hair. "The MCATs. Since I didn't know for a year that I wanted to do premed, I'm a year behind in taking the MCATs. There's one more test in September and maybe there will be some open slots in the med schools, so if I do really, really good, I won't lose any time. I mean, my mom and dad say I could do with a year off, go work at a doctor's office or something, but I'm already a year back, and if I can catch up, that'd be so great." She stopped, having either run out of words or breath. I wasn't certain which.

Old memories were slowly bubbling to the surface. MCAT. The Medical College Admission Test. The bête noire of many a premed student. Doing well on the MCAT is considered essential to getting into medical school and so creates a tremendous stressor for test takers.

"Is that what you're doing?" I poked at her backpack. "Studying for your MCAT?"

"Yeah. This is a great study guide." She pulled out the soft-covered textbook and thumped it on the table. The beast must have been a thousand pages long. "It's not as good as taking one of those tutoring courses, but those cost so much money. I mean like thousands. I'm doing pretty good on the practice exams, so I should do okay." She made the end of a sentence more of a question than a statement: ". . . I should do okay?"

I wanted to reassure her that she'd do fine. At the same time, I wanted to tell her that acing the MCAT didn't matter, that she could always take it again, that she didn't need to try so hard, that her parents were right, that taking a year off would be good for her, that resting for a year before heading off to the rigors of medical school might be the best thing for her. I wanted to tell her all of that, but I knew she wouldn't listen to any of it.

"Sara." I sighed. How was I going to say this? "You're going to make yourself sick, working so hard. That's why you were crying the other day, isn't it? You're wearing yourself to a frazzle, trying to do everything."

"It's just until I'm done with the MCATs," she said earnestly. "After that, I'll be okay."

"And what happens when you hit mid-terms? And finals?"

Her head went down again. "I can do it," she whispered.

"Yes, you can," I said. "But you shouldn't." I pushed Sara's backpack toward her. "Go home."

She blinked at me. "But I'm scheduled to work until close."

"Not anymore you're not."

"I'm . . . not sure what you mean."

"Sara, sweetheart, you need to quit working here."

"No!" Her eyes went wide, showing all white around the blue irises. "I love this store. I love everyone here and the books and the town and . . . and everything. I love working here, it makes me happy. I don't want to quit. Ever."

"Then you're fired."

Her lips trembled. "You mean, fired, fired? Like it'll have to be on my job applications?"

I sighed. "Of course not. I want you to stay, but I also think you're going to work yourself into exhaustion. This is a part-time job that doesn't pay you half of what you're worth. You're headed to medical school. What's more important, studying for the MCAT or working here?"

"But working here isn't like working. It's more like . . . fun." Her eyes pleaded with me. *Let me stay, keep me on, don't make me leave.*

I reached out and tucked her hair behind her ear. "Go home. Study. Get a good score on your MCAT. Get good grades this semester. Then, if you still want to, come back at Christmas."

"Oh, Mrs. K." Sara lurched forward and hugged me. "You're the nicest boss ever."

Tears stung my eyes. I wasn't that nice, not really, but it was kind of her to say so. "You're not so bad yourself."

She sniffed. "Can I really come back after the semester's over?"

"I'll be counting on it."

Chapter 9

After I'd walked Sara to her car, had another round of tearful hugs, and waved good-bye, I broke the news to Lois and Yvonne.

"You did what?" The unfazeable, nothing-shocks-me-anymore, jaded-to-the-core Lois stared at me with her mouth open.

"Fired Sara."

Lois reached out with a bony index finger and poked me in the upper arm. "Still flesh and blood. No, wait. Let me see your teeth. Come on . . . Okay, good. You're not a vampire. So the only possibility is that you've been possessed by . . . by the spirit of Auntie May." She smiled and nodded, obviously happy with her conclusion. "Auntie May's spirit can't stand being restricted to the confines of Sunny Rest and has reached out for a malleable soul that she can use to do her evil bidding."

It sounded reasonable. Except for one thing. "Auntie May likes Sara. Almost as much as she likes Yvonne."

Lois and I looked at Yvonne. "She just likes the books I pick out," she said. "That doesn't mean she likes me."

Her horrified tone sounded quite real. Which I could understand. The thought of having Auntie May as a close friend and confidante was not a comfortable one. Not only that, but the knowledge lurking inside Auntie May's head was generations deep and Rynwoodites of all ages hoped it would never be passed on.

"Anyway," I said. "Firing isn't really the right term. It's more like I encouraged her to quit for a while."

Lois put her hands on her hips. "Are you nuts? Sara's the hardest worker we have. She's willing to sort stickers and clean the bathroom, and she always wants to work during the big sales and on Saturdays and she's young and pretty and energetic, and how on earth are we going to get along without her?"

When she paused to roll her eyes, Yvonne said, "Beth's right. Sara needed to quit. She's been working too hard."

Lois glared at Yvonne, then at me; then the huff went out of her in a rush. She sighed. "So that means what? That I haven't noticed what everyone else around here has?"

"You said it, not me." I smiled at her. "And I told Sara to come back to work at Christmas, when the semester is over."

"Do you think she will?" Lois asked.

I thought about it, then sighed. "Not really."

Yvonne rubbed her arms, as if she were cold. "She'll come back to visit."

"Well." Lois sagged back against the counter. "So much for my theory."

"Which one was that?" I asked.

"That she's been upset because she was Dennis Halpern's illegitimate daughter."

"Oh, please."

"Hey, why not? There's good—"

The back door closed and a young man walked in. "Good afternoon, Mrs. Kennedy, Mrs. Nielson, Miss Ganassi." He stood a respectful distance away and smiled at us, his white teeth brilliant against his brown skin, black hair, and dark eyes.

Lois eyed him. "What are you doing here? I thought you were doing some sort of writing semester thing and couldn't be bothered to come back here to work until the end of the month."

"Yes, that is correct." Paoze made a nod that gave the impression of a bow. He'd been born in Laos and his family had immigrated to Wisconsin too late for him to learn English without hard work. Maybe because of this, he'd evolved into a literature major at the university and was sketching an outline for a novel based on his family's struggles. Recently, I'd found out that those struggles began about six hundred years ago. It was going to be a long book.

Lois put her hand to her forehead. "I always thought correct meant being, you know, right. Accurate. But now I'm wondering . . ."

I exchanged glances with Yvonne. Though Paoze's English grammar was better than most native-born Americans, there were language quirks that escaped him. And, in spite of working with Lois for almost four years, he remained slightly gullible. Lois lived to exploit this crack in his armor. Once, just once, he'd turned the tables on her, and it was clear that the episode still rankled.

"You need wonder no longer," Paoze said. "Mrs. Kennedy called me to say that Sara is unable to continue here. I am willing to help in any way I can until a replacement can be found."

Lois's hand came down with a snap. "Exactly. It is your job to find a new Sara."

I stirred. "Now, Lois—"

"Come, come," she said heartily, winking at me with the eye Paoze couldn't see. "You know it's the responsibility of the newest hire to find a new employee. Okay, technically Yvonne is the newest hire, but she's only lived in this state a year, so the responsibility transfers to you." She pointed at Paoze. "You've heard of the low man on the totem pole, right?"

"I have heard of totem poles." He eyed her warily.

"Actually," I said, "the lowest figure on the totem pole is—"

Lois ran over what was going to be a statement of fact. "Low man on the totem pole means everyone else is above you. You lack any real status, see, so you're the one who gets stuck making the new totem pole. Employee totem poles are a tradition in this part of Wisconsin. I'm surprised you haven't noticed them."

"An employee totem pole." His eyelashes came so close together that the brown irises couldn't be seen.

"Well, duh." Lois tossed her hair back in a middle-school move that didn't quite work for her. "How are we going to find a new Sara without a totem pole? Tell you what. Start with a small carving. Leave the very bottom blank and—"

Paoze turned to me. "You said Sara was working on the early readers. Shall I continue?"

"Hey," Lois said.

He gave her a blinding smile. "I do not believe in employee totem poles. Better luck next time, Mrs. Nielson."

Yvonne giggled. "He's onto you, Lois. Bet you never get him again."

"I'll get him," she said firmly. "Sooner or later, I'll get him. Count on it."

I wasn't so sure, but decided not to say so. No point in fanning the flames of her one-upmanship desires. Besides, I had something else I wanted to discuss with her, something serious, and I didn't want her distracted with planning her next attack.

"Yvonne?" I asked. "I know we have a troop of Girl Scouts coming in soon"—which was why I'd called Paoze in a mild panic and begged him to come in; thank heavens he'd been able to borrow a roommate's car instead of having to ride his bicycle—"but do you mind if Lois and I step out a minute?"

Knowing that the upcoming Girl Scout visit would be action-packed and loud, we chose to sit outside. I eschewed the sidewalk benches in favor of the quiet and sunny courtyard next to the town's new restaurant, Ian's Place. After years of scrimping and saving and begging for investors, Ian Byars, former cook at the Green Tractor, had finally raised enough money to open the bistro of his dreams.

Full of exposed brick, hardwood floors, frosted glass dividers, and pendant light fixtures that dangled from a high ceiling, the styling wouldn't have looked out of place in downtown Madison or even Chicago. How it would go over in little Rynwood remained to be seen. But Ian had Ruthie's full support—"I wish the kid luck. He's a great chef, and it's not like he's going to be competing with my cinnamon rolls and pea soup"—and though the food was expensive, area food critics were swooning over his Boursin-topped salmon, mushroom-stuffed chicken roulade, and his mustard spaetzle. I wasn't exactly sure what roulade was, and I kept forgetting to look it up, but if Ian was making it, it was bound to be good.

I went inside to buy two iced teas and came out to find Lois slouched into a wire chair and looking at the world with a sour expression.

"This sucks."

I looked around us. At the blue sky. At the tubs of small trees that twinkled with white lights in the evenings and would bloom white flowers in the spring. At the restaurant wall painted with a mural depicting farmers and artisan food-making. At the brushed-metal tables and chairs. At the tiny vases on each table crowded with local flowers. "Doesn't seem so bad to me," I said.

"You know what I mean."

And, of course, I did. "She would have left in the spring, anyway."

"Maybe not." Lois pushed her tea around the table, leaving a wide track of condensation. Though fall was almost upon us, today the temperature was in the seventies and the humidity was high. "Maybe she would have changed her mind about medical school and come to work at the store full-time."

"That is one of your worst maybes ever."

She sighed. "Yeah. I just don't want her gone."

"Me, either."

We sat a moment, wishing that things could be different, wishing that things could stay the same for a little longer, please. Not forever, that would be asking too much and would probably be boring anyway, but just a little longer, pretty please?

I picked up my tea. "Paoze is going to post flyers at the university, and I'll put an ad in the paper. Do you know anyone who's looking?"

"Not anyone I'd want to hire."

I slid her a glance but didn't say anything. Lois's extended family was large and varied and their exploits were just as likely to include overnight stays as guests of local law enforcement as vacations to Door County.

"We'll find someone," I said.

Lois grunted noncommittally.

"So." I put down my tea with a slight thump. "How serious were you about Sara being Dennis Halpern's illegitimate daughter?"

"Hey, it could have happened that way. Sara's smart

with math and chemistry and all that stuff that doesn't make sense to normal people. Dennis was smart with math and financial stuff, and most of that stuff doesn't make sense, either. Like father, like daughter, right?"

I studied her, but she looked perfectly serious. "Do you have any real basis for thinking this? Or are you just pulling a theory out of thin air, much like someone else we know?" Honestly, sometimes I wondered if Lois and Marina were twins, with Marina being cryogenically frozen for thirteen years until their parents were ready for another daughter.

"Mostly out of the air. Like this." She reached out and plucked a dust mote that had been wafting slowly over the table.

I shouldn't have been disappointed that Dennis hadn't been running around fathering children out of wedlock, but I was, just a little. "So Dennis didn't have a long-running reputation for . . . for . . . ?"

"For being a horn dog?" She laughed at my wince. "I didn't know him hardly at all, but one of his sisters ended up moving back to Rynwood and living down the street from me. Long time ago." She shook her head at the questions that were starting to tumble out of me. "She and her husband left for South Carolina years back, so everything I know is out of date. But."

She pursed her lips. "But I remember her saying that her little brother was quite the Romeo. That he always had a girlfriend hanging on him. Sometimes more than one." She shrugged. "Does that mean he did the same thing when he was older? Your guess is as good as mine. Better, probably. You're good at noticing things."

I nodded vaguely. Maybe Marina's notion of Dennis having a mistress wasn't as over the top as I'd thought. Still unlikely, but maybe not out of the realm of possibility. But . . . Summer? No. It couldn't be.

"Do you smell something?" Lois sniffed, looking around. "It almost smells like—"

The earsplitting noise of an air horn made us jump. A second blast was followed by a siren's up-and-down wail. A fire truck rushed past. On its heels was a fire engine, an EMT vehicle close behind.

We sat, tense, waiting for the sirens to wail off into the distance, waiting for the anxious sound to be gone, waiting for the afternoon calm to return.

But that didn't happen.

What happened was the sirens stopped midshriek. They couldn't be more than a block away.

Lois and I shared a quick, wild glance. Our mutual thought was so big and dreadful that it could almost be seen, writhing in the air between us.

The store!

We leapt to our feet and bolted from the table.

My fear for the store paled away to a wisp in comparison to my fear for Yvonne and Paoze. We pushed tables aside and tumbled chairs over in our race toward the sidewalk. If anything happened to either one of them, I'd never forgive myself. How could I have gone off with Lois when my employees were in danger? How could I have left them alone while I went gallivanting off to do more poking around into a death that the county sheriff's office was far more qualified to investigate?

We hit the sidewalk. The mass of fire trucks and revolving lights and emergency personnel was a block ahead. With Lois panting at my side, I ran hard as I could toward a sight I'd never imagined seeing in downtown Rynwood.

A fire chief with a bullhorn cracking out orders.

Firefighters pulling out hoses.

The metallic rattle of equipment.

The awful, acrid stench of fire.

Adrenaline kicked me along fast, and I started to pull ahead of Lois. Time slowed. Everything I saw was a brighter color than I'd ever seen. Everything I heard was crisp. Everything was sharper and more vivid than life.

And it was all terribly, horribly, frightening.

Business owners and staff were coming to their doorways and spilling out onto the sidewalk. Alice and Alan were in front of their antique mall, Alan holding a broom, Alice with her baking apron gathered up in her hands and pressed against her mouth.

Denise and her current crop of stylists stood at the window of the hair salon, scissors and combs in hand. Three women, plastic cutting capes tight around their necks, crowded next to them.

All had their eyes trained on the sight up the road; all had wide eyes and slack mouths.

Evan stood tall and straight in front of his hardware store. A curly lock of graying blond hair dipped down over his forehead, making me think to tell him he needed a haircut, but no, that wasn't any of my business, not anymore.

His head turned, and I saw the jolt of recognition when he saw me. "Beth, don't—" But whatever he'd wanted to say was lost in the blare of another fire truck and the pounding of my shoes on the sidewalk's dark red bricks.

Ruthie, order pad in hand, was side by side with her latest cook, a young woman with effervescent energy. Their worried faces made my feet move even faster. Ruthie didn't worry about much, and when she did, it was worth worrying about.

On and on I ran, every step an eternity, every step taking me closer to what I was dreading. What was I going to say to Paoze's parents if he'd been hurt? How was

I going to tell Yvonne's family? She was from California, how would I even find them?

I ran, pain stabbing a sword in my side, searing my lungs. But I had to know. I couldn't stop. I couldn't slow down. I had to find out.

On past Flossie, her arms wrapped tight around her body. Patrick had his arm around his great-aunt's shoulders, but it didn't seem as if she was finding much comfort.

But that didn't make sense. Flossie was the strongest person I knew. She would live forever. What I'd seen must have been a trick of the light. Yes. No need to worry.

On I went past Glenn Kettunen, hands in his pockets. He looked strange without a smile on his face. His staff grouped around him, small satellites to planet Kettunen. The tops of Melody Kreutzer's and Nicole Reilly's heads came up almost to his shoulder, and though the newest agent wasn't short by any means, he looked small standing next to Glenn. They stood, watching, spectators at the worst show in town.

I saw them ranged across the front of Glenn's building, I saw the fading flowers in their window boxes. I heard their murmuring comments. So many things I was seeing and hearing and so many of them I didn't want to see or hear or feel at all.

The raw fear for Paoze and Yvonne.

How could this have happened?

The shouts of the firefighters.

Why hadn't I been there to help?

The sound of spraying water and the sight of gawkers and spectators being held back to safety by police.

Please . . .

All my fears and hopes and prayers concentrated into one short word, repeated over and over again. *Please . . . please . . . please . . .*

And then I was there.

I slowed. Stopped. Gaped at the flames shooting to the sky. Blinked away the smoke. Coughed some out of my lungs.

Yvonne looked around. "There you are. We were about to send a search party after you two."

"Paoze . . . ?" I tried to finish the sentence, but couldn't find the breath.

"He's over there." Yvonne nodded at a cluster containing the waitstaff from the Grill, then, frowning, peered at me closely. "Are you all right?"

Lois arrived, panting. "Whoo-ee. I haven't run that fast since the day I was running after my youngest for eating the last piece of chocolate cake. I take it everyone's okay?"

"Well, yes, of course we are, why—" Her lips formed a small O. "You weren't here. You thought it was the store that was on fire. Oh, you poor things." She gathered us into an unusual hug. Yvonne wasn't given to displays of affection, public or otherwise. She smothered us with a hard squeeze, then let us go. "Paoze smelled it first. He went outside and looked around. When he figured out where the fire was, we called 911."

"You did the right thing," I said distractedly.

"Before we left, I made sure the store was locked," she said. "Should I go back and open up?"

But I didn't answer. Couldn't really. Because anything I might have said would have been drowned out by the crashing down of the flaming roof.

Of Dennis Halpern's office.

Yvonne, Paoze, and I watched the fire consume what had been an attractive office an hour ago. We watched the flames reach high and listened to the crackle and roar of orange tongues reaching out for more.

I hugged myself. "I hope . . ." But I didn't want to say the words out loud.

Yvonne touched my arm. "No one was inside. That's the first thing they did—go in and clear the scene."

"Hi there, ho there!" Marina joined our small group. "Hokey-malowkey, would you look at that?" Her long, low whistle was full of awe. "I mean, when was the last time we had something like this in town? This is just, like . . . wow."

I flicked a glance at her, then looked around. "What are you doing here? Where are—"

"Hi, Mom." Jenna materialized out of nowhere. "Did you know Mrs. Neff got a scanner for her birthday? You can hear all sorts of cool stuff."

Oliver bumped up against me. I put my arm around his skinny shoulders and hugged him. Not too tight, because there were other people around, but enough to let him know that I was there and always would be.

I eyed Marina. "Your birthday is in February. And you didn't have a scanner last time I looked."

She grinned. "A late present. Noah, here"—she patted the head of a young boy—"wants to be a firefighter when he grows up. What could I do but get a scanner? And when there's a five-alarm fire, how could I not pack up the kids and bring them to see things up close and personal?"

"This isn't entertainment," I said. "This is probably a very sad day for . . . for . . ."

"For who, exactly?" Marina asked. "Dennis is gone, the office was empty, and they're containing the fire so it doesn't spread any farther. Where's the tragedy?"

She had a point, but it didn't feel right to turn a building fire into a pursuit of amusement, even if it was done under the guise of career education.

"Okay," she said, "there might have been some files in

there that were crucial to someone, but if Dennis Halpern was the financial wizard everybody said he was, I'm betting everything really important was duplicated and stored off-site in a location more secure than that secret room in the Pentagon."

"What secret room?"

"Whichever one is most secret." She rolled her eyes at my skeptical expression. "You think they don't have secret rooms there?"

I let it go and asked about the rest of her day-care kids. Her subsequent description of two sick children that had been sent home contained way more information about stomach contents than I wanted to know, but it did explain why she was relatively footloose and fancy-free. Except . . .

"You should have called to make sure it was all right with me to bring Jenna and Oliver here. Did you—" I gestured at the boy next to her. Noah was clutching her hand fiercely, and I couldn't make out whether his facial expression was one of awe or one of terror.

"Of course I did. And I tried to call you, my sweet, but there was no answer at the store, and all I got on your cell phone was an invitation to leave a message. Naturally, I assumed that you were being held prisoner by terrorists who would come after your children next, so I brought them to safety." She beamed.

I wondered if she'd made up that story on the spur of the moment or if she'd been saving it for the appropriate occasion.

"Hey." Marina scanned the crowd, which was now even larger. "Where's the new guy? What's his name, the one opened that Midwest store."

"Lou Spezza."

"Right. Why isn't he here? Everyone else is."

I looked around. If there was any business being done

in Rynwood this afternoon, it wasn't downtown. All the business owners, staff, and customers were watching the fire. The afternoon was pleasantly warm, and I had a sudden image of the citizens of Gettysburg watching the battle. Which led me to think of casualties and soldiers and generals and the effects of heat on men in heavy fire-retardant coats.

"Jenna," I said suddenly. "I'd like you and Oliver to go get some bottled water from Mr. Jarvis's store. As much as you can carry." I dug into my purse. "Here's some money. And buy some of those protein bars, too."

She took the bills. "Can I get some potato chips?"

"One small bag. Oliver, you can get one thing, too. Everything else is for the people fighting the fire."

"Come on, Oliver," Jenna said. "Let's go."

But Oliver didn't move. He stood still as ice, staring at the fire.

"Oliver?" Jenna asked.

I smiled and put a hand on his shoulder. Only a few months ago, that gesture had me lifting my hand only a little above my waist. Now I was beginning to think that Oliver would end up taller than my six-foot brother. "I think we might have another budding firefighter in our midst. Marina . . . ?"

She saluted. "No need to fear when Marina's here, Cap'n. I'll take good care of him."

Jenna and I hurried down to Randy's store. He was outside, leaning against a gas pump, looking disinclined to move. Once I explained what I wanted, he pushed himself off and came inside.

We hauled three shrink-wrapped packages of bottled water, a pile of protein bars, chips for Jenna and a brownie for Oliver to the counter, but when we tried to hand over cash, Randy wouldn't take it. "No, no. It wouldn't be right to take your money."

"These are for my children." I pushed the chips and brownie aside. "At least let me pay for those."

He put the bars and the kids' treats into a plastic bag. "Your kids are good kids. I'll treat them just this once. But don't say anything to anyone, okay?" He winked at Jenna.

Before I even had to prompt her, she smiled and said, "Thanks, Mr. Jarvis. I won't tell, I promise!"

"Thanks, Randy." I hefted two of the packages of water and the bag of snacks. "I'll be sure to let everybody know that you donated these."

He waved us off, and my daughter and I, laden with the supplies, staggered back down the street. When we reached Marina and the two boys, I told Jenna to stay there and slowly went forward until I was within earshot of Gus.

"Chief!" I called. Which wasn't the smartest way to call for Gus, because both he and the fire chief turned. I hefted the water. "Fresh from Randy's store. A donation."

Gus came over. "Bless you, Beth. You know the fire chief, right? Beth Kennedy, Dave Lindholm. Dave, Beth." The fire chief was cut from the same cloth as Gus: short-cropped hair that may or may not have been gray and weathered features that could have been anywhere from forty to sixty years old.

We made mutual nice-to-meet-you nods and Gus said, "Here, let me take this." He relieved me of the water. "The bag, too? What's in . . . oh, the good ones with the chocolate-chip bits inside." He grinned. "Do I have to share these with his guys?" He tipped his head at the fire chief.

"Yes," Dave said. "You do. Either that, or—" The radio attached to the shoulder of his shirt squawked. He bent his head toward it. "Go ahead."

"Better call him in," the voice said.

Dave nodded. "I figured. Thanks, Gary."

The muscles on Gus's face went still. "Is that what I think it means?" he asked.

"Yes." Dave turned to face the ruins of Dennis Halpern's office, burned down now to short blackened walls. "There's a good chance this was arson."

Chapter 10

The next morning, I was in Oliver's room, making sure he had everything he needed for the upcoming weekend visit with his father, when the phone rang. I trotted down the hall into my bedroom and picked up the cordless phone as the fourth ring started up.

My slightly breathless "Hello?" was answered by "Hey, Beth. Gus here. Can you stop by the station this morning?"

"Stop by?" All my actions from the previous eighteen hours flashed before my eyes. Had I been distracted while driving and accidentally gone over the speed limit? Run a stop sign? Maybe bringing food and drink to working firefighters was against some health code. Or . . .

"And, no, you haven't done anything wrong," he said. "Unless you'd like to confess to something."

"A perennial guilty conscience, that's all."

"Join the club."

I hung up the phone, wondering what it was he wanted.

"Mom?" Jenna stood in the doorway. She looked over her shoulder, then came into my room and shut the door behind her. "What's the matter with Oliver?" she asked, sitting on the edge of my bed. "He won't play any games or laugh or anything."

When she was younger and had a question or a problem or needed comforting, she'd curled up in the middle of the bed, wrapped up in the shaggy blanket she'd dragged out of her bedroom. When she was a little older, she'd sat with her back against the footboard, legs straight out, our feet touching. Now she sat on the edge. I supposed it was a natural progression, but there was a tug at my heart whenever she did it. How long before she didn't sit at all? How long before she didn't talk to me?

I sat next to her. She leaned against my shoulder, so I put my arm around her and kissed the top of her head. "I'm not sure, sweetheart. I've tried to talk to him, but he doesn't talk back."

"Yeah, I know."

We sat quietly for a moment. Now would have been a good time to tell her that adults don't always have the answers, that growing bigger just means you have bigger problems, and that not even moms always know the right thing to do.

Instead, I kissed her again. "I'll ask your father to talk to Oliver."

She nodded. "Yeah. That's a good idea." But she didn't sound convinced. And for good reason. Richard was many things—smart, financially successful, able to speak in front of large audiences without breaking a sweat—but he scored slightly below average when it came to extracting confidences from his children.

I felt another tug. Evan would have been a good person for Oliver to confide in. I could just picture the two of them, their heads together over some project, Evan asking gentle yet probing questions, Oliver replying in short sentences that grew longer and longer, until eventually the dam broke and he told all.

I sighed. Had I done the right thing in breaking things

off with Evan? At the time I'd been sure it was, but now . . . now . . .

"Time to get going." I gave Jenna a hug and passed on the chance to tell her that being an adult can mean questioning your decisions months and years after they'd been made.

"Thanks for coming in, Beth." Gus pushed his rolling chair back and propped his feet on the edge of a drawer.

I perched on the front edge of one of his two guest chairs. The last time I was in, they'd been a scratched-up wooden variety with brass-tipped legs and flat arms. This time they were ladder-back chairs with rattan seats and plaid cushions. Comfortable enough, but I wasn't sure they belonged in the office of a police chief. "Where did Winnie find these?"

Gus's wife was the uncrowned queen of garage sales. Once I'd asked her how she'd managed to find a gorgeous coffee table at the garage sale where I'd seen only infant clothing and plastic dishes. She'd laughed and said garage salers weren't made; they were born.

Gus glanced at the chairs. "Someplace way east of town. I want the other ones back, but she says she wants to refinish them."

He sounded a little irked, so I made a soothing remark about Winnie's refinishing expertise, about how when she finished, the chairs would look brand-new and ready to go for another fifty years of service.

"Yeah, she's pretty good, isn't she?" He smiled contentedly, then chuckled. "And that's why I wanted to talk to you."

"About furniture?"

"About your instincts for people."

I looked at him. "Instinctively, I know that you're trying to flatter me so I agree to do whatever it is you want me to do."

"See, you can read people like they're open books."

"Only if the print is large. And pictures help a lot."

Gus looked at me, no humor in his face. Apparently, he didn't think I was as funny as I did. "Last night the investigator called me. The fire was confirmed as arson."

For a second, there was no air in the room to breathe. I'd spent the rest of yesterday afternoon and all of the evening trying to convince myself that an arson investigator was always called in when there was a fire. Due diligence and all that, just doing my job, sir. But to know for a fact that someone had intentionally burned a building, that someone had purposefully lit a match and set a structure ablaze . . .

Gus went on. "A cursory inspection indicates a slow accelerant. The fire had probably been started Wednesday night and took until the next afternoon to flare up hot."

And had whoever set the fire had been watching? Waiting? Hoping? I shivered.

"You read people," Gus said. "You watch and you listen and you make those sudden mental leaps that bring results."

"I . . ." I didn't know what to say.

He dropped his feet to the floor and sat up straight. "There's a firebug in our town. Maybe it has something to do with Halpern's murder, maybe it doesn't. Don't do anything, but listen for me, will you, Beth? Watch. We need to get this guy. Anything you think might be helpful probably will be. Can I count on you?"

Gus was asking me for help. Pleading, really, in a very chief of police sort of way. What choice did I have?

"Sure," I said. "I'll do what I can."

*   *   *

Friday mornings at the store were typically the second busiest morning of the week. Saturdays were the hands-down winner, but Fridays ran a close second. Why, I didn't know, I just knew it was true.

So between the elderly customers wanting to find the perfect books for their grandchildren and to whom I was happy to sell armloads of Paddington Bear books (stuffed animal separate but often a happy accessory), the homeschooling mothers with kids in tow looking for books that explained chemistry in a way that wasn't deadly dull, the callers checking on special orders, and the occasional wanderer-in, I didn't have time to think about Gus and his request until almost lunchtime.

Lois heaved a monstrous sigh. "If only Sara were here."

I looked at her. "Sara never worked on Fridays."

"Yes, but if she had, if she *did*"—Lois shot me an evil glare—"my feet wouldn't hurt so much."

"Or, how about this?" I asked. "You could wear shoes that didn't hurt your feet."

From across the room, we heard Yvonne giggle. "No comments from the peanut gallery," Lois called. Yvonne's giggle subsided into quiet snorts.

I'd found it hard not to giggle myself. Today Lois had chosen to wear a bright pink skirt and paisley pinkish blouse. Both of which were fine, if you liked polyester, but the shoes she'd found to match the skirt were satin with a small rhinestone heart clipped on the front. The heels were tall and spiked and not made for a day of retail.

"Where did you get those, anyway?" I asked.

"Back of my closet." She hitched herself up onto the counter and turned her feet this way and that. "Far, far in the back. They still look pretty good, don't they? I always knew I'd get another wear out of them," she said with smug satisfaction. "Just think of it. The shoes my sister made me wear to her wedding lasted longer than the marriage did. Say, have you heard what I heard about your PTA having a curse on it?"

"I doubt it," I said. "I'll be in my office. Give me a yell if it gets busy."

"Mmm." Lois was still admiring her shoes, but Yvonne gave me a nod, so I headed to the back. "Let me know when it's time for you to go to lunch," I said. "I'll come up front."

I sat in my creaky chair, wondered if I could commission Winnie to find me a cheap, uncreaky version, pushed around a pile of catalogs, moved a pile of packing lists, moved them back. Looked at the stack of invoices. Looked away. Clicked the computer's mouse and saw that there were twenty-three e-mails to read.

Bleah.

The whole town thought the Tarver PTA had a curse on it.

Double bleah.

I leaned back in my chair and closed my eyes.

Prioritize. What needs to get done first? What matters most? Separate the superficially urgent from the truly important. Think, Beth, think . . .

Gus had said to trust my instincts. Or at least that's what he had implied. And right now my instincts were insisting that I was missing something crucial. Par for the course, since it often took days of finger-snapping forgetfulness for me to remember to pick up a new bag of cat litter, but as bloodcurdling as the annoyance of a cat could be, it came up short next to arson. And far below murder.

The other day I'd shied away from something. It had been when I was looking at Halpern and Company's website.

It was time to face what I'd closed my eyes to. I fired up my computer's browser and got to work.

When I sat back from the computer screen, my back ached, my neck had a crick in it, and my stomach was shouting for attention.

I glanced at my watch. "Two o'clock?" I jumped to my feet and hurried out to find Yvonne helping a pair of customers and Lois unconcernedly rearranging the front window display.

"What happened to lunch?" I asked. "You were supposed to call me."

She shrugged. "You had that I'm-too-focused-to-hear-you look on your face, so we left you alone. And it hasn't been that busy since this morning. What were you doing, anyway?"

Um. "Research." Gus hadn't said to keep my observations to myself, but if I told Lois what I'd found, half the town could know by the end of the day, and that didn't sound like a good idea. "Finances."

"Finances," Lois said flatly.

"Sure." I cast about for something to say that she might believe. "Did you know that Albert Einstein said that the most powerful force in the universe is compound interest?"

"Uh-huh."

"And Benjamin Franklin said that an investment in knowledge always pays the best interest."

"Good old Ben." She smiled and shook her head. "How could a man who was so smart about so many things be so stupid about women?"

The sidebar quotes on Halpern's pages had saved the day. "Men," I agreed. "I'm going down to the Green Tractor to get a salad. Do you or Yvonne want anything?"

Safe and out on the sidewalk, I thought about the financial lectures I'd just sped through. Sped, because I'd turned the sound off. I hadn't been trying to gain financial knowledge, what I'd wanted to see was the people attending the lectures.

Because whoever set that fire might have killed Dennis. And maybe, just maybe, the killer had attended Dennis's lecture series.

Chapter 11

I stood in the small space, shivering inside my underwear. The rest of my clothes had disappeared and I could only hope that new ones would appear soon. I risked a glance down at my legs. Dimply, lumpy, and pasty white. I averted my eyes. Quickly.

What is it about women that we're hardest on ourselves when we're at our most vulnerable? Why can't we be proud of the mileage on our bodies? Why, when mostly naked and exposed to harsh overhead lights that must have been designed to highlight our flaws, do we insist on a critical self-assessment?

"Here you go," Marina called. There was a *thump*, and an armful of clothes appeared over the top of the dressing room door and started slithering toward the floor.

I half dove to catch them. "Men don't even try on clothes," I said, hanging Marina's selections on a hook. "Why do we have to?"

"Because we care how we look and they don't."

"That makes men sound smart," I muttered.

"What?"

"I said this outfit looks smart."

"Which one?"

There were three. I rapidly sorted through the selections and chose the least of the multiple evils. The first was a leopard-print blouse and skinny white jeans. I barely even looked at that one. White jeans? How could she possibly think that someone who ran a bookstore could wear white jeans without getting them filthy by midmorning?

The next outfit was a multicolor nubbly jacket that centered on orange hues, beige wide-legged pants, and a pink floral shirt that looked designed to remain untucked. I eyed it. Untucked, it would be longer than the jacket, and in spite of the number of young people wearing shirts out below sweaters and jackets, there was no way on this earth I'd ever do so.

Last was a pair of black pants, a black long-sleeved shirt, and a knee-length sleeveless vest made of wide red and black panels. I didn't have the panache to pull off wearing something like that, but I liked the look of it. "The red and black thing," I said.

"The duster?"

Whatever. I flipped over a couple of the price tags and almost choked. "Take them all away. Did you see the prices on these things? Bring my clothes back and let's get out of here."

"You don't get it, do you?" she asked. The leopard and the nubbly outfits slid away, but the red and black remained. "I never said we'd buy anything tonight, did I?"

I thought back. She'd said let's go try on some clothes. Silly old Beth for expanding that to purchasing. "What's the point of trying on clothes I can't afford?"

"To figure out what looks good on you."

"I don't need what looks good. I need clothes I can wear to work."

"Try it on," she commanded. "When I'm in Hawaii with the DH one month, three weeks, and five days from now, I want to know that my influence lingers."

I hugged my prickly skin and eyed the duster. If I actually wore something like that, I'd have the hem ripped out by the end of the day from standing on it when I crouched down to reach a low bookshelf.

"Say," Marina said. "Do you think the fire had anything to do with Dennis's murder?"

"You are the queen of the non sequitur." I held the duster up against me. Hung it back over the door. "It seems like a huge coincidence if they were separate crimes."

"That's what I think. So I was up half of last night watching those lecture videos on the Halpern and Company website."

"You were?" Had Marina and I had been friends so long that we were starting to think the same way? "Talk about coincidences."

"Did you say something? Anyway, I think I figured out who murdered Dennis. Pretty smart of me, to watch those videos, I'd say. Offering free financial advice was bound to cause problems, you know? And this is the best way to get rid of the nonexistent yet tenacious PTA curse, I'm sure of it. Solve the murder, end the curse."

My time in front of the computer screen had been spent scrutinizing body movements, facial expressions, the way each person had watched Dennis, the way they'd applauded at the end, and the way they'd watched other people ask questions. "I watched the videos, too. Did you notice that woman in the second row of the first lecture?" She had short spiky hair, a fierce expression, and she hadn't taken a single note.

"Here. Try this." A short denim skirt sailed over the top of the door, followed by a blouse whose fabric inspiration must have come from the garden at Giverny. "Nope, didn't see her. But did you see that guy in the front row? That tie? Oh. My. Word."

I added the recent arrivals to the reject pile. "How about the fourth lecture? Did you notice that young man? The one with the beard?" It had been the extreme neatness of the beard's trim that had caught my attention. Maybe he'd just come from the barber, maybe he just liked his beard trimmed tight. Either way, I'd noticed him and subsequently noticed his crossed arms and tapping feet. Why, if he was interested enough in what Dennis had to say that he'd attended the lecture in person, had he looked so hostile?

"Nah. But did you see the woman in the first video? Front and center? That lace shirt was just soooo nineties."

As most of the clothes in my closet were at least that old, I tried not to take her statement personally. "There was a man in the last lecture who creeped me out." He'd been seated at the far end of the front row. I'd watched every foot of video he'd been in and never once had I seen him blink. It had been fascinating, in an awful sort of way, but also disturbing. Eyes *have* to blink, it's what eyes do. About the only time they don't is when someone is concentrating intensely. And while the lectures had been interesting, not even a speech by Brad Pitt would keep me from blinking. So why hadn't that guy?

"Yeah," Marina said, tossing over a ruffled shell in an odd gray raindrop pattern, a red jacket, and white pants. "We're talking about that doofus with the plaid flannel shirt and the pocket protector, right? That was wrong on so many levels, I don't even know where to start."

What was it with her and white pants? I put it all aside.

"Would someone completely innocent wear that combination?" Marina was asking. "I think not."

"You're basing your who-killed-Dennis theory on clothes?"

"Hark! I hear the flag of doubt being raised."

All the way to the top of the flagpole. "I can't believe you're accusing people of murder based on the clothes they're wearing."

"Not accusing. We're declaring them persons of interest." She put a pair of black pants and a gold sparkly sleeveless top on the door. "Or should it be people of interest?"

I wasn't about to touch either those clothes or her question. Exploring the subtleties of grammar and punctuation with Marina was a pointless exercise.

"Okay, I can hear you in there," she said. "You're thinking that judging a person by her clothes is shallow and meaningless. That it doesn't matter what anyone wears, that clothes are in no way an accurate indicator of intent and action."

I fingered the gold spangles, just to see what it felt like. Not nearly as scratchy as I'd anticipated.

"So let me ask you this." The top of Marina's red head popped over the door and she skewered me with a look. "If clothes don't mean anything, why won't you let Jenna wear those tank tops with the spaghetti straps?"

"That's different."

"No, it's not." For once, Marina sounded completely serious. "It's exactly the same thing. You don't want her to wear clothes like that because they're not appropriate for her age. You don't want her to wear something that sends a message about her."

"That's . . ." I wanted to repeat myself, to keep saying that it was different, but I saw where Marina was going, and she was right.

"But that's what clothes are all about," she said. "Sending a message. Like it or not, that's what they do. Sometimes the message is I don't care about clothes"—her index finger snuck over the top of the door and pointed at me—"but it's still a message. Other people choose to have fun with their messages." Her head disappeared. "See?" A pink feathered boa flung itself over the top of the sparkly shirt. "How about these as part of a new store uniform? Maybe Paoze can wear a flamenco shirt. You know, with those sleeve ruffles?"

"There's nothing wrong with fun." Two small pink feathers drifted free, and one tickled my nose. I sneezed. "But you can't let it interfere with the things that need doing."

"You mean like alphabetizing your socks? Please. All work and no play makes Beth a drab duckling in deep need of a makeover."

Was Marina entering a new phase? Out with the Southern belle, and in with the fractured maxims. "Beth needs a makeover like she needs another ex-husband. What we do need, however, is a way to learn more about those people in Dennis's lectures, and I can't think how to do that." I'd watched six different videos and hadn't recognized a single person. The series had been in Madison, so I shouldn't have expected to see anyone I knew, and I hadn't, but I'd still been disappointed.

"Leave it to me," Marina said, flinging a sand-hued beaded jacket over the door. A white shell and silky brown pants followed.

"Leave what to you?" Certainly not my wardrobe.

"The people on the video. I haff vays ov vinding uut."

Suddenly, messed-up maxims didn't seem so bad. At least they were original.

"Speaking of ex-husbands," Marina said. "What is Richard doing with the kids this weekend?"

I unclipped the pair of black pants from the hanger. "Not sure. But I did call him last night and convince him to have a man-to-nine-year-old chat with Oliver."

"No improvement on that front, I take it?" The

beaded jacket and its friends disappeared. "I'd thought maybe the fire would snap him out of whatever funk he's in. I know, I know, it's a horrible thing to make hay out of another's dark cloud, but you can't blame a redhead for trying."

"When we took Spot for a walk last night, Oliver didn't ask any questions."

The rustling noise that Marina was making stopped. "None?"

I tugged on the pants. Tight, but not so tight I couldn't walk in them. Hunching down to get at a bottom shelf however . . . "There was a plumber parked at a house on the next block and Oliver didn't ask why he was there." My curious son always asked questions. Always. To see him glance at the truck, then look away with sparkless eyes had given my insides a hard, wringing twist.

Marina was silent. She'd known Oliver since the day he was born. She knew this was serious. "Do you think Richard will be able to help?"

I held the shiny gold shirt up to me. Put it back on the hanger. "He's his father."

"That's not an answer."

No, it wasn't. Unfortunately, it was all I had. "Let's just say I'll be working on a backup plan." All night and all weekend, if that's what it took. Finding out what was wrong with my son had escalated from oh-he'll-be-fine to it-might-be-time-to-interview-therapists.

I looked at the hooks full of clothes I didn't want and would never wear. Marina's intentions were good, but suddenly I didn't want anything to do with any of it. "Let's go home, okay?"

She must have heard the ache I'd tried to keep out of my voice, because she said, "Sure, honey. Whatever you want." My own clothes slipped over the door.

Never had jeans and a polo shirt looked so good. I

slipped them on and tried not to worry about Oliver. He was with his father. Richard was a great dad, and now that the problem had been brought to his attention, he'd work on getting Oliver to talk. It would all work out. There was no need to worry.

But I did, of course. Worrying was one of the things moms did best.

Chapter 12

I headed to the store bright and early the next morning. Saturday. The kids were probably already up and arguing about what TV show to watch. Richard, if our nearly twenty years of marriage had any bearing on his current habits, was sitting in his recliner, sucking down a pot of coffee, and growling at the headlines of whatever morning newspaper still existed. Richard was not a morning person.

Sipping at the travel mug of tea I'd brewed before leaving the house, I got out of the car. It was a chai tea, spicy with cardamom, cinnamon, and ginger. But even the pepper that gave it a hint of heat didn't do a thing to mask the smell coming from Dennis Halpern's former offices.

It was that burned-over smell you got from a campfire the morning after a beach party, only magnified a hundred times. A small breeze pushed the sour scent onto my face and I revised the number to a thousand.

The faint sound of footsteps turned me around. I started to say "Good morning," but didn't get beyond the first consonant because no one was in sight.

What, then, had I heard?

Who had I heard?

I shook my head to get rid of a vague sense of creepiness. I walked down the alley to the side street, then slowly made my way to the source of the smell.

Charred ends of blackened ceiling joists pointed skyward. Exterior walls, pushed in by the post-fire mop-up crew, flopped crazily on top of debris that littered what had been the floor. I made out the shape of what might have once been a filing cabinet, but it could just as easily have been a metal desk.

What a mess. There aren't many things messier than a fire. What the flames hadn't destroyed, the smoke had damaged, and whatever the smoke hadn't ruined had been taken care of by the water the firefighters had poured on.

When she was just out of high school, my older sister, Darlene, had dated a volunteer firefighter. I'd been shocked to hear him say that the fire department wasn't there to save buildings from burning. "We show up," he'd said, "to save lives and to keep a fire from spreading. Saving the house, the barn, the business, the whatever? Ain't going to happen. Not by the time we get there."

I'd told him that had to be wrong. Then I'd been summarily evicted from the room by Darlene and I'd gone to sit in my favorite tree to think about it. Eventually I'd come to the sad realization that he was right.

But I didn't like it then and I didn't like it now.

I tipped my head back and swallowed the last of the tea, gagging a little as the bottom sludge hit the back of my throat. After shoving the mug into an outside pocket of my capacious purse, I extracted my cell phone and pushed buttons.

"Hi, Pete. It's Beth." I suddenly realized it wasn't even nine o'clock yet. "Sorry to bother you so early. I didn't wake you, did I?"

"It'd be a crime to sleep in on a morning like this," he said. "What's up?"

I looked at the piles that had once been a small business. "Do you know anything about fires? In buildings?"

"I know they're the worst thing in the world to clean up. Most times you're best off bulldozing the whole kit and caboodle. Between the smoke and the water damage, there's usually not much worth saving, even if the place hadn't been even close to burning all the way down. Hard, for homeowners." He sounded pensive. "You want to save stuff. You know, the personal things that make your house a home. And maybe that photo album looks okay, but it's going to reek of smoke forever. You're better off just pitching it."

How horribly sad. The pictures of your children. Gone. The hair from their first haircuts you'd tied up with pink and blue ribbons. Gone. The necklace your father had given you on your sixteenth birthday, the Bible you'd received in third-grade Sunday School, the first Mother's Day card your child gave you, gone, gone, gone.

All just stuff, all just material things that shouldn't matter . . . but they did. They mattered very much.

"How long," I asked Pete, "until an arson investigator can go in and do his investigation?"

"You talking about the Halpern fire?"

If this was Evan I'd been talking to, back in our dating days, I would have tried to sidestep around the topic. Evan had wanted me to stay far away from anything that even dimly resembled meddling with police business. But this was Pete. He was a friend, not a boyfriend. Besides, he wasn't anything like Evan. "Standing ten feet from it," I told him.

Pete laughed. "Bet it stinks something fierce. Arson guys, well, it depends on the building, the kind of fire, how hot a fire. A day to a week, I'd guess."

Which was what I'd assumed. I'd just have to wait until Gus gave me the details, and that could be a while.

"Not much help, am I? Anything else I can not help you with?" He chuckled. "What are the kids up to today?"

"You're a big help," I said. "The kids are with their dad. And . . ." A lightbulb went off in my head. "And come to think of it, there is something you can do, if you don't mind."

"I live to serve."

I smiled. Funny, nice, and helpful. "Were you a Boy Scout as a kid?"

"Tried to be a Cub Scout once. They kicked me out for eating all the cookies."

"You're making that up."

"Sure am," he said cheerfully. "What can I help you with?"

My smile went flat. "It's Oliver. There's something wrong with him." I gave the symptoms. "This started about a week ago, and he won't talk to me about it. I've asked my ex-husband to find out, but I'm not sure that will work. Oliver thinks you're great and maybe you can get him to talk."

"You want me to talk to your son?"

I heard the surprise in his voice. "I'm sorry. It's too much to ask. Forget I said anything. Please. I'm sorry and—"

Pete ran over my babbling. "Beth. I'd be happy to talk to Oliver."

"You . . . would?"

"Sure. Anything I can to do to help, I will. He's a good kid. They're both good kids." He paused. "And—"

A woman's scream ripped the morning apart. Whatever Pete had been saying was lost in her anguish. I dropped my phone into my purse and ran.

Another scream tore at the air. The alley. It had come from the alley behind the stores on the other side of the street.

I ran hard as I could, fast as I could toward the sound, a sound layered over now with the barking of dogs. Hard, sharp yips that could mean anything from "Halt, intruder!" to "Hey, let's play!" More than one dog. Two? Three? I wasn't sure. However many, they sounded big.

My feet pounded over the narrow sidewalk between the hair salon and Glenn's insurance agency. Between the hard surfaces of the buildings, the noises of my running footsteps and panting breaths were larger than life.

Faster . . . faster . . .

I burst into the early sunshine flooding the alley. Two dogs, Lou Spezza's dogs, yipping and barking, their teeth showing white. A woman clutching the edge of a Dumpster, shrieking. Her silver hair shook wildly as her whole body quivered into reedy panic.

I plunged forward, not thinking, not anticipating, just doing. "Down, boy! Down!" I grabbed their collars and pulled them backward, trying to remember their names. Paired names. Twin names? Yes. "That's a good boy, Pollux. Good dog, Castor."

They each yipped one more time; then they subsided into happy dog grins. Tails wagging, they looked at me, at Flossie, and at me again, waiting for praise and pets.

"Sit," I commanded, and the dogs sat on the alley's cracked asphalt. "Good dogs," I murmured, looking around. I didn't see Lou—and where was he, with his dogs out here?—but I spotted a roll of garbage bags, the end trailing long on the ground, marking the spot where it had been dropped. "Stay." I held my hands in front of their faces. "Stay." They looked up at me adoringly, their fluffy golden-retriever-esque tails swishing back and forth.

I glanced at Flossie. She was clinging to the corner of the Dumpster, eyes closed. I wanted to go to her, but first things first. With one hand, I snatched up the roll. With the other, I drew out half a dozen black bags. In seconds I'd knotted together two makeshift leashes. One end of each I tied to their collars, the other ends I tied around the back wheel of the Dumpster.

"Good boys." I gave their heads one last pat. As Castor—or was it Pollux?—tried to lick my hand, I saw a piece of paper rolled around his collar and taped to itself to secure it. Odd. Maybe Lou had put it there until he could get a real dog ID made? Maybe it had his phone number on it. I untaped and unrolled it, thinking that I'd call him on my cell and—

My brain came to a screeching halt. I read the note through a second time. A third. And, since it was only a four-word sentence, I read it another time. Then I folded it up and slipped it into my pocket.

Flossie made a sad bleat of a noise. I went to her side and put my arm around her. "Come over here," I said. "Sit down on the step. It's a little dirty, but . . . Yes, there you go." I sat beside her, not letting go of her thin body. "Just sit a few minutes. The dogs are tied up and there's nothing to worry about."

She tried to talk, but all that came out was a stuttering breath.

"Shhh," I said, hugging her tight. "Shhh. You don't need to talk. I'll do it for you, okay? Then, when you feel a little better, you can tell me whatever you want to tell me."

So I babbled about nothing. About the weather, about the Super Bowl chances for the Green Bay Packers, about the color Lois wanted to paint the workroom, about what I'd eaten for breakfast, about the price of tea in China.

Finally, Flossie drew in a long, shuddering breath and sat up straight. I let my arm fall to my side and waited.

"Thank you, my dear. You are a gem and a treasure,"

she said, "and I will never forget what you did for me today."

I tried to deflect her thanks. What had I done, really, but save her from a licking by two overly friendly dogs?

She grabbed my hand so hard that I winced. "You have no idea what you did. I am deathly afraid of dogs. Have been ever since I was four. A neighbor's Alsatian . . ." Her breaths went short and sharp. "A neighbor's Alsatian attacked me. I . . . I . . ."

"Don't say any more," I said. "You don't need to relive it." Memories were surfacing, Flossie crossing the street whenever a dog was walking toward her. Her fixed smile when I plopped a big bag of dog food on the checkout belt and talked about Spot.

"No." She blew out a small sigh. "Thank you for not needing to hear the story."

"Just promise you won't ask to hear about the time I almost drowned."

Flossie smiled and the muscles at the base of my spine relaxed just a bit. She was going to be fine. She'd been surprised by the dogs, that's all. No need to worry about her. She was hale and hearty and she was in better condition at her age than many people ever were. She was . . . My throat tightened as my thoughts went deeper.

She was eighty-one. She was in great condition for her age, but she was still eighty-one. Old enough that she should be kicking back and spending some time on herself, not wearing out her body tossing the morning garbage into the Dumpster. But if I suggested that maybe it was time for Patrick to take over the heavier work, I'd get a smile, a "Thanks for thinking of me," and she'd go on doing what she'd been doing for the last thirty years. "I'm far too young to take it easy," she'd say.

When, I wondered, was it appropriate to interfere in someone else's life? When was it the right idea to speak up? How much did we owe our fellow human beings? Our friends? Our families?

I looked sideways at Flossie's thin frame. She shouldn't be working so hard, not when there was another way. Maybe I'd have a talk with Patrick. Suggest that he not talk to Flossie about a change, that he just go ahead and start doing some of the heavier chores. Was that too manipulative?

And this brought up the best question of all: Why was it so hard to figure out the right thing to do?

"Penny for your thoughts," Flossie said.

"Oh . . ." I realized I'd heaved a heavy sigh. "Um, I was wondering whether or not I should show you what was on one of the dog's collars."

Flossie glanced at the dogs, then away. "I saw you put something in your pocket. What was it?"

I really didn't want to show it to her. It wouldn't be right to keep it from her, but I really didn't want to. My natural inclination to tell the truth warred with my wish to protect her. "A note."

"For me?"

"It didn't have a name on it." At least I didn't think so. I pulled the notepaper from my pocket. No name. Just the four short words. Silently, I handed Flossie the note.

She read it out loud. "Keep quiet or die." She frowned. "What kind of note is that? Far too melodramatic and not at all specific. Keep quiet about what, for goodness' sake? How can I keep quiet if I don't know what not to say?"

I stared at her, then started laughing. "I can't think of anyone else in the world who would criticize the structure of a death threat."

"You would. You probably already have." She tapped the words. "You've probably already noted the eight-and-a-half-by-eleven piece of normal copy paper, the black ink from a ballpoint pen, and the block capital letters that could have been written by almost anyone."

She was right, of course.

"So the question," Flossie went on, "is what do I know that is a threat to someone?"

"Any ideas?"

She handed the paper back to me. "None whatsoever."

"The only thing that makes sense," I said slowly, "is that you know something about the fire. Or Dennis Halpern's murder." I read the note again. The straight lines of the letters were frightening somehow. Too bold, too forceful. I folded the paper and put it back in my pocket, trying not to think that the person who had killed Dennis had touched it. They were Lou's dogs, but did Lou have anything to do with the note? It would be extremely stupid if he did, and he seemed too smart for that. Still, they were his dogs.

"I don't know anything about the murder or the fire." Flossie ran her fingers through her hair, then patted it into place.

Three seconds of mostly unconscious action and her hair looked as good as if she'd walked out of the salon. Had she been born with that ability or had it come about from her years on the stage? My life was full of questions that I didn't dare ask. "Maybe you know something that you don't realize you know."

She smiled. "That sounds like an impossibility."

"And it doesn't sound like you're taking this seriously."

"A message wrapped around a dog collar?" She laughed. "There are more effective ways to send a threat, I should think. Whispered phone calls at midnight, perhaps. Or footsteps behind you in the dark. Or items in your home being rearranged. Or—"

Suddenly we heard heavy feet pounding toward us. I jumped up and stood in front of Flossie. She pulled at my hands, but I stood firm.

Lou Spezza came around the corner of the grocery store, arms pumping. "Beth!" he called. "Have you seen my dogs? They're gone, just gone and—" His eyes followed my pointing finger. "There you are!" He ran to the dogs and dropped to his knees, gathering them into his arms. "You good bad dogs. Yes, you're all right. Daddy's here."

The hind ends of the dogs waggled back and forth as their tails went wild. They licked Lou's mustache, making him laugh and bury his face in their fur. "Now, don't ever do that again, okay? Running away like that is bad for your old dad's heart."

He got to his feet. "Thanks so much for finding Castor and Pollux. I have no idea how they got out. I've been in the store since six, working on a new display. I went up to the apartment a few minutes ago to let the dogs out and the door was open." He stood, one dog on either side of him, their heads leaning against his legs. "I was sure I'd shut and locked it, but . . ." He frowned, then shrugged. "But I must not have."

He looked at Flossie, who'd come to her feet and was standing slightly behind me. "Flossie, right? Sorry about my dogs. I won't let it happen again."

"Thank you," Flossie said, and I wondered if I was the only one who heard the frost in her voice.

Lou laid a hand on each dog's head. "I really am very sorry," he said quietly.

So he'd heard it, too.

"Yes." Flossie nodded. "I can see that. So I will also assume you know nothing about the note?"

Lou's eyebrows drew together.

It was so obvious what his next words were going to

be that I preempted him by taking the note out of my pocket and holding it out.

"Keep quiet or die?" His frown deepened to the level where his mother, had she been around, would have warned him about his face freezing that way. "Where was this?"

"Around Castor's collar." Or was it Pollux's? "One of their collars, anyway."

"But . . ." Lou's black eyebrows drew so close that they touched. "But how did it get there? And what does it mean? Keep quiet about what?" He read the note again. Turned the paper over, saw that it was blank, turned it back again. "This doesn't make any sense."

I looked at Flossie. "How many people know how you feel about dogs?"

"My irrational and abject fear of the creatures, you mean?" Flossie smiled, but it wasn't a real smile. All surface and no substance. I started to say something, but she shook her head. "Almost everyone, I imagine. Certainly I've made a public spectacle of myself more than once."

I wanted to say that no one would think less of her for having a dog phobia, that everyone was frightened of something and her fear was just more visible than most people's, that's all. Most of all, I wanted to tell her that it didn't matter. But from the shadow in her smile, I could see that it did. She was embarrassed at her behavior, and if I knew Flossie at all, she'd probably tried to do something about her fear for years and failed.

So, yes, it mattered. Even if it didn't matter to anyone else, it mattered to her. And what should I do about it? I thought through the possibilities. How would I want to be treated if it were me?

Easy enough.

"It could be worse," I said. "You could have an irrational fear of broccoli. I've heard that's impossible to get over."

Flossie blinked at me, then barked out a laugh. "You're right. It could be worse."

"Yeah," Lou said, chuckling. "It could be a fear of canned goods."

"Or cardboard boxes," Flossie said.

"Pennies."

Smiling, I looked from one of them to the other as they got sillier and sillier. When they'd reached the point of inanity, I sighed and brought the conversation back to earth with a hard thud. "Lou, so you don't have any idea how the dogs got out? Or how the note got on Pollux's collar?"

"How they got out, it must have been an accident," Lou said. "The only thing that makes sense. Must have been I didn't shut the door tight. I mean, do you know for sure that you shut and locked your door this morning?"

I had been, until that very second. Now, of course, I was going to have to call Marina and ask her to go check. "And the note?" I tried to ask the question in my best possible Gus imitation, but I sounded more like a mom questioning a child about a broken window.

"No idea," Lou said, looking at his dogs. "The boys were running around loose, and someone . . . well, I don't know why anyone would have done that."

A thought popped into my head. "Do you think they could get a fingerprint off the collars? Even a part of one might be worth something."

"Not a chance," Lou said quickly. "Not those nylon mesh collars. Those won't take a print at all. Leather ones, maybe, but not that nylon. And the buckles are way too small to get anything worthwhile."

Flossie and I looked at each other. Had he been playing the "I'm a guy, so I may be making this up, but I'm going to say it in such an authoritative way that you won't think to question me," card? Maybe. But it made sense. Still . . .

I held out my hand and Lou gave me the note. A thought flitted through my head; would he have done that if he'd written the threat? Another thought followed fast; everybody's motives are a mystery, even your own, so don't think you can guess anyone else's.

"We should take this to the police," I said.

The reply came in unison: "No!"

I looked from one to the other. "Why not? This is a threat, Flossie. Maybe it's something to worry about, maybe it isn't, but Gus and the guys should know about it."

"No fussing." Flossie stood tall as if the top of her head were attached to an invisible string in the sky pulling her taut. "You go to Gus and Gus will talk to Patrick, and the next thing you know, I'll be shut into Sunny Rest with nothing to do except knit hats for the great-great-nephews and -nieces I don't yet have."

"It was probably kids," Lou said. "I seen these three punks hanging around the last couple of weeks. They looked like trouble, the kind that would do something like this."

I remembered the tongue-lashing Melody had given the Harvey brothers. From what I'd heard of them, they were more the type that would break into vacant houses than the death-threat type, but they did have that dog, so maybe.

"What if," I said carefully, "what if I talk to Gus in confidence? Just ask him to keep an eye out. Not make a formal report or anything?"

"No." Flossie snatched the note from my hand and ripped it in half. I protested, but she ignored me and ripped the note in half a second and a third time. She tried for a fourth, but the papers were getting too thick, so she tossed the scraps into the Dumpster. She turned to us, dusting her palms together. "There. All taken care of, yes?"

Lou gave her an admiring grin. "No fuss, no muss. I like that."

I studied Lou. "You don't think going to the police is a good idea? Not even for Flossie's sake?"

His mouth opened. Shut. Opened again. "If that's what she wants. But it's up to her."

Flossie nodded. "And my decision is not to bother anyone with any of this. Thank you, Lou. And, Beth, I'll thank you to keep this episode to yourself. Do I have your promise?"

"Are you sure?"

Lou smoothed his mustache, right side first, then the left. "She sounds sure to me. I think you should respect her decision."

Flossie laid a hand on my arm. "Please, Beth."

I looked at her hand. Flossie was smart, talented, beautiful, and kind, but she wasn't someone to instigate physical contact. Not the hugging type, not the air-kiss type. For her to do this . . .

"Whatever you want," I said, then couldn't decide who looked more relieved, Flossie or Lou.

Chapter 13

On Sunday morning, the church sanctuary was filled with slanting sunbeams. The sunshine lit the little faces gathered up front for the children's sermon with a soft glow that was worthy of a portrait artist. An intense longing for my own children stabbed at me, and it faded only when the minister got up to the pulpit and began to speak. Distraction can be a good thing.

I whiled away the afternoon by taking a long walk with Spot, trying to enjoy the sound of other family's backyard games, and welcomed Jenna and Oliver home with hugs and warm cookies fresh out of the oven.

Weekends without the kids were sometimes very, very long.

Monday morning's weather was a shocking reversal from the sun and warmth we'd been enjoying. Rainy and cold and dark, it was a reminder that October was fast on its way. The multiple mugs of tea I downed did little to warm me up, and I spent the morning shivering and wishing I'd worn something warmer than thin dress pants and an Oxford shirt.

Lois had clucked at my clothing. "Light blue over navy? That has to be the most boring color combination in your closet. And look at you, not a single accessory. No bracelet, no scarf, no necklace, not even a pair of earrings."

I glanced down at my practical, reasonably priced, no-iron clothing. "Tell me again that you and Marina aren't in cahoots."

Lois twirled one end of her fuzzy scarf. It was a multicolored hand-knit gift from a niece, and the multiple hues almost went with the olive drab pants and deep purple top. None of which matched the light pink sneakers, but color matching wasn't ever one of Lois's primary concerns. "Why, is she on you to get out of your mom clothes rut?"

"We were at the mall on Friday night. You should have seen some of the stuff she was tossing over the dressing room door."

"Ha." Lois grinned. "Wish I could have seen you in some of her picks." She narrowed her eyes as I rolled mine. "Don't tell me you didn't try anything on."

"One."

"Gold lamé sheath dress?" She raised her eyebrows. "A spangly tube top?"

I flashed back to the single thing I'd taken off a hanger—the black pants—and pointed at my watch. "The first interview will be here in a few minutes."

Lois sighed dramatically. "I know. I know. You want me up front and you and Yvonne will interview her. Why don't I ever get to have any fun?"

I held up two fingers. "Two answers. Number one is that you're not to be trusted around potential new hires due to your penchants for hyperbole and mischief. Or you can choose option two, which is you're the person I trust most to run the store while I'm otherwise occupied."

"Hmm." Lois rubbed her chin. "I choose option three."

I looked at my two fingers. "What's that?"

"That it's both one and two."

She was right, of course, and we both knew it. "Option four," I said. "We could skip the interviewing thing and hire Marcia back."

I said it matter-of-factly, as closely as I could to sounding serious. Lois stared at me. "You're joking, right? Tell me you're joking. You must be . . . right?"

"If I called, I bet she'd come back in a heartbeat."

Lois fixed me with a hard glare. "Option three it is." She spun around and marched off, muttering, "Marcia. Ha. Marcia Trommler wasn't worth the toner her paycheck was printed with, let alone the paper. Marcia. As if."

Smiling, I retreated to my office to get ready for the first job applicant.

Twenty minutes later, the office felt even smaller and more cramped than it was. Not only were three people occupying it—two more than the fire marshal would have liked to see—but the comfort level was down to an all-time low.

"So, April." I smiled at the girl. Well, young woman, technically, since she was a recent high school graduate and a part-time student at a nearby community college, but she didn't look much older than Jenna. Her straight dark blond hair parted in the middle, she wore black pants that bore a striking resemblance to the ones I'd tried on the other night and a knit shirt she kept pulling down. That, plus her anxious expression all contributed to an overall impression of youth, innocence, and a complete inability to work in a children's bookstore. "What books did you like to read when you were in school?"

The three of us had been sitting here for a fifteen-minute eternity. It had taken me less than sixty seconds to realize that April wasn't suited for the job, but it would have been cruel to end an interview that quickly. Instead,

I'd plowed ahead with my questions, and for the last five minutes Yvonne had been casting me panicked looks that could only mean "You're not seriously thinking of hiring this kid, are you?"

I tried to send her comforting glances, but she still looked nervous. Not nearly as nervous as April, though. The poor girl was so soft-spoken that every time she talked, I had to ask her to repeat herself. And even then, I caught her words only half the time. Sadly, I'd found my mind wandering even as the girl was talking about the books she'd loved as a child.

While April whispered about staying up until midnight to buy Harry Potter books, I worried about my son. Richard hadn't been able to get Oliver to talk at all, and Pete had been called out of state on a big cleaning job he couldn't afford to turn down. "I'm really sorry, Beth," he'd said, talking on his cell phone while he was driving west. "I can call him if you want, but I'm guessing that won't work as well."

I'd reassured Pete that it could wait, but last night Oliver had woken up, shrieking with nightmares that he wouldn't talk about.

What on earth was I going to do? My hugs and kisses might help temporarily, but what about tonight? And the next night?

"After I was done with Harry Potter," April said, so softly that Yvonne and I were on the edges of our seats, straining to hear, "then I started reading the Twilight books. You know, Stephenie Meyer?" She looked at us doubtfully, didn't look reassured when Yvonne and I said that we did, in fact, know about Stephenie Meyer, but went on with her recitation of the books that had changed her life. "It was, like, beautiful, you know?"

Meanwhile, I wondered if Marina's list of suspects had any value whatsoever. Did clothes really reveal so much about us? Did those FBI profilers—if they actually existed—take clothes into account when looking at . . . at whatever they looked?

But under all those thoughts was the steady question that ran low and slow and treacherous: What had Lou been hiding? Because as surely as boys loved to play in the mud, Lou hadn't wanted to talk to Gus. And whyfor would fair Lou not want to talk to law enforcement? One reason only. Because he was hiding something.

All of which led to the obvious question of: What was he hiding?

I tugged at my lower lip. I liked the man, I really did. But people had liked Ted Bundy, too, and if Flossie was in danger . . .

"Beth?" Yvonne asked.

I blinked. Both Yvonne and April were looking at me. Um. "Thanks so much for coming in, April," I said, putting on a fast smile. "We have a number of applicants to interview. We'll let you know."

We watched her make a fast exit. Yvonne hummed a few notes of indecision, then said, "She seems . . . like a very nice girl."

I sighed. "Yes. Unfortunately, nice isn't enough."

"No."

We sat a moment longer, thinking our own thoughts, which for both of us probably ran along the lines of "It's too bad that nice isn't enough, and wouldn't it be a wonderful world if it was?"

Finally I pushed back from the desk. "I'll call the library. They're doing a complete inventory next month. She'll be perfect for that."

Yvonne's smile brightened the room. "You're a nice lady, Beth," she said. "I'm proud to work for you."

She left, but I continued to sit in my chair, staring at nothing.

Nice. It wasn't enough, and never would be. I needed far more than nice, and I was afraid I didn't have any idea how to get it.

Whatever "it" was.

That night was the first meeting of Summer's committee. I'd called her on Saturday from the bookstore. "Summer, it's getting to be the end of September. Your committee is supposed to have a proposal to the PTA board by the November meeting, remember?"

"Oh, so you think we should meet soon?"

I couldn't decide whether to shriek at her like a harpy or fall to my knees sobbing. "Yes," I said, with all the patience I could muster. "We should meet soon."

Another pause. "Are you mad at me?"

Apparently, the patience at my disposal hadn't been enough. Deep, calming breath. "No, I'm not angry. All I'm saying is we need to get going. Putting together a proposal like this could take a lot of meetings."

"Oh. You really think so?"

More deep breaths.

"Beth?" she asked. "Are you still there?"

"Let's just say this *could* take a lot of meetings. Maybe not, but we have to assume it will."

"Okay. I guess I see what you mean."

I rubbed my forehead. The Summer I knew was smart and sharp and quick to pick up on things. This indecisive, please-give-me-direction Summer I was hearing at the other end of the line was not the woman I'd come to consider a good friend. "Are you okay?" I asked. "You're not getting sick, are you?"

"What? Oh. No. I'm fine."

"You sure?"

"Sure, I'm sure," she said. "It's just . . ."

I waited for her to finish. Nothing. "Just what?"

"Oh, nothing."

I'd started to ask her what was wrong, if she was troubled by the murder accusations hanging in the air, if Claudia was becoming too much for her, to say that if she needed someone to talk to or a shoulder to cry on, I could do the job. But just as I'd started to say so, she'd chirped up. "Okay, committee meeting. You and me and Marina and Carol Casassa. We can meet at my house first, then decide if we want to rotate. How does Monday night sound? Let's say seven."

And now it was Monday night at seven and the four committee members were seated around a card table in Summer's living room, four notepads in front of us, each with a pen in hand. Summer and her husband, Brett, were in the middle of expanding the kitchen and dining room of their 1960s ranch house, and the dusty evidence of renovation was everywhere. Summer had apologized for the mess, but why would I mind mess in someone else's house? As long as I wasn't responsible for the cleanup, I didn't mind a bit.

I glanced over at Marina's pad. She'd written "Artsy Ideas" at the top of the page and was playing tic-tac-toe everywhere else.

Carol was sitting across from me, but even from that distance I could see that her pad was empty. To my left, Summer's pad looked a lot like mine. "Ad Hoc Committee for Fine Arts Expenditures" at the top, then nothing.

I glanced at the clock. Almost seven thirty. All the kids were downstairs in the Langs' family room. Laughter and random thumps filtered their way up the stairs, but so far there'd been no screams and no crying. Long may the peace reign.

"So," I said. Three heads popped up. "We need some ideas. Some inexpensive things, some expensive things. Priorities. A short-term plan and a long-term plan." As I talked, Summer was scribbling away. When I paused, she stopped, and I could see that she'd been writing what I'd said. "Summer," I said, "we don't need verbatim minutes of this meeting."

"We don't?"

"No. A summary will be fine."

"Oh." She drew lines through her handwriting. "Sorry. I didn't know."

"No need to apologize," Carol said. "It's the first committee you've chaired. There's no way to know how it's done until you've done it."

Summer looked at her notepad. "But the chair should be doing something, right?"

"Leading discussion," Marina said, letting her X's beat her O's. She drew another frame and put an O in the middle square.

I looked at her. That had been a little harsh.

Summer's face crumpled, then smoothed out. "You're right. I should be. So . . . does anyone have any ideas? About fine arts spending of the storybook money, I mean?"

"Music teacher." Marina added pointy ears, a nose, and whiskers to the O, making it a tiny cat face.

"That's right." Summer nodded vigorously. "Music teacher," she repeated, writing the words.

"We'll need to find out how much hiring one costs," Carol said. "And what instruments and any other equipment she'd need."

I started making a list. "Wouldn't hurt to work costs for a full-time teacher and a teacher at half-time. Maybe at a quarter-time, too." Was there such a thing as quarter time?

Marina drew another circle and turned that one into a puppy face. "Percussion is big with kids. We should make sure the music teacher can teach drums."

"Great idea. Boys especially do that drum thing," Carol said. "I know mine was crazy for us to get him a drum set. Nick got him a weight set instead. I'm not sure he used it much, but at least it was quiet. Drums?" She closed her eyes and shuddered.

Marina laid her palms flat on the table, then starting a rolling drum solo. "In a gadda da vida, baby," she chanted.

I raised my voice to be heard over her unauthorized cover of the Iron Butterfly song. "Any ideas other than a music teacher?"

Marina's drum solo decrescendoed to a dull patter. "In a gadda da vida, honey."

"Um . . ." Summer looked around her living room. "Um, I know I had a bunch of them. Ideas, I mean. And I thought I wrote them down, but I can't find them anywhere."

Carol shrugged. "I can come up with estimates until the cows come home, but I'm not an idea person. You know that."

When Marina and I and the kids were walking over, I'd asked her for her ideas and she'd said I was the guts and she was the glue of the operation, which I'd interpreted to mean that I was supposed to be doing the brainstorming.

"Summer?" I asked. "You can't come up with any more ideas?"

"Um, I think one was something about an August . . . no, that can't be right. We don't have PTA events that time of year." Her voice was strained.

I slid a look at her. Were those tears? "Let's call it a night," I said. "We've made a decent start."

Marina looked at her notepad. "We have?"

"Summer, what do you think about meeting a week from tonight?" I asked.

"Um, sure." She rubbed her face. "I mean, yeah. Next Monday at seven. That sounds good."

I put on my best Erica voice. "And next week we'll each bring a list of ideas, right, ladies?"

The three of them blinked at me.

"A long list," Summer said.

Carol nodded. "Sure. I'll think of some things."

"Aye, aye, Cap'n!" Marina saluted.

I crossed my eyes at her. "Then I say this meeting is done. I hope someone brought treats."

We walked back to Marina's through a soft dusk that filtered both light and sound to a golden hue. The stuff of memories, I thought. Marina was at my right, and Oliver was at my left, holding my hand. Jenna and Zach were up ahead of us, playing some sort of tag game with the maple trees that lined the street. The slanting light held dust motes that sparkled and danced. I watched as Oliver tried to catch one with his free hand.

My son, my love. What is making your heart sore? Why won't you talk about it to the one person who will love you unconditionally the rest of your life and beyond? When will I see that brilliant smile of yours again, the smile that lights up the world?

I held his hand tight. He looked up at me, question marks in his eyes. I smiled at him. "How are you doing, Ollster?"

He looked down. "Okay," he said, then pulled his hand out of mine. "I'm going to play with those guys, okay?" Without waiting for an answer, he ran ahead.

Marina watched him. "Still no change, is there?"

No change, no hint of what had caused the change, no nothing. "Richard couldn't get a word out of him last weekend."

She hummed a short, tuneless song. "Think it's girl

trouble? And don't tell me he's only nine years old. Zach had girls calling him in kindergarten."

"I asked him about that, but he said no."

"What does his teacher say?"

I'd called Mrs. Sullivan this afternoon, but she hadn't had any insights either. I told Marina as much. "Weird," she murmured. "This is not like the kid at all." We walked half a block in silence, watching our children circle around maple trees, their backs to the bark, then dash onward to the next tree and circle the tree trunks with their fronts to the bark.

"About the meeting," I said.

"Yeah. Is Summer going to work out as chair? We didn't get a whole lot done. One idea? We need a freaking truckload of ideas." Marina spread her arms wide.

"They'll come," I said. "Summer just needs to focus."

"Good luck with that. Everyone's still saying that she's the one who killed Dennis. Must be driving her nuts, being talked about like that."

I nodded. Being the object of gossip was an awful thing. I'd run into my share of it and knew well how the sideways glances, smirks, and choked-off conversations could sneak into your dreams and ruin your sleep.

"Plus there's the whole curse thing," she went on. "I can't believe anyone's taking it seriously, but I keep running into people who ask what horrible thing is going to happen next. It's just nuts. This is the twenty-first century, for crying out loud!"

I nodded, agreeing with her wholeheartedly. "What's with the drums?"

Marina looked about, frowning. "I don't hear any drums. Maybe you need your hearing checked. Matter of fact, when was the last time you saw a doctor? Since before the divorce, I bet. Richard may be as boring as a beach with no water, but at least he made sure you took care of your health."

I bypassed the impossibility of calling something a beach if it lacked water. "I'd like to talk about your insistence that the music teacher be able to teach drums. Is pushing for that the reason you volunteered for the committee?"

"Moi?" She laid her hand flat on her chest. "Would I do something like that?"

"Just tell me the truth." I wasn't in the mood for her game playing.

"You are no fun." She scuffed at the sidewalk. "Would you believe me if I said being on the committee was a guaranteed way to spend more time with you?"

"No."

"Then I guess you'll have to live without knowing the answer. Say, I'm pretty sure I know who killed Dennis."

I gave her a stony stare.

"C'mon, don't be mad. Guess who I think it was?"

"Claudia."

Her face fell. "How'd you know?"

"Precedent. You always want it to be Claudia. Every time there's a death in town, even if it's a ninety-five-year-old man who died in his sleep, you want it to be Claudia's fault. If some kids spray paint their names on the school wall, you want it to be because of Claudia. If a baby cries, you figure it's because Claudia is in the neighborhood."

"Could be her perfume. Did you smell that stuff at the last meeting?" Marina held her nose. "Hope it was a gift," she said nasally.

"Claudia didn't kill Dennis."

"And you know that how?"

"She's too self-centered."

Marina started to object, so I said, "Claudia thinks too much of herself to mess around with anything as icky as murder. She wouldn't go to the trouble, that's all. She's passive-aggressive with a reflex to retreat to passive whenever there's anything anywhere close to a confrontation." Marina didn't look convinced. "And what happened to your theory that the clothes tell the tale? Your names of people from the video, remember? On Friday you said to leave it to you."

"That's right, dah-ling, Ah did." Marina had sashayed straight into Southern-belle mode in a single step. "And Ah meant every last word of it."

I counted on my fingers. Four words weren't very many words to mean.

"Trust me," she said, threading her arm through mine.

And, strangely enough, I did.

The next day began as one of those mornings in which nothing whatsoever goes right and you get that tumbling, neck-tightening feeling that the day is going to get worse. Sure, you know that you're creating a self-fulfilling prophecy, so for a time you do your best to fight the pull of negativity, but the evidence continues to pile up and by midmorning you've accepted your unfortunate fate.

This particular Tuesday began with the classic homework argument. We were at the kitchen table eating a marginally nutritious breakfast of cold cereal and reconstituted orange juice. "Is your homework packed?" I asked, glancing at the bulging backpacks.

Oliver nodded at his cornflakes. Jenna shrugged. "It's all done," she said.

I looked at her. Twelve years old now, she'd measured five feet tall on her birthday in June. Just five inches shorter than her mother. I flashed on an image of a seventeen-year-old and six-foot-tall Jenna in front of the goalie net. Six three on skates. No. She wouldn't grow that tall. Would she? "I didn't ask if it was done," I said. "That I knew last night. The question was, is it packed?"

She stuffed a large spoonful of Cheerios in her mouth, her go-to stalling technique since she knew I wouldn't force her to answer with a mouth full of food. Which led me to an obvious conclusion. I pulled her bowl out from under her chin. "Jenna, you know the rule. No breakfast until all your work is packed and ready to go."

"But I'm hungry!" Small drops of milk splattered across the table.

I pointed to the ceiling. "Go to your room and get your homework. Your hunger can wait two minutes."

"But—"

"Go," I said.

Her lower lip rolled out. "I don't see why I can't finish eating."

"You know the rule."

"It's a stupid rule! Why do I have to go by stupid rules?"

For a half second, I considered entering into a debate about the importance of rules and regulations and laws and ordinances. But since I often had debates with myself over that very issue, I quickly decided to leave it alone. Maybe when we had more time. And less preadolescent angst. Which meant we'd talk about this in ten years.

"Go," I said. "Your breakfast will wait."

"It's getting soggy."

"And whose fault is that?"

I saw her mouth start to form that dangerous word— "Yours"—but luckily for all of us, she stopped before it got out. "Fine," she snapped, shoving her chair back. "But if I'm late to school because of this, I'm going to need a note."

She stomped off. Oliver and I tracked her movement with our eyes. Up the stairs. Down the hall. Into her room.

I looked at my son. "Are you going to have any fun in school today?"

He shrugged and aimed an overloaded spoon at his mouth.

Briefly, I wondered why it was that bad habits spread so easily. Good habits, on the other hand, took root so slowly as to be invisible. Why did it all have to be so hard?

Then I heard an echo of Marina's voice in my head. "If it was easy to be good, everyone would be doing it."

Once again, she was right.

The morning continued to be marked by a series of accumulating annoyances. Stoplights turning red in front of me, dropped keys at doors with rain dripping down, typos found in a store flyer after I'd printed five hundred copies, the bottom falling out of a box of books, sending them thumping onto my toes, and worst of all, sour milk for the tea.

I took one sniff of the milk and slammed the carton into the small sink. "Can anything else possibly go wrong today?"

Yvonne glanced over from her self-appointed job of dusting the light fixtures. "What's the matter?"

"Oh, nothing." I rinsed out the carton. "Or everything. Some days it's hard to tell."

There was a faint groaning noise as Yvonne stood on her tiptoes, her arms stretched to their limit. Since I'd done the job myself for years, I knew for a fact that it was the worst job in the store. If you didn't use the ladder, you ended up straining your neck and wearing out your shoulders. If you did use the ladder, you ended up spending an hour traipsing up and down the ladder's steps . . . and wearing out your shoulders. When Yvonne volunteered to take over the dreaded duty, I'd protested halfheartedly, saying we should rotate the chore. When she'd said she didn't mind, the rest of us gave her a standing ovation.

"I think it's a pretty good day," Yvonne said cheerfully.

Shame flooded my face. Of course it was. My children were healthy, the rest of my family was fine, I had good friends, great employees, the store was turning a small profit, and I was keeping off the weight I'd lost last spring. Why had I let my mood be colored by things that didn't matter?

"Thanks, Yvonne," I said.

"For what?" She stretched to reach the far side of the light fixture. "I didn't do anything. Did I?"

I grinned. "Nope." Nothing, other than kick my priorities back to where they should be. Nothing, other than show by example that whining never did anyone any good. Nothing, other than be yourself. "I'm off to get some milk. I'll be right back."

Outside, I ran from store awning to store awning, trying to stay out of as much rain as possible, wishing I'd thought to bring my umbrella. "Dumb," I told myself. "It may be only a block, but you're not that good at dodging raindrops."

"Excuse me?"

I came to an abrupt halt. It was the salt-and-pepper-haired man who'd caught me talking to myself last week. "We have to stop meeting like this," I said, laughing. "And it's absolutely not true what they say about people who talk to themselves."

He looked at me with eyes far too sad for his face. "I'm sure you're right," he said politely, and walked away.

I watched him go. "You know," I said, "I don't think he believed me."

The grocery store was crowded with morning shoppers. In addition to purchasing milk, I'd wanted to see how Flossie was doing, if she was suffering any ill effects from the incident with Lou's dogs. When I walked in, though, she was at the cash register, ringing up purchases and chatting with customers lined up three deep.

I watched her for a moment, then wandered over to the dairy case, thinking hard as I checked the sell-by dates. I could discount the dark circles under her eyes as the result of a night or two of poor sleep. Understandable after a scare like she'd had. But her shoulders were sloping, and that made her look . . . well, old. Never ever had I seen her with anything except perfect posture. That alone told me—

My hearing twitched and a prickling went up the back of my neck. Something wasn't right. Not right at all. But what was it?

I turned slowly, oh so slowly, and saw nothing but grocery store. Brandishing the plastic milk jug, I peeked around the end of the cereal aisle. Nothing. I walked softly to the next aisle and peered through the racks of bread loaves. Nothing.

Huh.

The tension leaked out of me. Once again, I'd given in to my overactive imagination. I paid Patrick for the milk and walked back to the store, talking to myself all the way.

"Chill," I said. "No one's out to get you. Maybe it's not paranoia if they really are out to get you, but there is no 'they,' so just cut it out."

Then again . . .

I started making a mental list. Dennis Halpern was

dead. His office lay in smoking ruins. Flossie had been attacked. Not that those dogs would have done anything more than cover her with canine saliva, but someone had taken advantage of Flossie's fear, and to me that counted as an attack. Lou Spezza was hiding something. And . . .

As I came in the front door, jingling the bells, Lois slammed the phone into its cradle. "That's the third time this week," she growled.

"What?"

"The third time someone's called and *breathed* at me." She made huffing and puffing noises. "I tell you, it's creeping me out. Why is it we don't have caller ID?"

"Find out how much it costs," I said. But while I listened to her go on and on about how crank phone calls were the first sign of serious psychological disturbance, I was finishing my mental list.

Lou Spezza was hiding something.

And we were getting anonymous phone calls.

Chapter 14

Late that morning, I hauled a half dozen boxes of books out to the trunk of my car and sailed off into the wild blue yonder. Well, I drove, and the sky was a low, leaden gray, but my spirits were more in keeping with the freedom of the high seas.

Thanks to Yvonne's unintentional intervention, I'd cast off my feelings of doom and gloom in spite of my fears about an unknown enemy. It wouldn't last, of course, but that was no reason not to enjoy my current perky frame of mild.

My mood endured through the deliveries to various homeschooling mothers and parochial schools, survived the deliveries to three day-care centers, and made it all the way through to my entrance into Sunny Rest Assisted Living.

"Morning, Beth," the receptionist said. "No, wait, it's afternoon, isn't it? Are those for Judy?"

Judy Schultz was Sunny Rest's activities director. We'd come to know each other fairly well over the course of last spring's story project. When I'd mentioned my selection and delivery service, her ears had pricked up and I'd added the facility to my regular route.

I hefted the box. "The whole kit and caboodle. Is Judy in her office?"

"Probably. But you could leave them here, if you want."

I clutched the box tight to my chest. "Um, no thanks." While I fully trusted that Judy would fulfill her job responsibilities in a prompt manner, if Mr. Meagher didn't get his copy of the latest Lee Child thriller as soon as was physically possible, my head would be on the chopping block. "I'll see if she's in."

The carpeted hallway kept my footsteps quiet. Most of the rooms were empty due to the noon hour, but the brightly lit dining area was filled with the clatter and chatter of a meal.

I slowed, trying to remember where Judy ate her lunch. The receptionist had said she was in her office, but hadn't Judy once said something about eating in the employee lounge? I shifted the heavy box in my arms, thinking that I shouldn't have stayed so long at Tiny Tots Day Care.

But who can resist those chubby little smiles? And since I knew almost all of the parents, it was almost an obligation to stay for a few minutes. Our school superintendent and his wife had had a late-in-life baby—a *very* late in life baby—and at eighteen months, she was as cute and adorable as any toddler ever.

"Beth!" A voice came at me from the far end of the hallway. "Can I talk to you for a second?"

I squinted and saw a woman and a dog walking toward me. "Hey, Summer. Did you know there's a great big dog on your left?"

She laughed. "We come here once a week for dog therapy. The residents like Zeppo a lot, don't they, boy?"

The pair reached me. When Summer stopped, the dog sat and she rested her hand on his black head. He looked mostly black Lab, but the shagginess of his tail and the way his ears were set made me think there was more than one breed in his ancestry. Maybe lots more.

"Zeppo?" I'd known Summer's family had bought a dog a few months ago, but I'd never met him. Last night he'd been with her husband and oldest offspring at a Boy Scout meeting. Or was it Cub Scouts? Oliver wasn't interested in scouting, so I'd never learned the age divisions.

"Yup. He's the best straight man ever."

I shifted the box again, trying to ease the growing ache in my arms, and looked at the dog's face. Eyes alert and watchful, ears pricked slightly, he looked the picture of doggy intelligence. "He doesn't look like he'd miss much."

"Not a thing. Say, can I ask you a question about the PTA minutes?"

I smiled. This was more like the Summer I knew. Whatever had been biting at her heels yesterday had vanished. "Fire away." And after that, I thought, we'd have a little chat about how to run a committee meeting. No need for me to worry about having to step in and run the committee myself. She'd be fine with a little guidance.

"It's when motions are made," Summer said. "Some of the old minutes have it in bold and centered on the page, but some of them have the motions italicized and indented. Which way should it be?"

I looked at her. This was what she was worried about? Methodical and rut-bound as I was, even I had never thought that how a motion was positioned on a page mattered a hill of beans. "What matters," I said, popping my hip forward to let the box rest on it instead of my forearms, "is that the text of the motion is accurate."

"But there's got to be a right way to do it." Her brow furrowed. "Isn't there someplace that says?"

"A handbook for PTA minutes?" I laughed. "Sorry. If there is one, I've never—" I stopped. "What's the matter?"

Summer was staring over my shoulder. "It's her," she whispered. "I knew I should have left through the maintenance door."

I turned and saw Auntie May Werner barreling toward us, full steam ahead in her purple wheelchair. "Hold it right there, missy!" she yelled. "Don't you move a muscle till I have my say."

Neither Summer nor I so much as twitched. With all my might, I was hoping that Auntie May was yelling at my friend and not me. Shameful, but true.

"I got a question to ask," Auntie May called, pushing at her chair's rubber wheels fiercely, "and I won't go away until it's been answered, got it?"

Summer and I glanced at each other. The urge to flee was strong, but the knowledge of Auntie May's subsequent wrath glued us in place. And still we didn't know which of us Auntie May had her beady little eyes fixed on.

"You." Auntie May was close now, close enough that I could see a copy of the *National Enquirer* sitting on her lap. She rolled right up to us, stopping only when her small front wheels ran onto Summer's feet. Well, one ran onto one of Summer's feet. The other would have run over Zeppo's toes, but he scooted backward out of the way just in time.

Auntie May thumped the arm of her wheelchair with her fist so hard that the beads of her multiple Mardi Gras necklaces rattled together. It was months past Mardi Gras, but May liked how the colors matched her wheelchair. "I want to know and I want to know right now!"

Now that I was out of the firing line, my voice came back. "How can we help, Auntie May? Is there something we can do for you?"

I was ignored so completely, I wasn't sure I'd even

spoken. "You." Auntie May pointed a remarkably long and very knobby index finger up at Summer. "I want to know if the talk is right. Tell me true, girl, you know I'll get it out of you one way or another."

"T-talk?" Summer stammered. "I'm not sure what you mean."

The elderly woman aimed her gaze straight along the length of her arm, narrowing her eyes as if she were sighting a rifle. "Don't mess with me, missy. I'm not going to live forever, and I don't want to die without knowing the truth."

I tried again. "Auntie May, why don't we—"

"Did you do it?" Auntie May shook her finger. "Did you kill Dennis Halpern?"

"I . . ." Summer's face twisted and crumpled. Zeppo whined and leaned against her leg. "I . . ."

The finger dropped. "Ah, she didn't do it." Auntie May sounded disgusted. "That girl," she said, finally looking at me, "wouldn't smack a spider if it were climbing up her arm." She eyed me up and down. "Not sure you would, either. Bunch of lily-livered, namby-pamby, soft-skinned pansies running the world these days, I tell you."

I thought about all the things we had to deal with that earlier generations hadn't. The disappearance of pensions. The proliferation of computers. The explosion of information, all of it demanding attention. The rapid change of . . . of everything. Blink once and you'll miss a news cycle. Blink twice and you won't recognize the clothes your daughter wants to wear to school.

Auntie May made a snorting noise in the back of her throat. "Now she's crying. Can't take the heat, get out of the kitchen, I say."

I'd had enough. "You're the one who fired up the broiler," I snapped. "Do you do anything productive around here, or do you just make people unhappy?

Come on, Summer. There's a reading room just down the hall." I tugged on the weeping woman's elbow. Two tugs, and she and Zeppo came along.

Trailing after us was Auntie May, who was sounding suddenly conciliatory. "Now, Bethie, you know all I wanted was to find out about Dennis."

I ignored her. "Just sit a minute, Summer." I put the ten-ton box on a table and steered Summer to a cushy chair. "I see a sink right over there. Let me get you a glass of water, okay? That's it; just sit. You'll feel better in a minute."

She sank into the chair's deep embrace. Her dog looked at her, tilted his head, then lay down and closed his eyes.

I gave the purple wheelchair a wide berth, ran the water cold, and came back with a paper cup two-thirds full. The way Summer was still crying, I was sure she'd spill a full cup.

"Here." I sat in the upholstered chair next to her. "Drink."

"B-but I don't want—"

"Drink," I said, gently but firmly.

Using both hands, she took the cup from me and sipped. Sipped again.

I relaxed a little. Why this worked, I did not know, but in my experience getting overwrought people to drink helped ease the transition back to coherency. Maybe it was the act of holding something. Maybe it was the swallowing. Maybe it was something else entirely, and some researcher would someday spend five years analyzing the cause.

Summer took a few more swallows, then wiped at her tears with the back of her hand. "Thanks, Beth," she said with a weak voice. "I'm sorry I fell apart like that. It's just . . . been so hard."

"What has?"

"Pretty much everything." Her head dropped down.

Despair spread out from her, great circles of darkness that I wanted to duck away from, to hide from, to run fast and far from. Instead, I gritted my teeth and let it crest and wash through me.

"No," I told her. "Whatever is wrong can be fixed. No, don't say it can't be, because I know it can." At least I hoped so. But since I was certain she hadn't killed Dennis, almost all other problems were mere details. "Now. Tell me, in your own words, specifically, what's been so hard."

"Besides everything?" The small laugh she managed didn't last long. "Brett doesn't know any of this. I don't want to bother him, he's so busy ..."

Her voice trailed off. I could see why she wouldn't want to share gossip with her husband, but if it was gossip that might lead to being questioned by the police and could possibly lead to ... to much worse things, it seemed to me that Brett should be the first person she'd turn to.

"He's your husband," I said. "Shouldn't you tell him?"

The tears started falling again. I dug a tissue out of my purse and handed it to her. "Thanks," she sniffed. "I know I should, and I almost have, lots of times, but he'd be mad and he was mad enough about Destiny."

Auntie May cackled. "Getting mad about that is like getting mad at the weather. Ain't no point. 'Course, that don't stop people from ranting and raving their fool heads off."

Summer frowned. "Destiny is my friend."

"Oh, sure." Auntie May nodded, making her neck wattles sway. "Easy enough to say when you're young. Harder to say when you're stuck in one of these." She whapped her elbows on the wheelchair arms. "If I'd know this was my destiny, I might have made sure I had more fun in my seventies."

I tried to erase an image of a seventy-five-year-old Auntie May doing the Macarena in high heels while wearing a spaghetti-strapped tank top and short shorts.

"No, you don't understand," Summer said.

"What, you think I'm stupid?" Auntie May narrowed her beady little eyes. "Girlie, every thought you've ever had in your tiny little pea brain I've had at least hundred times over. Don't tell me I don't understand, because I been there, done that, and have the scars to prove it."

But not tattoos, I thought. Please, not. If there was one thing I didn't ever, ever want to see, it was body art etched into the small of Auntie May's back. Although if she did have a tattoo, what would it be? A snake, maybe. Or a dragon.

"Of course I don't think you're stupid." Summer dabbed at her eyes with the tissue. "You're one of the smartest people I've ever met. I wish I had a memory like yours."

"Years of practice." Thanks to Summer's compliment, Auntie May turned into Lady Bountiful, showering her adoring crowd with condescending compliments. "Live long enough and you might remember half the things I do."

"Destiny is a girlfriend of mine," Summer said. "It's her name. She lives over in Madison, near the university."

I thought back to what she'd said a minute ago. "Why was Brett mad about your friend Destiny?"

"Oh . . ." A tear streaked down Summer's cheek. "It's the money, see? How can I tell him about the money?"

Auntie May and I exchanged glances. "What money, honey?" she asked, then grinned. "Hey, that —"

I cut her off. "Does this have anything to do with Dennis Halpern?"

More tears. Lots of them, accompanied by wails I

couldn't quite make out. I dug more tissues out of my purse and waited. May started tapping the arms of her wheelchair until I reached out and put my hands firmly on the red, white, and blue glittered fingernails.

May's whine of protest died when she saw my hard glare. She yanked her fingers away and made a dramatic show of folding her hands on her lap.

Summer finally put enough sounds together to get out an entire sentence. "It's a secret."

"Sweetie," I said, "your secret is safe with me. You know I won't tell."

The two of us looked at Auntie May. She put her nose up in the air. "What, you think all I do is flap my mouth all day? I can keep my trap shut if I have to."

"Then consider this a 'have to' moment," I said, "or Summer and I will go talk about this in private."

Auntie May crossed her arms. "Fine, but what about him?" She jerked her chin at Zeppo, who was lying at Summer's side, eyes closed.

"Dogs," I said, "are almost as good as cats at keeping secrets. Summer, if you don't want to tell us, don't. But if you think we can help, we're here."

She nodded and took another sip of water. "I won so much money," she said, gulping the words out one by one. "Destiny and I went to a casino and I won so much money and I don't know what to do with it all and my mother can't know and Brett can't know and the kids know something's wrong but they don't know what and now everyone in town hates me and . . . and . . ." She pulled in a long breath. "And I don't know what to do."

"Back to the beginning," Auntie May said, rotating her index fingers in a circle. "To Destiny. She's the stir stick, right?"

I looked at her, frowning.

She shrugged. "With a name like that, how could she not be?"

Summer either hadn't heard the exchange or she ignored it. "Brett doesn't like Destiny, but she was begging me to take a girls-only weekend trip to that big casino up north. Her favorite band was playing up there and she promised it would be a lot of fun, and it did sound like fun."

"Was it?" Auntie May asked.

"Oh, yeah." Summer grinned. "Or . . ." Her smile faltered. "At least it was until I won all that stupid money."

In my experience, there were a lot of descriptors that could be stuck in front of the word "money." "Not enough" being first and foremost, followed closely by "where-are-we-going-to-get-the." There were a few others, like "*how* much," and "that's an awful lot of," but nowhere had I ever heard anyone use the phrase "all that stupid money."

Auntie May cackled out a laugh. "Slots? No, roulette, I betcha. I can see you and your little friend at the roulette wheel, drinking umbrella drinks and watching that ball go around and around, squealing like stuck pigs. Bet you bet on red, didn't you?"

And I'd never imagined that Auntie May had darkened the door of a casino. "You gamble?" I asked.

"Every time the Sunny Rest bus heads to a casino, I'm the first little old lady on it." She closed her fist and shook it. "Give me seven out, baby, seven out!" She tossed her imaginary dice out across the invisible table.

"Blackjack," Summer said. "We played in junior high during lunch hour. I won back then, so I figured I'd try again."

"What are you, some sort of card counter?" Auntie May *tut-tut*ted. "Casinos hate that, you know."

"I can barely remember my own phone number."

Summer rubbed her nose with the now-damp tissue. I handed her a fresh one. "Thanks. How can anyone count cards? They use like six or seven decks."

We were getting a little far afield. "So you won a lot of money?"

"Gobs of it." Summer sighed. "And I can't tell Brett. He'll hit the ceiling."

Auntie May snorted. "What, he doesn't like money? What kind of idiot is he?"

"He's very smart." Summer sat up from the slouch she'd sunk into and put the cup and tissue on a side table. "But see, Brett doesn't know where I went. He thought I went to visit my mother up in Sheboygan."

All was becoming clear. "So he doesn't know you were with your friend Destiny," I said.

"And he doesn't know you went gambling." Auntie May slapped her scrawny thighs, chuckling. "A pretty pickle you got yourself into, missy. What are you going to do about it?"

"I don't know," Summer said, sinking back into the chair. "I tried to talk to Dennis Halpern. He was supposed to be this financial genius, I figured he must know a way out of this mess."

Things were becoming so clear that I could see the exact shape of Summer's problems. "You asked Dennis if there was a way to hide the money."

"Yeah." She propped her elbows on the chair arms and put her head in her hands. "Right after the trip, you told me Dennis had agreed to come to that meeting. I called and talked to him, and he told me ... You know what he told me?"

To tell your husband, I thought. "What?"

"He told me to tell Brett!" She put her hands over her face. "I said there must be some way. Switzerland, maybe, or aren't there banks in the Cayman Islands?"

"Um . . ."

"But Dennis said the casino has to report winnings to the IRS, that there's some goofy form, W-G or something—"

"W-2G," Auntie May supplied.

"That's it, a W-2G. So unless Brett and I file our taxes separately—and we don't; that's just nuts—there's no way I can keep Brett from knowing." A sob caught in her throat. "He's going to find out. What am I going to do?"

Something here wasn't making sense. I glanced at Auntie May for corroboration, but she was still playing her ghostly game of craps. Or at least I thought it was craps. There were huge gaps in my life knowledge, and a thorough understanding of casino games had a special and very empty shelf.

"Why," I asked slowly, "will Brett be so angry?" Though I didn't know Summer's husband very well, he'd always seemed to be a reasonable man. Amiable, even. If I remembered correctly, he managed half a dozen or so retail stores that sold . . . something. Lighting fixtures? Plumbing fixtures? Car parts?

"Because he thinks Destiny broke up his brother's marriage."

"Aha!" Auntie May chortled. "Now, that's more like it. Dirt, and good dirt at that. So did she?"

"Of course not!"

Auntie May pressed on with the skill of a seasoned investigator. "Then why does your Brett think she had anything to do with it?"

"Because he's an idiot!" Her cheeks flared red. "Destiny is friendly, that's all. So she likes to hug people. What's the big deal with that?"

If she's hugging both men and women, I thought, not much of a deal at all. But if she's hugging only men, and hugging them at the least provocation, then there is a very big deal.

"And maybe she likes to show off her body," Summer said. "She's worked hard to get back into shape. Why shouldn't she show off her abs?"

No reason. Or lots of reasons, depending on your point of view.

"And she likes to have a good time." Summer's hands were fists. "Why is that such a horrible thing? Why shouldn't I go out and have fun with her every once in a while? Why shouldn't I get to have fun, too?"

I could see that Auntie May was about to put her two cents in, so I jumped in ahead of her. "Is Destiny married?"

"Not anymore. That was why she wanted to go up to the casino, to celebrate her divorce. How could I say no? I mean, maybe I promised Brett I'd stop seeing her, but she's not a bad influence; she's just fun."

The final cloud vanished, leaving the sky clear and blue and bright.

Summer looked from me to Auntie May and back to me. "Brett's wrong about her, he really is. She's a nice person, and I don't see anything wrong with what I did." Her gaze darted around my face, analyzing my expression. "You . . . you don't, do you? Think I did anything wrong?"

How do you tell a friend that she's being an idiot without hurting her feelings? How do you find the words to say that, yes, you think she's wrong? How do you manage to ride the zigzag line that divides honesty and acceptable social truths?

But at the end, all of those questions collapsed into one. How good a friend was I?

Auntie May, of course, had no such questions in her head.

"You're an idiot," she said.

"I . . . what?"

"Let's see." Auntie May squinted. "Your so-called friend Destiny got you to lie to your husband. She got you to break a promise to him. And now you're stuck with all those stupid lies and you don't know how to get out of it. Is there much smart in any of that?"

"But . . . Destiny *is* my friend. Why shouldn't I be able to spend time with her?" Summer started to look mulish. "She's fun! Why can't I go out and have some fun every once in a while? Because I'm a mom, I should never have any fun? Is that it?"

I started to say something, but Auntie May beat me to it.

"No, it's because you promised your husband." She stared at Summer hard, and for a second I thought she was going to pull out her index finger again, but she didn't. "I bet you two had a huge fight over this Destiny person, right?"

Summer looked at her knees and didn't answer. When Auntie May lashed out with her shoe and caught her in the shin, Summer said, "There might have been an argument."

"Uh-huh. And I bet in the end you said you'd stay away from Destiny."

"Okay, yeah, but—"

"But nothing. A promise is a promise and you don't go messing around with promises unless you want to get treated the same way."

I looked at May with something very close to admiration. If I'd thought for a month, I wouldn't have been able to come up with such a succinct delivery. I wanted to write it down so I could tell it to the kids.

"And now what are you going to do?" Auntie May leaned forward, her purple and green necklaces clinking together. "Stuck good in that stupid lie. Kids today." She poked Summer's knee. "That's you, missy. A kid. And kids today are about as stupid as they come."

Summer twisted her knees out of reach, but she didn't try to get up. The time for her to flee had long gone, and now she was trapped until Auntie May was done speaking her piece. "Dennis should have been able to figure something out," Summer muttered. "He's not much of a financial genius if he can't figure out how to hide a little money."

Which didn't sound like Summer at all. I looked at the depth of her pout and thought that Brett was right, that Summer shouldn't spend much time with Destiny. And again I wondered about the easy spreading of bad habits.

"Ha." Auntie May thumped back in her wheelchair. "Bet that's what you were fighting with Denny about that night he was killed."

"There should be a way," Summer said. "There must be."

"Don't be stupid. Didn't you pay any attention to what he said? Casinos report straight to the IRS. What did you want him to do, break into the IRS and steal your form?"

"No, of course not," Summer said, but she looked thoughtful.

This wasn't going anywhere good, so I asked, "Have you told the sheriff's office any of this?"

Summer's eyes flew open wide. "What? No way! How could I?"

"It explains your fight with Dennis," I said. "Clear that up and maybe people will stop saying . . . well, you know."

"But I can't." Summer was sliding into the whining zone. "If I tell them the truth they'll go talk to Brett and then . . . then he'll know!"

"Denny was right," Auntie May said.

"He certainly was." May Werner and I, joined together in complete agreement. Note the day on your calendars, folks, this event is history in the making. "You have to tell Brett. You can't hide something like this from your husband."

"Face up to the music now," Auntie May said, "or you'll end up seeing your kids Wednesday nights and every other weekend."

"That's nuts," Summer said. "We're not going to get a divorce because I won some money."

No, I thought, *but you might end up in divorce court because you're lying to your husband.*

"Ha," Auntie May said. "What would you do if things were flip-flopped? If he made a promise to you, broke it, then lied about it? Eh? What would you do?"

"I . . ." Summer looked around wildly. "I . . ." Her gaze met mine. I looked at her, steady on, and once again the tears started flowing. "I've b-been s-so stupid," she sobbed. "Why am I so dumb?"

"Because you're a moron," Auntie May said in a "duh" tone of voice.

"But in a very nice way," I said quickly, patting Summer's shoulder and glowering at Auntie May. She shrugged.

"What am I going to do?" Summer wailed.

"You're going to tell Brett," I said. "And then you're going to talk to Gus."

"Oh . . ." She bent over as if she'd been punched in the stomach. "Do I have to?"

"Should have done it a long time ago," Auntie May said. But she said it sotto voce, so there was a good chance Summer didn't hear.

"Yes, you have to." I squeezed her shoulder and let go. "Sit Brett down tonight after the kids are in bed and start at the beginning." I considered, then reconsidered. "Maybe not at the very beginning. Start with an apology."

"Get him liquored up first," Auntie May said. "Worked like a charm with my husband."

Summer shook her head. "Brett doesn't drink."

Auntie May sighed. "I tell you, this generation is a mess and not going to get any better."

"Tell him tonight," I urged. "Putting it off just makes it worse."

Summer was still shaking her head. "It's bowling night. He won't get home until late. I'll do it tomorrow. Or this weekend. This weekend will be good."

Auntie May looked at the ceiling. "Listen to her. She's going to put it off until doomsday."

Maybe all Summer needed was a push in the right direction. "Two days," I suggested. "Do it within two days or . . . or . . ." I thought fast and hard for a motivator. "Or I'll go talk to Gus myself."

"No!" Summer's hands fluttered in her lap. "Don't do that. I'll tell Brett, I promise. And Gus, too. Give me three days."

"Summer . . ."

"Please? Just three days? Today's Tuesday, and it's like half over, so by this time on Friday, I'll have . . ." She swallowed. "I'll have told Brett."

"And Gus," I said.

She nodded. "And Chief Eiseley. I'll talk to Brett, um, Thursday and stop at the police station after I drop the kids off to school on Friday morning." Her gaze darted over to me. "Is that okay? Three days is okay, right?"

I sighed. I was such a sucker. "Okay. Three days."

"You're the best!" She jumped out of the chair and wrapped her arms around me. "The absolute best. I won't disappoint you, I promise! Zeppo, let's go, boy." Woman and dog trotted out of the room.

And there I was, alone in a room with Auntie May. I instantly started making ready-to-go movements, but I wasn't fast enough. May started talking. "Girl's a bad influence," she said.

Of all the things Summer was or might be, naming her as a bad influence had never occurred to me. "I don't agree. A little misguided, perhaps, but that's far from being a bad influence."

Auntie May narrowed her eyes in my general direction. "And when did you get so much gumption, missy? Two years ago you hardly said a word, and now you're telling me"—she thumped her chest—"telling *me* that I'm an idiot?"

"Just because we disagree about something doesn't mean we have to think the other person is stupid."

"Huh," she said. "Could have fooled me."

I let that go in favor of returning to the previous subject. "Summer may be going through a rough patch, but I don't see how that translates into being a bad influence. She's a hard worker, she's willing to take on responsibility, she's—"

"Whoa there, Nelly." Auntie May waved me down. "I ain't talking about Summer. I meant her little playmate there, what's-her-name. Denise. No, it's Della. Wait, I got it. Deirdre!" she said triumphantly.

"Destiny."

"Whatever. Summer's a nice girl, but if she keeps on lying to her husband, she's going to be in a world of hurt."

I agreed, but I didn't want to venture into the land of gossip with Auntie May at my side. Within seconds, I'd learn far more than I wanted to about people I dealt with on a daily basis, and I was still trying to wash away the image of a young and skinny-dipping Mack Vogel that she'd suggested into my head months ago.

Auntie May pushed her wheelchair around so she was staring straight at me. "Who do you think killed Dennis Halpern?"

"That's for the sheriff's office to figure out. Now, if you don't mind, I need to—"

"Don't give me that." She rolled forward to where I couldn't stand up and take a step forward without falling into her lap. "You must have some idea. You and that Marina catch more criminals than Gussy Eiseley and his crew put together." She smirked. "Women been catching people in lies for thousands of years. Only now we're finally getting some notice for it."

I smiled. Now that we could agree on. But . . . Gussy? Never once had I heard anyone call him that. Not even his wife.

The wheelchair rolled forward onto the tips of my shoes. "You got a list of suspects somewhere, don't you?"

It took an act of supreme will not to glance at my purse.

"Well, your list don't matter squat," she said. "I know who killed Denny."

I looked at her inquiringly. "Did you know him?"

"Babysat the little brat, didn't I? Kid was forever asking questions. How do you get to be president? How does a radio work? Where does that road go?" She rolled her eyes. "I told him Toledo and he went to get an atlas. Yep," she said with satisfaction. "Another one I outlived."

Curiosity won over politeness. "Are you keeping score?"

"Of course I am. What else do I got to do in here?"

"Well, there's—"

"Yeah, yeah. Activities every day. I know all about it." She made a gagging noise. "I think they schedule that stuff just to keep me out of their hair."

Since I happened to know that there was a large element of truth in her statement, I made as noncommittal a noise as I could, then asked, "So you think you know who killed Dennis?"

"Don't think. I know."

Riiiight. "Don't tell me, you think it's Claudia Wolff."

She snorted. "That's just dumb. Why the heck would she kill Denny?"

"Then who did?"

"The janitor," she said, triumph ringing loud and clear.

"Harry? Why would Harry kill Dennis?"

"Motive ain't my concern."

I started to point out her hypocrisy, but she cut me off. "The janitor's like the butler in all those movies. No one really suspects him because it's too plain, see? The perfect crime."

I tried to move my feet, but they were pinned down by the wheelchair. "So the reason you think Harry did it is because of some old movies."

"Ooo, listen to the expert, tearing down my case." She tried to roll forward, but this time I put out my knees to prevent any further incursion on my toes. "Now, girlie, don't be getting all feisty on me. You got any better ideas?"

I thought back to Saturday morning. "Do you know Lou Spezza? He opened that Made in the Midwest store."

"Brought in some chewy cherry bars," she said, nodding. "Tasty, but he'll probably go broke with a store like that. Not enough scope, you know?"

"Do you know anything about him?"

"Hey," she said, her face lighting up. "You think Lou killed Denny, don't you? Sure, why not? New guy in town gets in an argument with the hometown kid, he loses his temper and bam!"

"Kid?"

"Honey, just about everybody is a kid to me."

She had a point. "I don't think Lou killed Dennis," I said.

"Then why you asking?"

"Because . . ." Think, Beth, think. "Because he's practically my neighbor downtown and I haven't heard a bad word about him." All true. "And if there is anything bad to be heard about him, you'd be the one who'd know. So, if you don't know anything, there probably isn't anything." Maybe.

"Gotcha." She tapped the side of her head. "I'll keep my ears open. Say, do you carry?"

Again with the handguns. "No, but I have the best weapon of all," I said, giving her wheelchair a light push.

Rolling slowly backward, she squinted at me. "Better than a .44 Magnum?"

"Too obvious." I picked up my purse by the shoulder strap. "What man would see this coming?" Moving forward half a step, I spun, whirling the purse around. It smacked into the side of the chair. *Thwap!*

Auntie May cackled out a laugh. I picked up the box of books and made my escape.

A short hour later, I'd eaten a fast lunch of peanut butter and jelly, worked on the details of an upcoming author visit, paid invoices I should have paid a week before, and was playing with numbers in an effort to figure how the store could afford to replace the increasingly worn carpet when Marina banged into my office.

"Hi ho, Ms. Works-too-Hard. Let's go find a groove for you to get on."

I looked about for small children, but saw none. "What did you do with your day-care kids?"

"One is home sick, one is at a doctor's appointment

with his parents, and the other . . ." She peered at the ceiling. "What did I do with the last one? Oh, yes. Her mother is off work because of a plant shutdown, so she's not with me this week. All accounted for, Cap'n." She saluted.

"Well done, First Mate."

"Yes, sir, thank you kindly, sir. Now, let's scoot. We have an appointment."

I looked at my desk blotter calendar. "No, we don't."

She picked up a pen and reached across my desk to scribble something. "Now we do. Let's go."

I squinted at her upside-down writing. "Who's Marcus Lombardo?"

"Remember at the mall, when you were rejecting all my clothing choices? By the way, those navy blue pants you have on today are sooo late eighties. Pleats? Puh-leese."

"My pants *are* from the late eighties."

"Huh. The only thing from that decade that I can still fit into is a pair of earrings. Anyway, remember that I said leave it to me? Remember the guy in the video who sat in the second row in the middle? Fortyish, short brown hair, short-sleeved dress shirt that only grandpas should wear, took lots of notes? Well, I had to check, but that guy used to work with the DH, and we're going to talk to him. The guy, not the DH."

"Used to work?"

Marina came around the desk and put my purse into my hand. "He's a civil engineer and got laid off a couple years ago, like half the other civil engineers in the country. Come on. We were supposed to be there seven seconds ago, and you know how engineers are about being on time."

"Be where?" I asked.

But she didn't answer.

*   *   *

Two minutes later, I knew why she hadn't said where we were going. Marcus Lombardo had switched careers with a vengeance. No longer a member of cubicle world, he was now a manager for a Rynwood retail business. The local hardware store. The store that was owned by my former love interest.

Marina breezed up to the six-foot-four Evan. "Hi. We need to talk to Marcus for a few minutes. We have some . . . hardware questions. He said he'd be checking stock in the basement this afternoon, so we'll just toddle down there, if that's all right with you. We'll be in and out of here in a flash. Thanks!"

Evan looked at me. "Beth. How are you?"

"Fine." I nodded. "And you?"

"Oh, for crying out loud." Marina grabbed my arm. "He's fine; you're fine; we're all peachy-keen fine, okay?"

She pulled at me and, after a moment, I went. "Don't know what you ever saw in that man," she muttered. "So what if he's as rich as Midas? So what if he's good-looking enough to star in his own television series? So what if he wined and dined you like no one's done before or is likely to do ever again?"

"How nice that you're so optimistic about my romantic prospects."

"What's that? Speak up if you want me to hear what you're mumbling." She released my arm and started down the broad stairs.

I made a face at the back of her head. She'd heard me well enough, she just didn't want to respond. But if I was going to be truthful with myself—and I always wanted to be, even if I hardly ever was—I knew what she meant. What I'd seen in Evan was all surface. He was a very nice man, but there was no deep connection between us. No sense of . . . of oneness. We'd gotten along well enough, but it was more the getting-alongness of friends.

"We never should have dated," I said softly.

"And if I'd said so, would you have listened to me?" Marina asked.

"How can you hear me when I'm practically whispering but not when I'm speaking in my normal tone right next to you?"

"The acoustics are weird in here; haven't you noticed?" We reached the bottom of the stairs and walked across the ancient black-and-white linoleum tiles to a counter where a man was standing, tapping away on a laptop computer. "Hey, Marcus."

As we approached the thinnish man, he held up his index finger. "Marina Neff. Greetings. One moment, please."

I looked at her. She shrugged and laid her elbows on the counter, crossing her arms and looking as if she could stand there for hours. With ease. "So," she said. "What'cha doin'?" All she needed was some bubble gum to snap and she'd be fourteen again.

Marcus flicked her a short look, then refocused on the computer screen. "If I recall correctly, and I'm sure I do, you have a tremendous capacity for tenacity."

"Yup." She inched closer to him. "Say, what would happen if I, you know, accidentally of course, pulled the plug on your doohickey here?"

His face, still impassive, nonetheless gave the impression of long-sufferance. "I am coming to the conclusion that it will be faster if I halt my work on redesigning the layout of the store's plumbing fixtures, let you speak, and then return to work than try to continue working with you here."

She grinned. "You're pretty smart for a boy."

The middle-aged boy made a few more taps on the keyboard, then stepped back from the counter and folded his arms. "What is it you wish to know?"

Marina made the introductions. "Beth, Marcus. Marcus, Beth."

"Does Beth have a surname?" he asked.

"Kennedy," I said. "I own the Children's Bookshelf."

He nodded. "You used to have a relationship with Evan Garrett, correct?"

"Yes," I said. "That's correct." I waited for a cold shoulder, for a knowing glance, or at least a quiet snort, but he gave me nothing except: "I've never met anyone with the last name of Kennedy. Odd, as it is a relatively common surname."

Marina bumped me with her elbow. "Marcus collects names. He remembers the names of everyone he's ever met."

The term "pencil-neck geek" popped in my brain, and I didn't know how to get it out. *Think about Marcus as an infant,* I told myself. He must have had a nice fat baby neck at six months old. But try as I might, all I could picture was a miniature version of the adult man, reaching out for his mother's smartphone and downloading an app to play "Itsy Bitsy Spider" at his vocal cue. Not that there were cell phones when he was that age, but the image felt right.

"I used to collect rocks," I blurted out. "Little ones." I used my index finger and thumb to indicate an object about an inch in diameter.

"Igneous?" Marcus asked. "Metamorphic? I assume not sedimentary, not for something that small."

Actually, what I'd filled my pockets with were the pretty ones. Sparkly had been best, but I'd liked the red ones, too. "It was a long time ago." Marcus gave me a long look. I gave him a bright smile. "So," I said. "My friend Marina here says you attended all of Dennis Halpern's lecture series last summer."

"That's correct."

"And can I assume that you know Dennis has been killed?"

"You can."

"So . . ." I was suddenly stumped. How could I convince Marcus here to share information that might possibly incriminate people who might possibly be his friends?

Marina placed her forefinger on the counter and pushed hard enough to send it into a backward arc. "Point one. The police have not arrested the killer." Her middle finger went down next to the first finger. "Point two. Local law enforcement is asking people to speak up if they see or hear anything that might help catch said killer." Her ring finger joined the pair. "Point three. Beth and I think it's possible that someone who attended those lectures might have killed Dennis. Point four. You were at all the lectures." Her hand went flat on the counter. "Point five. We're thinking you can help."

His arms crossed in front of him. "If you think I killed Dennis Halpern, why haven't you gone to the police?"

Marina's eyes opened wide. "What? No! That's not it at all!"

"I suggest," he said coldly, "that you make your accusations after you have some semblance of proof."

"No, I . . ." Her mouth opened and shut a couple of times. No words came out, only small pathetic squeaking noises.

"Leave it to me," she'd said. "I have ways of finding out," she'd told me.

"Look, Marcus," I said, pulling my list out of my purse's outside pocket. "Here are descriptions of the people I'd like to know something about." I pushed the paper over to him. "I'm sure you've heard of kinesiology. Using some of those techniques, I studied the videos and came up with three people who fit the parameters of actions committed while under stress."

Marcus nodded. "Applied kinesiology is gaining ground as a science. There are some respected researchers doing work in the field. Though it's not a hard science, of course."

"Of course," I murmured.

He scanned the paper, turned it over and saw the blank back, then turned it over again. "These are the people you've selected as possible suspects?"

Marina pulled a crinkled piece of paper from her own purse. "These, too."

He lined up the lists side by side. Read them both, then reopened his laptop. As he tapped on the keyboard, Marina pushed herself forward on her elbows to see what he was doing. "Good idea," she said. To me she whispered, "He's going to the Halpern website."

Marcus's head rotated between the lists and the computer screen, at the speed of someone watching a very slow game of tennis. "This man"—he pointed at my description of the man with the short beard and tapping feet—"has been in China for the last month. He spent an inordinate amount of time during breaks on his cell phone making the arrangements. This man"—he tapped Marina's description of the man in the flannel shirt and pocket protector—"is my cousin, and I'll vouch for his character."

He eliminated my description of the man who didn't blink by saying he'd moved to Montana the week after the last lecture to take up a career as a fly-fishing guide. Which left two people.

"These two," Marcus said, "are possible."

From my list, the woman with the fierce expression. From Marina's list, the man with the horrendously ugly tie.

"One of mine and one of yours." Marina clapped her hands. "Hooray, we both win!" We grinned at each other.

"However," Marcus said, "I'm afraid I don't know their names."

Our grins fell to the floor. "You ... what?" Marina asked. "But you know the name of everybody you've ever met. How can you not know their names?"

He shrugged, the most human thing I'd seen him do. "I didn't meet any of these people. It was a lecture, and we weren't introduced. I have to be formally introduced to someone to collect a name."

Marina started to say something, but I jabbed her in the ribs with my elbow. "Thanks for your time, Marcus. We appreciate it." I headed for the stairway.

"Now what are we going to do?" Marina said, sending Marcus a stink-eye look of which he was completely oblivious. "I was sure he'd have those names. What kind of dumb rule is that, to not learn someone's name unless they're officially introduced?"

We started up the stairs, and Marina continued to grouse about the stupid rules of Marcus's name game. When she ran out of breath, I finally got a word in. "Don't worry about it."

"*You're* telling *me* not to worry?" She stopped halfway up the stairs. "Has the world ended and no one texted me about it? We need those names and we have no way of getting them, and you're saying not to worry?"

"That's right." I smiled. "Leave it to me."

Because I had an idea.

I abandoned Marina to her own devices and returned from whence I'd come, back to my office. Once seated, I pushed aside the stacks of work that were calling my name and fired up the Internet. In the three seconds it took Halpern's website to load, a small mountain of questions piled into my brain.

What if this didn't work? What if I couldn't remember how to do it? What if, in the five minutes since we'd left Marcus, the web designer had uploaded a site revamp and all the videos were gone? What if . . .

The site came live on my computer screen, links to the videos in full view. "Quit with the worst-case scenario," I said out loud. But I never would. Moms the world over had cornered the market on that habit eons ago and they'd never relinquish their grip.

I played the video that showed the intense woman, then tweaked the PLAY and STOP and REVERSE buttons until the best view of her was displayed. I leaned close to the keyboard, scrutinizing each button. "I know it's here somewhere," I muttered. "Somewhere . . . ha!" There, in teensy-tiny print, on the obscure seldom-used upper-right part of the keyboard, was a key marked PRT SCR. For "print screen," a misnomer if there ever was one. Create-a-digital-image-of-what-you-see-on-the-screen-and-then-hide-it-in-an-undisclosed-location was more like it. I whacked the key, spent a few minutes figuring out where the file of the screen image had been sent, then printed it. Rinsed and repeated for the guy with the tie.

Step one, complete.

I slid the pictures into a vinyl-covered clipboard I'd been given at a long-ago booksellers conference and picked up my purse. Step two was about to commence.

Half an hour later, after I'd made some vague explanation to Lois and Yvonne about an urgent errand, I walked into the Madison offices of Halpern and Company. I eyed my surroundings. If I'd had enough money to think about investing in anything other than a savings account, this place would inspire me to hand over my cash. It could all be an interior decorator–inspired illusion, of course, but the wood-paneled walls, subdued lighting, and original artwork spoke of success and trust.

"Good afternoon." The receptionist, sitting behind a large and very solid dark wooden desk, gave me a polite smile. "How may I help you?"

My heart warmed to the woman. Anyone who properly used the word "may" was worthy of respect and admiration. I smiled back at her. "Well, I have a question."

The woman, her hair in a smooth French twist, nodded. "Answering questions is one of our favorite things here at Halpern."

I desperately wanted to ask if the air of somber quiet was permanent or if it was due to the death of the company's founder, to ask how the company would manage without Dennis, to ask if the remaining partners would carry on or if they'd sell to the highest bidder, to ask if she had any ideas about who killed her boss. Instead, I trotted out the lines I'd rehearsed during the drive to downtown Madison.

"My name is Beth Kennedy. I own a children's bookstore in Rynwood, and—"

The woman's face lit up. "The Children's Bookshelf? I love that store!"

"You . . . do?"

"Oh, sure. It's been a few years since I've been there, my kids are grown now, but I'm hoping for grandchildren soon." Her polite smile slipped into a real one. "My name is Valerie. Beth, you said?" She held her hand out over the desk.

As I shook her hand, the story I'd so carefully composed fell to bits. No way could I ask this nice lady to look at the pictures and say I was afraid that these two people had been sitting beside a friend of mine who had just been hospitalized for a horrible disease that had an extremely long incubation period and could I have their names, please, because they should be contacted right away.

"You have a wonderful store," Valerie said. "It must be great to work with books all day. Children's books, especially. Lots of happiness in children's stories. A few problems, but no death, no—" She came to a sudden stop.

But I knew where she'd been headed. "No murder?" I asked, as gently as I could.

She studied the desktop. "You're from Rynwood, so you must know about . . ." Her hands made a small gesture that told of sorrow and pain and a deep reluctance to talk about Dennis's death.

"Yes," I said. And since I had a similar reluctance to talk about it, because any more talk and I'd have to mention my role in his appearance at the PTA meeting during which he'd been killed, and if she was astute in asking questions, I'd end up telling her that I'd let his killer escape. No, I definitely did not want to talk about it.

All of which meant that instead of the made-up tale of diseases and hospitals, I told her the truth. "The police have asked for help. If anyone thinks they might know anything about the killer, we're to contact them right away."

Valerie shook her head slowly. "But I don't know anything. There were detectives in here, asking everybody questions, but I don't think any of us here helped at all." She looked up at me, her face crumpled with the effort not to cry. "We all loved him."

"Loved?" I echoed. Maybe Marina had been right about the mistress thing.

"Not *love* love," Valerie said. "Dennis swore up and down that Vicki was his best and last and forever wife. No more divorce, he said. He'd finally found the woman he'd been looking for all his life. I meant we loved him like a brother. An uncle." She looked unhappy with her word choice, so I supplied the right one.

"A friend."

She swallowed. "He was our boss, but he was our friend, too. And if any of us knew anything about his murder, we would have told the police already."

I opened my clipboard and slid the two pictures across her desk.

"Who are they?" she asked.

"Both of these people attended the lectures that are up on your website. One or both of them might have something to do with Dennis's death."

Valerie's eyes thinned as she studied the pictures. "Right. I'll call the police and let them know."

Ah. That hadn't been my plan, exactly. It might be the right one, but I spun out the future conversation in my head. Valerie would talk to the sheriff's office, and they'd call me and ask why I thought these two people had anything to do with the murder. I'd have to say, "Well, Officer, it's like this: I'm a mom, and I can tell when people are lying or uncomfortable and these two people . . ."

There wasn't a chance in a kazillion that I'd be taken seriously. What I needed was a teensy bit of evidence. But how to tell Valerie that? There was only one way. The truth.

"Um . . ." I explained the dilemma, but toward the end, when she could see where I was going, Valerie started shaking her head.

"I'm sorry, but I can't tell you. They're clients, and it's confidential. I'm really very sorry."

I'd suspected as much. Maybe I should have stuck to the disease story. I thanked her for her time, picked up the papers, and turned to go. But before I got halfway across the room, Valerie asked, "Are you on Facebook? You know, that social media site?"

"Sure." The bookstore had a very active presence. I posted regularly about author signings, new books, and sales of all shapes and sizes.

"Halpern and Company is on Facebook," she said. "And we have a lot of friends." She arched her eyebrows. "A *lot* of friends."

Light dawned. "It's good to have friends," I said, a grin spreading wide.

Valerie's crumpled look returned. "Yes, it is."

I wished there was something I could do to ease her pain, but there wasn't. "I'm so very sorry," I said quietly. And left.

That evening, the phone rang while my hands were covered in egg wash and bread crumbs. "Jenna, could you get that, please?" I asked.

My daughter was at the kitchen table, chewing on the end of a pencil eraser. A week earlier, she'd announced to her startled mother that she wanted to get her homework done before dinner instead of after, and would it be okay if she did her homework in the kitchen instead of up in her bedroom?

The phone rang again. "Jenna," I called a little louder. "Answer the phone, please. My hands are all gooey."

"Oh. Okay." She slid off the chair and walked over to the phone. "Kennedy residence, Jenna speaking." After a moment, she plopped the receiver back into its home and went back to her homework.

"Wrong number?" I asked.

"No one there." She shrugged. "Mom, if the prefix 'dis' means the opposite of whatever the rest of the word is, how come 'parage' isn't a word?"

"Because the English language was made to torture middle schoolers."

"Hardy har har." But she said it with a smile. "Do

you—" The ringing of the phone interrupted her. This time after she answered, she said, "Sure. She's right here. Hang on a second, okay?" She clunked the cordless phone onto the table. "It's Mrs. Neff."

I put the boneless chicken breast on a wire rack, quick-washed my hands, and had them half-dried on a towel by the time I picked up the phone. "Did you call just a minute ago?"

"Non, mademoiselle."

"Since when did you start speaking French?"

"I am practiced in ze language," she said in what even I knew was a horrible accent. "I have many words in ze French. Croissant. Baguette. Champagne. Merlot. Éclair. Quiche. Crepes."

"I notice that your French is heavy on the pastries."

"Yeah." She sighed. "Heavy is the word."

"How about this word? Genius."

"A lovely word," she said, "especially when applied to me."

"Nope. Elsa Stinson and Kyle Burkhardt."

"Who are they?" She stopped. "Wait a minute. Are they . . . ?"

"Yep. The names of our suspects."

"How did you do that so fast?" she demanded.

"I have my ways."

Marina started to sputter. I enjoyed the sound for a few sputs, then took pity on her and explained. "It took me half an hour of looking at tiny pictures to get Kyle's name. Five minutes later, I had Elsa's."

"I get Kyle," Marina said quickly.

"What are you talking about?"

"They each need investigating, right? I get Kyle; you get Elsa."

I turned and stared in the direction of her house. Which I couldn't see because it was a mile away and night was coming on fast, but there's no controlling instinctive reactions. "Why?"

"Do you need the truth, or can I make up something?"

"Did you really need to ask that?"

"What if the truth makes me look silly?"

"Especially then."

"Yeah," she said glumly. "I figured. Truth, then. Say, remember that old show *Truth or Consequences*? How about if I—"

"Just tell me. I need to get dinner in the oven."

Her next words came all in a fast whooshing rush. "That woman scares the crap out of me."

"Elsa Stinson?"

"See, even her name is scary! Please don't make me investigate her, let me do the tie guy, please, please, please."

I didn't care one way or another, but . . . "What's so frightening about El—"

"Don't say her name!"

"About that woman?" On the video she'd looked intense, fierce even, but scary?

Marina mumbled something.

"What was that?" I asked.

She heaved a huge sigh. "She reminds me way too much of this girl I knew when I was a kid. Toni Cregar, her name was. All through elementary school, she pushed me around."

"You got pushed around?"

"Hard to believe, I know. But I was short for my age back then and very shy."

"That is also hard to believe," I said dryly.

"Toni the Tiger was queen of the playground and I . . . I wasn't." There was a short silence. "I suppose it would be good for me to deal with someone who looks like her. Get over that childhood stuff once and for all."

She was right. It probably would be good for her. Then again, it would probably be good for me to wear a feather boa at least once in my life, but I didn't see it happening. "I'll do Elsa," I said. "Getting over stuff is overrated."

"You're the best." She made a loud kissing noise. "Gotta go. Zach and the DH will start chewing the flesh off my bones if I don't serve dinner in the next five minutes."

I hung up, wondering what childhood wounds Jenna and Oliver would carry with them into adulthood. The divorce, certainly, and the murder of their school principal two years ago. But did they have playground incidents I didn't know about? Were there—

The phone rang, and since I was still standing there, lost in thought, I picked it up. "Kennedy residence, Beth speaking." I heard traffic noise, a sharp intake of breath, then nothing.

"Was that Mrs. Neff again?" Jenna asked.

"No." I put the phone back into its cradle. Absentmindedly, I brushed at the back of my neck, trying to wipe away a feeling of trickly unease. "Sounded like someone's cell phone is calling us by mistake."

Jenna, buried in her homework, made a grunting noise and I went back to cooking dinner. Cell phone, I told myself. These things happen. Just a coincidence that the store is getting hang-up calls at the same time we were getting them at the house.

Pure coincidence.

Oliver was moving the last plate from table to kitchen counter when the phone rang. This time it was hot, sudsy water with which my hands were covered. "Oliver, could you get that? I'm all wet over here."

The phone was in midring when Oliver picked it up. "Kennedy residence, Oliver speaking." Pause. He repeated himself, then looked at me. "Mom, no one's there."

"Just hang up," I said. Coincidence. They happened, after all. "Third time's the charm, right?"

"What do you mean?" He put the phone away and scrambled up to sit on one of the kitchen island stools. Not as much of a scramble as it had been a few months ago, though. My little boy was growing fast.

I smiled at him. "That's the third time we've had a hang-up call tonight. I'm sure it's just—" He jumped down from the stool in an awkward heap, his eyes round. "Oliver, what's the matter?"

"They're after me," he whispered, staring at the phone.

"They who?" I asked.

"The . . . the . . . guys."

"The bad guys?"

He shut his eyes tight and nodded.

I wiped my hands dry on my pants and hurried to his side. "No one's after you. You're safe at home with me. With your sister. With Spot." I laid my hand on top of his head.

He jerked away. "No, no, you don't know! They're after me and I can't let them get me!" His voice went high and thin. "Don't let them take me, Mommy!"

I dropped to my knees and hugged him tight. Oliver hadn't called me Mommy in years. "Shh, Ollster. Shh. I won't let anyone take you. You don't need to worry."

"But what if—"

"Shhh," I said. "There's nothing to worry about. Mommy's here. I'll take care of you. I'll always take care of you, forever and ever."

He buried his face in my neck. Wrapped his arms around me and held me with a strength I hadn't known he had. "Please don't let them take me away. Please, Mommy."

"I won't, sweetheart, I won't." But even summoning all the mom powers at my disposal, it took a long, long time to calm Oliver down from near-hysteria, and through it all, he wouldn't say why he was so scared.

I kissed him and held him and made soothing noises. And I made my decision.

Tomorrow I'd call in the big guns.

Chapter 15

The next morning, I dropped Jenna off at the middle school, dropped Oliver at Tarver, drove around the block to give Oliver enough time to get inside and out of sight, then parked in a spot marked VISITOR just outside Tarver's front door.

I hurried into the front office, got a quick introduction to the gorgeous new vice principal, Stephanie Pesch, and was soon sitting in the school psychologist's office, pouring out my concerns. Millie Jefferson listened for the fifteen minutes it took me to tell the tale, asking quiet questions when they needed to be asked, giving small nods of encouragement when my words slowed.

Finally, there was no more to tell. "So what do you think is wrong?" I asked. "I've talked to the mothers of all his friends and they don't know. Marina Neff is his day-care provider, and she doesn't know. His father doesn't know."

"How would you like me to help?" Millie asked.

"Well." I shifted. "I was thinking maybe you had a magic wand in your desk drawer."

She smiled, making her comfortable round face look even more like a fairy godmother's. "I save that for the truly difficult cases."

Hope sprang up inside me. "You don't think there's anything really wrong with Oliver?"

"Anything is possible, but judging from what I know of the boy, I'd say no."

Relief was a great wave, washing worry out of dark nooks and crannies, cleansing me of the concern that had been weighing me down. "You have no idea how glad I am to hear you say that."

"I'd say nothing is seriously wrong," Millie went on, "but obviously something isn't right. If my years in this field have been at all worthwhile, it will be my working theory that he's feeling guilty about something."

"Guilty? Oliver?"

"How has his schoolwork been the last few weeks?"

I thought back. "Fine. Better, if anything. That's one reason why . . . um . . ."

"Why you didn't come to me earlier?" Millie asked gently.

Shame colored my face. It was true. The quality of Oliver's homework had been a prime factor in my reasoning that whatever was wrong with him was just a small bump in the road. If anything had been deeply amiss, his grades would have slipped. Every mom knew that.

"Don't worry." Millie sat back in her chair, suddenly looking less like a fairy godmother and more like a multidegreed psychologist. "It's a typical reaction for parents. Don't blame yourself."

But I would. Of course I would. I nodded, indicating external agreement. "What should I do next?"

"Go to work," Millie said, moving her reading glasses from the top of her head to her nose. She made a few fast squiggly notes. Shorthand, I realized. How pretty it was. "With your permission," she said, "I'll talk to Oliver. See what I can see. Today is Wednesday . . ." She turned to her laptop and tapped keys. "My schedule is full today and I'm not due back to Tarver until next Monday. Will that be soon enough?"

"Oh." Somehow I'd thought she'd be able to pull Oliver out of his classroom, have a cozy chat, and figure it all out before lunchtime. "Well, sure. If that's the soonest you can, that's the soonest you can."

Millie studied my face. I don't know what she saw, but she said, "I'll see if I can fit him in today. Not a full session, but we can get comfortable with each other. That will help for Monday."

The tension in my shoulders eased a fraction. "Thank you."

"It's what I'm here for." She smiled, back to being a fairy godmother. "I'll call you tomorrow and let you know how things went."

I thanked her again and left, worry seeping back into those cracks and crevices. Tomorrow. It suddenly seemed like a million miles away.

Lois and I and a young man named Cody sat around the table in the workroom. Yvonne said she'd rather not do interviews, if I didn't mind. Lois had put her hand on her heart and promised to be good, but I was starting to think that her definition of good and mine were quite different.

Cody looked around. "Like, this is where you sort all the books and stuff?"

"And stuff," Lois said. "Absolutely. We do lots of stuff back here."

Lois had taken against the boy even before he'd walked into the store. She'd noticed him walking down the sidewalk a few minutes before his interview. "Another fine piece of youth," she'd said, pointing. "Why on earth do they buy pants that long if they're just going to let them drag in the dirt? And all that black. They think they're in New York, or what?"

I'd looked up from the stack of special orders I was sorting. "He's clean-shaven and his hair's combed."

She'd snorted. "A five-year-old can do that much."

I'd started to point out that five-year-olds don't shave when he'd walked in the door. Now the interview was five minutes old and going south fast. "So," I said heartily, smiling as sincerely as I could. "What makes you want to work in a children's bookstore, Cody?"

"Uh . . ." He pulled at his lower lip. "I need a job, like, real bad. My mom says she's not making any more of my car payments until I start doing something."

Lois leaned forward. "So you know how to read?"

"Well, yeah. Like, I graduated high school, you know. It's on my application."

Before Lois could get going on her soapbox about the current state of public schools, I asked, "What reading have you done outside of school assignments?"

"Uh." More lip pulling. "I guess there's a couple of those graphic novel things that I read once."

"Have you read any Harry Potter books?"

"Nah. They're too long. I don't got time for that. I saw the movies, though." His face gained some animation. "Like that first movie was cool, you know, when the chess pieces came alive and—"

"You didn't read any of the books?" Lois asked.

"Nah. Are they any good?"

"How about the Percy Jackson books?" I asked. *"The Lightning Thief? The Last Olympian?"*

"You mean like the video game? I didn't know they'd made a book out of it."

I laid a hand on Lois's arm. "Thanks so much for your time, Cody. Do you have any questions you'd like to ask?"

"Uh, yeah. You're that PTA president, right? I hear you guys got a wicked curse going. That's fierce, man, fierce."

"There's no such thing as a curse," I said.

"Yeah, whatever." Cody inched forward on his chair. "And you're the one who keeps finding dead people, right? What do they look like? Do they look like they've been murdered, you know, all bug-eyed and scared?" He widened his eyes and made them stick out as far as they could. "Or do they look more like they're sleeping? My buddy and I have this bet, see. I figure murdered people got to look scared."

I stared at the table. At the pad of paper I'd brought in. At the blank paper.

Don't listen to him. Don't go back in time. Don't relive the awful horror of finding your friend Sam strangled to death. Don't see the red blood staining Dennis's shirt, don't see his too-still chest. Don't, don't, don't.

Lois stood up. "We're done, kid. Don't call us, we'll call you, okay?"

"But she hasn't said which—"

"Out!"

"Oh, man, this sucks," Cody muttered. "I was so close." But he slouched to his feet and scuffed out.

"You okay?" Lois asked.

"Fine," I said automatically. "I'm fine."

"No, you're not. But I'll make you a mug of chamomile that'll fix you up fast." She patted my shoulder. "Come with me. We'll drink tea and make fun of him the rest of the afternoon. I can't wait to tell Yvonne what he said about Percy Jackson."

I got to my feet and trailed after her.

Don't go back. Don't see it. Don't relive it.

But, of course, I did.

*   *   *

Since it was Wednesday and Richard was done giving his seminar, I stayed late at the store. When Richard had the kids on a weeknight he was dutiful about dropping them off at school the next morning, dressed and breakfasted, their homework done. There was no reason for me to worry about them. None at all.

Not so very long ago, Evan and I had spent Wednesday evenings together. Those nights had passed quickly, but now that I was footloose and fancy-free, I'd begun working late, long past closing time. A salad from the Green Tractor served well enough for dinner, and I hardly ever spilled dressing on anything important.

And it turned out that I liked working late. The store, dark and quiet, felt comfortable around me. The shelves were filled with books I knew and loved, books waiting for new owners to pick them up and take them home.

I shook away the thought. The concept felt right, but it wasn't something I'd risk saying out loud in a public setting.

When I finished my To Do list—or at least finished the tasks I had a realistic chance of completing—I got up and turned off my office light. I'd been in there so long I hadn't realized that the sun had set long ago. Shelves and books were lit only by what was trickling in through the front windows, streetlight leftovers.

Huh.

Since it was unlikely that I'd get through the mostly dark store without crashing into something, I flicked on the rear bank of overhead lights. Immediately, I was distracted by the new crop of early-reader books Yvonne had put out, and it took me a good fifteen minutes to make my way to the back entrance. I reached for the light switch, turned it to off . . . but nothing happened.

Huh.

I flicked it a few times, but the lights stayed on. Bugger. I tramped back through the store, turned the lights off at the other switch, hoped I'd be smart enough to remember to get the broken switch replaced soon, and picked my way carefully across the darkness.

When I opened the door, I finally recognized the faint noise that I'd been hearing for the last two hours and hadn't paid much attention to.

Rain.

Which meant wet.

I liked being wet just fine when it was intentional, but not so much when it was forced upon me. "Rats," I said.

The rain continued down.

"Double rats."

I stared into the alley. The sole city streetlight was burned out, and the only other illumination came from a few business owners who left the lights over their alley entrances on all night. The asphalt seemed to attract any stray ray of light and absorb it without reflecting it back. What if this alley was something out of a Dean Koontz novel and it was going to suck in every last particle of light in Rynwood, in Wisconsin, in the country, in the world . . . ?

"Stop that," I muttered, and yanked my imagination out of the dark and stupid direction it wanted to go. "Butterflies, kittens, and rainbows." Much better. "Sunshine, ice cream, and—"

The sound of footsteps interrupted my positive thoughts. "Lou?" I called. "Is that you?" The sound stopped. "Hello?"

I peered into the rain, trying to see who it was. Suddenly, all the odd events of the last few days piled up together in my memory. The hang-up phone calls. The footsteps I'd heard Saturday morning.

Fear sizzled down my throat. I shrank back into the

doorway and felt for the knob. If I could get out my keys without making a sound, I could get inside and call the police. Gus would come to my rescue, and . . .

And the guy would be long gone and I'd look like an idiot. Gus would be nice about having to come out in the rain, but I'd feel head-patted.

I hated that feeling.

So instead, I sank into a crouch and crab walked down the single step. Moving silently in my sensible shoes, I skirted the side of the building, stayed low while moving around my car, and edged behind the Dumpster we used for cardboard recycling. From here, I had a sight line that would let me see anyone walking down the alley.

Rain dripped off the roof and down the back of my neck. I put up the collar of my light coat and wished I'd ignored Marina's scoffing when I'd wanted to buy a jacket with a hood.

I stayed down and waited. Soon, my thighs started screaming at me to "Stand up; we're not used to this!" but I ignored them.

The rain came down.

I waited. He was out there. I knew he was. All I had to do was wait. I could wait; waiting was something moms did every day.

More rain.

My thighs screamed louder.

More waiting.

When my calf muscles had cramped almost to the point of no return, the footsteps came again, shuffling forward through the river of rain now sheeting off the asphalt.

There he was. I saw a foot, a leg, a second foot and leg, a rain-coated body, and . . .

My right foot slipped. I fell forward, my shoulder

crashing hard against the Dumpster, the thudding noise reverberating off the buildings, the concrete, the asphalt. The figure turned my way. I gasped.

It was Staci Yost.

We stood in the store's kitchenette. I'd rummaged through the cabinets and come up with a handful of clean dish towels. Staci was rubbing at her hair with a terry-cloth rooster and apologizing like crazy.

"I was so horrible to you at Dad's visitation. Ryan tried to stop me, I know he did, but I wouldn't listen. All those things I said, it would serve me right if you never forgave me. I'm sorry, Beth, I really am. I can't believe I was so mean to you in front of all those people!"

Murmuring something about grief and the pain of loss, I handed her another towel.

"Look at you," Staci said. "You should be yelling at me for being such a jerk. Instead you're helping me dry off."

I took our wet towels, hung them over the edge of the sink, and tried to think of something to say. I wasn't mad at all; I was just relieved that the person in the alley hadn't been a man with a stocking mask over his face and a gun in his hand.

"Anyway," Staci went on, "I've wanted to apologize ever since. But every time I picked up the phone, I just didn't know what to say, so I hung up."

"You called?"

She dragged her fingers through her wet hair. "Ow. I guess I called a few times. Here and at your house, too. I'm really sorry. You probably thought I was a stalker or something. You know, like that woman who was after my dad."

The world, which had been moving at a rapid clip complete with sounds, smells, and textures, came to a sudden and very quiet stop. "What woman?"

"Dad—" A small noise came out of her, a tiny whimper of pain. I started to move toward her, to offer what comfort I could, but she shook her head and stepped back. "I'm good. It's okay, thanks. Dad said some woman kept bugging him. He thought it was funny, I think."

"Bugging him about what?"

She shrugged. "He never said. Because of client confidentiality maybe? Not sure. But I don't think he took her very seriously. He said any woman who wore that much jewelry wasn't to be trusted. And then he'd laugh." Her smile came and went so fast, I wasn't sure I'd even seen it.

"Did you tell the police about this woman?"

"Well, no. There wasn't anything I could tell them, not really." She blotted the ends of her hair with the towel. "Do you think I should?"

"You never know what will be important in a police investigation." Then, because that had sounded far too Richard-like, I added, "If you want, I could talk to Chief Eiseley. Tell him what you said and ask him if he thinks you should talk to the sheriff's office."

"Really? You'd do that for me?" Staci's eyes looked moist. "After what I said?"

I handed her a plaid towel. "Here, your hair still looks wet." Surely no one could cry with a plaid towel on her head. "That's nothing compared to what my kids put me through every day."

What might have been a sob was swallowed up by a laugh. "Ain't that the truth. And my mom says I'm the one who turned her hair gray, so I guess what goes around comes around."

I was pretty sure it had been my sister Darlene who'd been the cause of my mother's hair change, with some blame laid at the feet of my sister Kathy, and a little bit at my brother Tim's door. I'd been the quiet kid, the good kid, and I couldn't remember doing a thing that would have cost my parents any sleep. Well, except for the time in high school when I snuck out to go to *The Rocky Horror Picture Show*. That might have worried them a little. And there was the time that—

"So I just wanted to say I'm sorry," Staci said. "And I hope you'll forgive me both for making a scene at the visitation and for scaring the crap out of you."

I bowed. "Lady Staci of the Yost, thou art forgiven."

She curtsied in return. "Thank you, Lady Beth of the Kennedys. Your kindness is deep and boundless and you set a shining example as our PTA's president."

I smiled. She was sweet. Misguided, deluded, and wrong, but sweet. I shooed her off home and swore on a stack of Hunger Games books that I wouldn't mention the incident to a soul. But as I got into my car and started home, there was a *click* in my head. Staci had been the hang-up caller, but tonight was the first time she'd come to talk to me in person.

Whose footsteps, then, had I heard last Saturday?

The next morning was Thursday, the day before the tell-your-husband-and-Gus-or-I-will deadline I'd given Summer, and I'd spent more time than I should have wondering if I'd done the right thing. Had I been too hard on her? Auntie May thought I hadn't been hard enough. Did such a thing as a happy medium really exist?

Half an hour before the store opened, I was sitting at my desk, drumming my fingers on a stack of invoices, thinking about footsteps and dogs and gunshots and the reasons behind murder. Sure, TV and newspapers and radio were heavy with reports of people committing murder for horribly banal reasons, but that all seemed far removed from Rynwood, Wisconsin. No one in my town would kill for something so trivial as a pair of sneakers.

At least that's what I wanted to think, and until I was proved wrong I'd continue to think that way.

Then, before my brain could talk my hand out of it, I picked up the phone and dialed Summer's number. After the standard good-morning-how-are-you's, I girded my mental loins. "Have you had a chance to talk to your husband?" I asked. "I need to see Gus today, and I could give him a heads-up on your situation."

"Um, about that," she said. "Brett's been really busy. There hasn't been a good time to talk to him."

I rested my head against the back of the chair. "Okay, but don't forget that you promised you'd tell him about the casino by Friday noon. That gives you the rest of today and all tonight to find time."

"Sure, but he's got this big presentation at work Friday morning, and I don't want to bug him with anything until that's done. He'll be up late working on it, and I don't want to distract him. If this presentation goes well it could mean a big promotion."

"Summer . . ."

"This weekend," she said quickly. "I'll do it this weekend. We'll have lots of quiet time on Sunday. His parents are taking the kids to the zoo and we'll have all afternoon."

I sighed. I should tell her that every day she delayed telling Brett about her trip with Destiny would be a day filled with unnecessary anxiety. Instead, I said, "I'm calling Gus on Monday, even if you haven't told your husband."

"Sunday afternoon," Summer promised. "I'll sit him down and tell him all about it."

And since I wanted to believe her, I did.

"Hey, have you heard the rumors about a curse on the

PTA?" she asked. "About how there's all these deaths, that it's turning dangerous to be in it. That maybe it's time to dissolve the group, or something. Makes you wonder, you know?"

When I didn't say anything, she gave a short giggle. "You don't think there's anything to this curse thing, do you?"

"No," I said shortly. "I don't." And I hung up. After I said good-bye, of course. There's no excuse for rudeness.

Later that morning, when I was getting a headache-by-invoice, the phone rang. Paoze's voice called out, "I will get it, Mrs. Kennedy," but a moment later he appeared in the office doorway. "It is a Dr. Jefferson. Would you like to take the call?"

I snatched up the phone. "Millie, how are you this morning?"

"As fine as caffeine can make me," she said. "Do you have a minute?"

I shoved aside the papers, catalogs, and files on my desk and reached for pen and paper. "All the time in the world."

"Spoken like a good parent. Now. Oliver and I had a nice chat yesterday."

"And?"

"And he's a very nice and polite young man. You have good reason to be proud of your son."

On the days when I wasn't worried sick about him, yes.

"Something is definitely troubling him," she went on, "but it's too soon to say what."

"Oh." I deflated. "How long do you think?"

"Beth," she said, "this isn't like going to the emergency room."

"I know, it's just . . ." But I couldn't say what I wanted to say. It would sound too stupid.

Millie filled in the gap. "It's just that you're worried about your child and you want to fix everything and make it all better as soon as possible."

Exactly. "A little unrealistic, I suppose."

"But understandable," Millie said. "You said your ex-husband hasn't been able to get Oliver to confide in him, correct? Is there another man that he's close to? A grandfather or an uncle?"

"Well," I said slowly, "there's a friend of the family who might help out."

"See if you can get them together," Millie advised. "Ask him not to force a conversation, but to open the door for communication, if you see what I mean."

Open the door? I'd burst it wide open with a bulldozer, if that's what it took to help my son.

The rest of the day passed uneventfully, and I spent the evening helping the kids with homework, doing the laundry I'd put off for too long, and worrying about Oliver. Friday morning, I opened my office e-mail and found a message from Marina. "Kyle is the killer," it said. "You know that tie he wore at the lecture? You should see the rest of them. No way could an innocent man have a tie collection like that. None."

I rolled my eyes. No way could Marina know what Kyle Burkhardt had in his closet. None.

But the e-mail was serving as a reminder that I hadn't done a lick of research on scary Elsa Stinson. I fired up my new favorite research tool and got to work.

At lunchtime, Marina called. "You didn't waste any time looking up stuff about Elsa the Horrible, did you? Kyle's the killer, I tell you."

"You just like the alliteration."

"It is fun, yes, but this time I'm right about who did it."

"There's a first time for everything," I said. "And please tell me that your e-mail about his tie collection was pure imagination?"

"Nope," she said cheerfully.

"You went into his house?" My heart suddenly felt too big for my chest. "How?"

"Easy. I made up some business cards and rang his front doorbell. Said I was a home organizer and that I was giving free advice on closets."

"You did what?" I shrieked.

"Quit with the yelling, already. I was perfectly safe. Zach was waiting in the car with a cell phone and instructions to call 911 if I didn't come out in ten minutes. Plus Kyle's wife was home."

I groaned. Her idea of perfectly safe and mine were not on the same page. Not even in the same chapter.

"Anyway," she said, "that's that. I'd say no more proof is needed."

"What if I told you Elsa Stinson was in the army and spent two tours of duty overseas in the military police?"

"An MP? Wow, girls really can do anything, can't they?"

"After she left the army, in which she won numerous shooting awards, she spent four years with the Milwaukee Police Department. She wrote a book called *The Girl's Guide to Army Life,* and now she's a private investigator for one of the largest firms in Wisconsin."

"Good heavens," Marina said faintly. "How did you learn all this?"

"You wouldn't believe what people put on Facebook." And LinkedIn and Pinterest. Send a friendly invitation, and bingo bango bongo, you have a new friend. I felt a little guilty about the deception, but I doubted I'd lose sleep over it. Not much, anyway.

"Gotcha," Marina said. "Remind me to warn my children about the dangers."

It was too late—I'd looked up her older offspring months ago—but I'd decided to save that conversation for another time. Like when the world froze over.

"So she knows how to handle a gun," Marina mused. "Interesting."

"And as a private investigator, she knows how to find people. She has all the skills the killer has."

"Okay, you got me there. But Kyle is a gun guy. There was one of those big gun safes in the corner of the bedroom. And he had dead deer heads mounted all over the living room."

So we still had two suspects. Both had the skills and weaponry required; either one could have killed Dennis. The what, where, when, and how questions were answered, and we were closing in on the who part.

Which left the biggest question of all: *Why?*

Chapter 16

Oliver and I huddled together against the cold of the Agnes Mephisto Memorial Ice Arena. Huddled in a general sense, anyway. We were both sitting on the same aluminum bleacher, on the same folded-up blanket, and our laps were covered with the same green-and-gold Green Bay Packers blanket, but we might as well have been at opposite ends of the arena for all the closeness I was getting from him.

I looked at my son, perched there on the far end of the blanket, and wondered what I was doing wrong. Was this the price I was paying for the divorce? Sure, that had happened three years ago, but maybe the full reality of the situation was finally hitting my son. Or maybe this was a reaction to my breakup with Evan? That had been months ago, but—

"Go! Go!" The crowd of parents, stepparents, siblings, and friends were on their feet. Oliver and I rose with them. "Go!" A girl from Jenna's team had broken away from the rest of the players and was skating for all she was worth down the ice. Blades scraping hard, head up, stick flashing left and right keeping the puck in line. Close to the net now, she pulled her stick back and slammed a shot straight at the net.

The goalie flung herself onto the puck and stopped it cold.

"Ohh . . ." Half the crowd dropped back to their chilly seats. "Nice save!" shouted the other half.

"Where's Mrs. Neff?" Oliver asked. "She almost always comes to Jenna's games."

Marina enjoyed the rough and tumble of hockey, but even more she enjoyed what happened after the game. What she really liked was watching girls, who twenty minutes before had been outfitted in skates and helmets and hockey pads, come out of the locker room dressed in purple and pink.

The contrast tickled her, and if she couldn't attend the entire game, she tried at least to see the last period. This Saturday, however, Marina had been obligated to attend the college homecoming activities of her second-youngest offspring. I told Oliver this, but he didn't look overly interested. He didn't even ask what homecoming was.

My son, my son. What is wrong? Why won't you talk to me?

I sighed, snuck an inch closer to Oliver, and tried to concentrate on the game.

This time it was the bad guys who had the puck. Number two—who, under all her equipment had the cutest freckles and the most adorable pointed chin ever—snuck around the back of the right defenseman and skated toward the goalie. Toward Jenna.

My darling daughter lunged toward the puck, and the freckled pixie instantly whipped her stick the other way and slapped a shot toward the goal, sending the puck flying through the air, right toward the exposed part of the net.

But Jenna hadn't committed herself; her action had

been a feint. Quick as a wink, she dug her skates into the
ice and pushed herself in the opposite direction, arm
outstretched, glove open . . . and caught the puck smack
in the middle of her palm.

The parents around me leapt to their feet, cheering
my daughter.

But I just sat there. Jenna's first move had been a
feint. A fake. A ploy. A ruse. A gambit.

What if the murderer was doing the same thing? What
if I'd been thinking about the incident with Flossie and
the dogs all wrong? What if that didn't have anything to
do with the murder?

I took the kids to Sabatini's for a victory pizza, where
Jenna relived each of the twenty-two saves she'd made,
complete with NHL-style commentating and slow-
motion replays with Oliver gladly playing the part of the
puck. Thanks to precedent set at other victory pizza
lunches, I'd asked the hostess to seat us in a corner, distant from any other diners. Far better to let Jenna work
off her post-game excitement in a commercial establish-
ment built for abuse than at home, where I'd spoil her
stories with mom-admonishments.

Back home, while Jenna was unpacking her hockey
bag in the laundry room and Oliver was out with Spot in
the yard, I made the phone call. "Ready," I said.

"Give me ten minutes," he said.

"Ready for what?" Oliver asked as he and Spot came
in the back door.

I slid my cell phone into my purse and smiled brightly.
"For anything," I said. "What would you like to do this
afternoon? Climb every mountain? Pick a pocket or
two? Row, row, row your boat?"

Usually my nonsense made him giggle. Today,
though . . .

He shrugged.

A vision of the future struck me cold. If Oliver was this uncommunicative when he had a problem at age nine, what would he be like at thirteen? Seventeen?

I shook away the image. No. It would be fine. It had to be.

Soon, the front doorbell rang. In the olden days, Jenna and Oliver had fought over whose turn it was to answer the door. Today, no kid went flying, so I went myself.

I opened the door to see Pete Peterson and his young niece, Alison, standing on the front porch. "Hi, Pete," I said. "Thanks for doing this."

"Hey, not a problem. Anything I can do, you know?"

"Hello, Alison." I smiled at the eight-year-old standing next to him. "What have you been doing today?"

She held up a plastic shopping bag. "Mommy and me went to the dollar store."

"That sounds like fun. Why don't you go inside and find Jenna; then we'll look through your bag together. And could you please tell Oliver that I need him? Thank you."

Pete and I watched as she scampered inside, her dark blond curls bobbing. "She's a little sweetheart," I said. He made a noncommittal guy noise, but his smile belied his pride. I knew that Pete's sister, Wendy, had been through a bad divorce and that Alison rarely saw her dad. Not many men would have stepped up to become the father figure for a young girl, especially not many single men. I was about to say so when Oliver came up behind me.

"Hi, Mr. Peterson."

"Oliver, you are just the man I need," Pete said.

My son stared at him. "I am?"

"What I need is some help at my house. Some guy help." He winked broadly. "Well, not in the house, exactly. The garage. It needs cleaning like crazy, and I could do with an extra pair of hands."

Oliver pulled his hands out of his pockets and eyed them. "I'm not that strong," he muttered. "Or very big."

"Ah, big is overrated," Pete said. "I'm not what you'd call tall, and I make out okay. And I bet you're strong enough to move paint cans around, aren't you?"

"Um, I think so."

"Scraps of wood? Piles of newspapers? Boxes of nuts and bolts that don't fit anything I own?"

By now, Oliver was grinning. "I can do all of that." He looked at me. "Can I, Mom? Go with Mr. Peterson, I mean?"

I put on a frown. "Seems like you should do that in your own garage first."

"Pleeeeeaase!" He gripped his hands tight together and held them up to me. "I'll help clean our garage next weekend. And I'll be able to do a better job if I help with Mr. Peterson's garage first. I'll learn how to do things."

I looked at Pete, trying not to smile. "Well, I suppose it'll be all right. You're sure he won't get in the way?"

"Oliver?" Pete asked. "He wouldn't know how."

Beaming, Oliver nodded vigorously. I shooed them out, telling them to be back by six thirty for hamburgers and hot dogs. I found Alison and my tomboy daughter at the kitchen table, their heads together as they examined the dollar store purchases.

"This one's all glittery," Alison said. "And pink. I think it's my favorite. Which one do you like best?"

"Um . . ." Jenna sounded uncharacteristically indecisive. "I've never done this before."

"Let's see." Alison squinted at Jenna, peered at the purchases, squinted at Jenna. "I think this color would be good on you." She picked up a bottle of purple fingernail polish and held it next to my daughter's face.

I stifled a snorting giggle. The day Jenna tried finger-nail polish would be the day—

"Okay," my daughter said.

—would be today. I stared at Alison. How had she done that?

"Mrs. Kennedy, what color do you want to try?" the pint-sized pied piper asked.

"Color? Me?" I started to back away. "Oh, sweetie, I have a number of things I have to do this afternoon. Why don't you and Jenna work together and I'll view the beautiful results."

Alison grabbed a bottle and jumped to her feet. "This color. Here, see?" She thrust a bottle of dark red polish at me. "You'll look gorgeous. Just like Sandra Bullock."

"Yeah, Mom." Jenna grinned at me. "Just like."

I looked from one face to the other, both of them full of youth and enthusiasm and fun, and I felt my own face spread wide in a smile. "Well," I said, "if you're sure about the Sandra Bullock thing . . ."

In answer, Alison grabbed my hand and pulled me to the table. "We'll do Jenna first, okay? If she doesn't like the color, we can take it off and try again. Or maybe we should do a bunch of different colors, just to see."

Their happy chatter drowned out my plans for the afternoon. No laundry was going to get done, the kitchen floor was going to remain unmopped, and the upstairs bathtub was going to stay slightly gunky.

But I didn't care. At all.

Late that night, after the dishes were washed and put away, after the card game, and after the good-byes and the bedtime stories and the good-night kisses, I prowled around the house, tidying and thinking.

During dinner cleanup operations, Pete had pulled me aside and told me that Oliver had been an excellent assistant and that he'd seemed to have a good time, but that no confidences had been forthcoming.

"Thanks for trying," I said. Realistically, it had been too much to hope for. Some days I wasn't overly fond of realism.

Pete scratched his head. "There was a time or two when it seemed like he wanted to say something. Once he asked if I could keep a secret. And when we were sweeping up at the end, he asked if I'd ever done anything really bad."

Fear clutched at me. What had Oliver done? "What did you tell him?"

He shrugged. "That, sure, I could keep a secret. My mom still doesn't know how the front window got broken that one time. And I said I've done a couple of sort of bad things, but that it always helps to talk about it."

Bless the man. I looked at him, smiling. "Sort of bad? How bad were they?"

"Now, see," he said, "that's where keeping secrets comes in handy."

I'd laughed, the kids had come rushing in with two decks of cards, and the evening had moved on. Now I stood in the family room, folding the blanket that had fallen off the back of the couch, wondering. How could Oliver be thinking he'd done something bad? His teacher wasn't aware of anything. Marina didn't know of anything. The mothers of his friends didn't know. His father didn't know. I didn't know. What could—

The ringing of the phone interrupted my circling thoughts. I picked up the handset of the old princess phone, the family room phone, the one manufactured decades ago when phones were still built to take physical abuse. "Kennedy residence, Beth speaking."

There was an odd tinkling noise, a sharp intake of breath, and the single hoarse word, "Don't!"

The line went dead.

Slowly, mechanically, I hung up the phone.

For the next couple of hours, and once every hour after that until morning, I checked and rechecked that the doors and windows were locked. Front door, garage door, back door. Upstairs windows, first-floor windows, tiny basement windows. Locked solid, every time, yet the compulsion to make sure drove me around the house, over and over again.

A hundred times I reached out to call Gus; a hundred times I pulled back.

Monday. I'd promised Summer I'd wait until Monday. I could wait that long. After all, even though it was still dark, it was already Sunday, with church and Sunday school and choir and a Sunday dinner to cook and homework to oversee, and Sundays weren't appropriate, really, to tell Gus what needed to be said.

But maybe I needed to. Maybe it was time to tell him everything. About Flossie and the dogs and the note and how it might be a feint and the footsteps in the alley and Elsa and Kyle and the hang-up calls. I could tell him all that, couldn't I?

Yes, I could. And then he'd ask, "Is there anything else?" and I'd think about Summer and the casino and say, "No, that's it," and Gus would hear the lie in my voice and press me to tell him and I'd resist but he'd keep pressing and I'd end up telling him.

No. I'd promised. And why was I so scared, anyway? Someone had called, said "Don't," and then hung up. Not exactly worthy of a police car visit, lights spinning and siren blaring.

But still . . .

Monday. It couldn't come soon enough.

Chapter 17

Thanks to Jenna-induced panic ("But I don't *remember* where I put my shoes!") and an Oliver-created sulk ("Why do I have to wear a good shirt? School pictures are dumb!"), my arrival at work was late and rushed, and my intention to call Gus first thing was curtailed when I found the note I'd written and taped to the top of the computer screen.

"Interview, take three, nine o'clock Monday morning."

I glanced at my watch. Not nearly enough time to call Gus. Besides, I needed to call Summer first and see if she'd followed through with telling her husband.

"Hidey ho," Lois said, appearing in the doorway, one hand held behind her back. "It's off to another interview we go. I say this is a fine morning for"—she whipped her hidden hand around her body and brandished a white bag—"a hearty dose of Alice's cookies, guaranteed to rejuvenate body, mind, and soul."

And to expand the hips, but there was something to be said for the psychological benefits of an extremely good cookie. I picked out a coconut chocolate chip and took in today's sartorial display.

A Madras plaid shirt over a bright pink T-shirt. A beige skirt and shoes of apple green. Leather, they looked like.

Lois watched me eye her ensemble. "Comments?" she asked.

A line from an old folk song whispered in my ear. What was the title? Ah, there it was. "I know where I'm going." I didn't have dresses of silk, but who wanted clothes that were dry-clean only, anyway?

"Huh. Must be nice. Want some tea?"

At nine o'clock sharp, the interviewee rapped her knuckles on the front door. Lois went to let her in and I slugged down a last swallow of tea. Ready, Cap'n. Steady as she goes.

We settled around the workroom table. Taylor Eaton was a recent college graduate and was dressed for success in pants ironed to a sharp crease, an understated jacket, and a white shirt. Small gold earrings and a new-looking watch were her only jewelry.

"So, Taylor," I said. "What was your major in college?"

"Business administration." She smiled. "My plans are to get an MBA within the next five years."

Lois kicked me under the table. I ignored her and continued to smile at Taylor. "And what do—"

The purse the young woman had placed on the table jiggled. "Oh, I'm so sorry. I thought I'd turned that off. I must have accidentally set it to vibrate." Her cheeks went slightly pink as she unsnapped the bag and pulled out the phone. "I'll turn it off."

Her eyes went still as she looked at the smartphone's screen. She darted a glance at me. At Lois. Back at the phone. "Wow. I, uh, wow. Awkward."

Lois kicked me again. Awkward how? I wondered. In that she was committing the faux pas of answering a phone call while in a job interview? In that her boyfriend was breaking up with her over the phone? Proposing to her over the phone? In that she—

"Um." Taylor flicked me a quick look, then pushed a few buttons. "It looks like I just got a job."

—or, in that she'd accepted a job working for someone else before Lois got a chance to reject her.

Still pushing phone buttons, Taylor named the largest bank in Madison. "I interviewed there last week for a management job. I didn't think I had a chance of getting it, so I thought I'd come talk to you."

Ouch.

Lois grinned. "Well, best of luck to you. We're sure you'll be very happy over there in cubicle land. Ow! Beth, quit kicking me."

As soon as the door shut behind Taylor, I told Lois that we'd dissect the interview after Yvonne came in. Before she could think up a counterargument, I retreated to my office.

Summer's phone rang three, four, five times. Just as the answering machine started making clicking noises, Summer's breathless voice came on the line. "Hello?"

"Hi, it's Beth."

"Oh, wow, just the person I wanted to talk to."

I took an easy breath. She'd done it. She'd talked to her husband, she'd confessed all, and now was ready to come with me to the police station to see Gus.

"You know the committee meeting we're supposed to have tonight?" she asked. "Do you think . . ." She stopped. "Uh, do you mind hanging on a second?" The phone clunked down.

I hummed the *Jeopardy!* song. I pushed my cuticles down. I thought about what to make for dinner. Just when I was ready to hang up, she came back to the phone.

"Sorry," Summer panted. "And I'm really sorry about

tonight, but I can't make the committee meeting. My daughter's running a fever and she's just not settling down. She hardly slept at all last night."

My irritation had been mounting all through her absence, but the mention of a sick child popped the bubble. And if Summer's daughter hadn't slept, neither had she. "We can reschedule for next Monday. I'll let Marina and Carol know."

"Would you? That'd be great." She blew out a breath. "I'm being a horrible committee chair, aren't I?"

Yes, but at least she was acknowledging the fact. "Sick kids come first."

"I knew you'd understand. Well, I have to go, okay?"

Not so fast. "Did you talk to your husband yesterday?" No reply. "About the casino?" Nothing. "About Destiny and the money and why you were fighting with Dennis Halpern?"

Summer's voice was small. "She got sick so fast. I didn't have time. Really, I didn't."

And once her daughter was healthy, there'd be another reason. And then another. "I'm talking to Gus today," I said.

"Oh." There was a short silence. "I suppose you're going to tell him about . . . you know."

"Don't you think it's time?" I said softly. Past time, really. And not just for the information Summer had; Gus should have known about Flossie and the dogs long ago. You never knew how one additional piece of the puzzle could change the shape of an investigation. Or so all the TV shows indicated.

"Today?" Her voice went thready. "You're going to talk to him today?"

"This morning," I said. "Right now."

"Oh, but—"

"I'm sorry, Summer. This has waited too long already."

She sucked in a short breath, then let it out. "Yeah. I guess it has. See you later."

The line went quiet. I held on to the phone, wondering if I'd just lost a friend, trying to think what I could have done differently. If only . . .

I sighed, then replaced the receiver and went to talk to Gus.

The young man standing behind the high counter looked up when I walked in. "Good morning, ma'am. Welcome to the Rynwood Police Department. How can I help you?"

I gave him a quick once-over and tried to make an honest estimate of his age. He had to be older than sixteen, didn't he? Of course he did. "You're new here, aren't you?"

"Yes, ma'am. Officer Ford at your service." If his spine had been any straighter, it would have started arching backward. "I started with the department last week."

One more in the long line of young officers the city council hired cheaply and who moved to greener and richer pastures as soon as possible. Well, maybe this one would be different. "Is Gus in?"

"Yes, ma'am, sorry, ma'am. He's in a chief's meeting."

An image of a group of men dressed in buckskins and feathered headdresses bounced in and out of my head. "Police chiefs, you mean?"

"Yes, ma'am. From all over the east half of the county."

"How long will the meeting will last?" My sense of urgency had only increased during my walk to the station. Now that I'd finally made the move to talk to Gus, my need to tell all was starting to hurt my head.

"Most of the morning, is what Chief Eiseley told me."

Now what? I twisted my mouth to the side, trying to remember the name. All I could come up with was bar stool, which couldn't be right. "Barlow," I said.

"Huh?" the youngster said. "I mean, excuse me, ma'am?"

"You've been a big help." I wanted to reach across the counter and pat his cheek, but smiled and thanked him instead.

I retraced my steps and was back in my office in five minutes by dint of telling Lois that "I have to make a quick phone call," as I hurried past her.

Flipping through the pages of the phone book, I found the number I needed in the government section.

"Dane County Sheriff's Office, how may I direct your call?"

"I'd like to speak to Deputy Barlow, please." Or was he a detective?

"One moment, please."

A hum, then a click, and "Hello, this is Detective Barlow."

"Hi, this is Beth Kenne—"

"I'm afraid I'm away from my desk now, but please leave a message and a phone number and I'll get back to you as soon as possible. If this is an emergency, please dial 911."

Beep.

"Uh . . ." I left a long babbling message in which I sounded like a moron, but I recovered enough presence of mind to leave my phone number. "Okay, then, thanks," I finished lamely. "I'll look forward to your call."

After hanging up, I slouched in my chair, frowning at the world. I'd primed myself to do something and hadn't counted on chief meetings and voice mail. I was itchy with action. I wanted to *do* something.

But what?

                           *   *   *

What I did was go to work. Good hard work would
surely take my mind off all the questions that were poking at me. Would telling Detective Barlow about Summer and Dennis make any difference? Next, who had
called Saturday night and scared the bejeebers out of
me? Was it the same person whose footsteps that had
given me the mild creeps the Saturday morning after the
fire? And what was troubling Oliver?

Around and around and around again, question tail-
ing into question. It wasn't until Lois was standing in
front of me, hands on her hips, that I realized what I was
doing.

"What on earth are you doing, young lady?" she asked.

I looked at the racks that held the rolls of brightly
colored stickers so loved by the preteens. "Um, making
sure all the rolls are lined up." We both studied the perfectly aligned rolls, the raw edge of each one in the exact
same position, all the way down the rack.

"I can see that," she said. "The question is why are
you doing it?"

And a very good question it was. "If I answer 'why
not,' will you leave me alone?"

"What do you think?"

I spun a roll of smiling bunnies. Around and around
they went. "There's a lot on my mind right now, that's all."

Lois snorted. "And that would be different from every
other day in your life how?"

"Today's stuff seems . . . bigger."

"It's the kids, right? They're get bigger and their problems get bigger, too." She spun a roll of bright green
stars. "What, is Jenna talking about tattoos?"

"No, but . . ." I stopped before a pent-up flood of
words poured out.

But everything's all wrong, I wanted to shout. *Dennis*

is dead. Flossie isn't right. Summer is having husband troubles. Oliver is having Oliver troubles, and I have no idea how to fix any of this.

"You know what you need?" Lois asked.

"A brain that functions properly," I muttered.

"What you need is a new pair of shoes."

I glanced down at my brown loafers. "These are fine."

"Fiddleheads." She picked up her right foot and pointed her shoe of fine green leather at me. "You need something like this. Go."

"Lois, I—"

"Right now."

"I do not need green shoes."

"Then get some pink ones."

Me, in a pair of pink shoes? A smirk started climbing up one side of my face. Now, that was something Marina would pay to see.

Lois smiled back. "See, even the thought is perking you up. Git!"

I let her shoo me outside. Though the day was bright with sunshine, a light breeze was pushing me eastward. Coming soon, the radio had told us cheerfully, were clouds and rain and thunder and lightning. Just the thing for the last day of September.

When I was halfway down the block, a burst of wind blew at my back. I shivered and stopped to put on my coat. After I'd zipped it up, I noticed a man sitting on the bench just outside the antiques mall. It was the man I'd seen a few times in the last weeks, him of the salt-and-pepper hair, the man I'd dubbed Mr. Sad. Even though he was dressed for success in a suit and tie, he didn't look any happier today.

My feet started moving before my head realized it had made a decision. "Hello," I said. "Do you mind . . . ?" I gestured at the empty half of the bench.

"No," he said wearily, as if uttering that single short word was almost more than he could manage.

"Thanks." The wooden slats made a comfortable creaking noise underneath me at I sat. "My name is Beth. Beth Kennedy. I own the Children's Bookshelf down the street."

His shoulders rose and fell. I watched as he worked through the situation, and I could almost answer the questions without him asking them out loud. *Yes, I'm going to keep talking. Yes, I'm going to make you talk back.*

"Bruce," he finally said.

I nodded and wondered what to say next. All I wanted was to see him smile. Even a little one would do. Discussing the weather was not going to do the job. I was a horrible joke teller, and—

"Oh, no," I breathed, and sat up straight. Not her. Not now. The last thing I needed was a conversation with that woman.

Bruce inched slightly away from me. "Problem?" he asked politely.

My back filled with tension as I tried to make myself small. Doom approached . . . and then went into Faye's Flowers. "She's gone." I relaxed. "Auntie May, I mean. She's gone into a store."

Bruce smiled. "That woman could strike fear into the heart of a saint."

Aha! So he was from Rynwood. "She loves my store," I said glumly.

"You have my sympathies."

It was the most sincere thing I'd heard him say. "And you've had mine," I said. "I've noticed you the last few weeks, looking so terribly sad, and I've wished there was something I could do for you."

"Do something?" He turned to look at me, surprise

written in the lines of his face. "You don't even know me."

"Can't I care about the pain of a stranger?"

My question caught at him. "Of course you can." He frowned. "It's just . . ."

"Strange?" I offered. "Odd? Intrusive?"

He smiled a second time. "All of the above. But also kind. Thank you, Beth. It is very nice of you to be concerned."

"You're welcome."

We sat, comfortable in a tentative sort of way, watching the sun shine. After a while I said, "If you'd like to talk about anything, I'm willing to listen. Don't feel obligated," I added hurriedly, "but I am willing."

The sun moved a little bit farther in its track across the sky; then Bruce started to talk.

"My business is bankrupt," he said. "There's no way out. I was just turned down for a loan by the last bank who would talk to me. I'm going to have to close the business and lay off my employees. Fifty of them — " His voice cracked.

I ached to reach out, to touch him, to help him, but I knew I couldn't.

He turned his sob into a cough. "Excuse me. Fifty people who have depended on my business to pay their mortgages and put food on their tables and make their car payments, and now I have to shut the doors."

I wondered what business it was. But I supposed it didn't really matter. "I'm so sorry," I whispered.

He went on as if he hadn't heard, and maybe he hadn't. "If only I'd listened, if only I'd done what he said. My wife said he was a financial genius. She said he'd be able to keep the business afloat, but I couldn't do what he said. Lay off thirty percent of the work force? How could I do that? And now they all have to go." Bruce sighed. "They're all losing their jobs and he's dead."

For a short moment, the world stopped. There was no movement, no life, no air, no sound. Nothing existed except that last, cold word. " . . . Dead?"

Bruce nodded. "Remember the man who was killed out at the elementary school two or three weeks ago? Dennis Halpern, Halpern and Company? He saw immediately how to keep the business alive. Told me what I had to do. And I didn't do it."

I stared at him. Realized what I was doing and turned away before he sensed how my gaze was searing the side of his head.

Was this the *why* I'd been trying so hard to find? Would anyone kill over good advice not taken?

Then again, it wasn't a question of whether I thought a motive was realistic or not; it was the matter of finding out if the motive had created action. So, more specifically, had Bruce killed Dennis?

"Do you blame Dennis?" I asked. "For the bankruptcy?"

Bruce shook his head emphatically. "Not in the least. It's my fault, from beginning to end. Mine and mine alone."

That seemed a little harsh. Surely there were other people involved.

I said as much and he half smiled. "Kind of you to say so, but I'm the owner. The captain of the ship, so to speak. And the end of the day, I'm the one who's responsible. I'm the one who's supposed to make sure everyone gets off the ship safely." He stopped, then added, "But they're not. They're all going down with me."

The despondency was back.

"I have no idea what I'm going to do." His shoulders, which had straightened a bit when he'd smiled, bowed forward. "My wife . . ." He dropped his head in his hands.

I wanted to say that his wife would be supportive and understanding, that together they'd battle through this rough spot and come out on the other side, but since I had no idea who his wife was, I couldn't say that. "Your wife?"

He rubbed the sides of his face. "She has no idea that I didn't take Halpern's advice."

"She . . . doesn't?"

"No." He gave a deep sigh, gusting out grief and despair. "She thinks I did exactly what he advised, so she blames Halpern for the bankruptcy. But how can I say I didn't follow his advice? She was so sure he'd fix everything."

I was getting a very bad feeling about this.

"And look," Bruce said, his voice low. "There she is. We were going to meet for coffee after my meeting at the bank. What do I tell her? What am I going to do?"

Walking briskly toward us, bracelets jingling, was Melody Kreutzer.

Chapter 18

I stammered a greeting to Melody, made a short remark about the weather, and beat a hasty retreat to the bookstore.

Safe inside, I stood for a moment, breathing in the scent of new books. A comforting smell, hinting of things to learn and stories to hear. "And happy endings," I murmured. "Lots and lots of happy endings."

"I don't see any new shoes," Lois said severely. "I thought I told you not to come back until you'd found a fun pair of shoes."

At least that's what I think she said. Her voice came to me from a long distance, as if miles separated us instead of a few feet. She was just across the room, but it felt as if she weren't even there.

Melody Kreutzer. Had she . . . ?

"Hey, are you okay?" Lois dropped the scolding-mother tone and come close. "You look a little . . . weird."

I shook my head. *Yes, I'm fine. No, I'm not. No, there's nothing you can do for me. No, I'm not going to burden you with this. Yes, I'm going to keep this trouble to myself. Yes, I need to think this through on my own.*

"Was that a yes or a no?" Lois asked.

I worked up a smile. "I'll be fine." Eventually. "I need to do some things in the office. Paoze will be here soon, but knock if you need me." I pushed past her look of concern and completed my retreat by closing the office door.

The small room suddenly seemed even smaller. Cozy, I reminded myself. And quiet. Just what you need.

I sat in my chair and slouched down, letting my head be supported by the chair's high back. Closed my eyes. Tried to clear my mind. Tried again. Gave up and started thinking about what I'd learned from Bruce Kreutzer. Tried to come to a different conclusion.

Didn't.

Once, twice, and three times, I started over in my head, and each time I ended up in the same place. Melody had killed Dennis.

Did I have any proof? Of course not. All I had was supposition and conjecture.

I opened my eyes and unslouched myself. There was only one thing to do, really. I picked up the phone.

"Good morning, Rynwood Police Department."

It was still morning? "Hi, this is Beth Kennedy. I'd like to speak to Chief Eiseley. Is he still in that meeting?"

"No, ma'am, the meeting is over. But he's out on a call. Can I help you?"

The dear child. "Thanks, but I really need to speak to Gus."

We agreed that leaving a voice mail message would be the best thing. At the appropriate beep, I told Gus I had some information that might be pertinent to Dennis's death and to please call me when he had a chance. I paused, then said, "It's not urgent, but it might be important. Thanks, Gus."

I hung up, thought some more, then called Detective Barlow at the sheriff's office. Once again, I was sent to voice mail.

"Stupid voice mail," I muttered. It was far too easy to

ignore a voice mail. Much harder to ignore a pink message slip taped to your computer. Even harder to ignore
a person standing in your office, but that didn't seem to
be an option right now.

Now what?

"Tomorrow morning," I said. "Ten o'clock." If I
hadn't heard back from one of them by ten tomorrow,
I'd go find a law enforcement office in which to stand.
But after all, as I'd said to voice mail number one, this
wasn't urgent information. What difference could one
day make?

That night, after the homework and dinner dishes were
done, after Spot had been walked, fifteen minutes into a
game of Apples to Apples and five minutes after I'd
thought it was time to start the kids toward bed, the
phone rang.

Jenna jumped off her chair while I was still looking at
the phone and remembering too many things.

"Kennedy residence, this is Jenna." Pause. "Sure, she's
here. One moment, please." She held out the phone. "For
you," she said unnecessarily.

If it had been Marina on the other end, Jenna would
have told me. If it had been anyone she knew, she would
have said. Therefore, this wasn't someone Jenna knew.
Which told me something, but not enough. Time to add
"Who's calling, please?" to the phone etiquette list.

"Hello?" I asked. "This is Beth."

"Lou Spezza. Sorry to bother you at home."

His apology took away the sting of fear. Not that I
was scared of the phone, of course. "No problem. What
can I do for you?"

"Well, it's like this. I was out with the dogs—stayed far
away from Miss Flossie, just so you know—and I saw
some lights were on in your store. In the back, you know?

Those aren't normally on. The dogs and I talked it over, and we figured it'd be good to say something."

I smiled. He and the dogs had discussed this. "Thanks for calling, Lou. Someone must have left them on."

"Yeah, that's the weird thing," he said. "Because they weren't on when the dogs and I started out. When we got back, they were on. Maybe somebody stopped by for something, is what I figured."

"Thanks, Lou. That must have been what happened." When I hung up the phone, I stood there, thinking.

"Come on, Mom." Oliver tapped his cards on the table. "Let's play."

Twenty minutes. That's all it would take to drive downtown, unlock the store, turn off the lights, lock it back up, and drive back home again. Twenty minutes.

"What's the matter?" Jenna frowned. "You look funny."

What I looked like was a mother about to change the course of her children's lives. This moment had been inevitable from the time they'd been born, but inevitability wasn't making the reality any easier.

"I need to run to the store," I said. "We left some lights on and I don't want to leave those hot halogen lights on all night."

"Because of fire?" Oliver asked.

"Because they're expensive to have on," Jenna said.

I smiled. "You're both right. And since you're both so smart, I'm going to leave you alone here in the house while I'm gone."

"You are?" Oliver's eyes went big. "Ow, Jenna, that hurt!"

"No kicking," I said. Maybe this was a bad idea. Maybe they weren't ready. But Jenna was twelve and I'd only be gone twenty minutes. I'd been babysitting toddlers at thirteen, after all, and Richard was always telling me I wasn't giving the kids enough responsibility.

"I'll be gone less than half an hour." I ducked into the study and grabbed my purse off the desk chair. "Jenna, here's my cell phone."

She held it in her hand, looked pointedly at the cordless phone that was perhaps eight feet from her head, then looked back at me. "And I need this why?"

"Because I'll feel better if you have it. Now, it's time to start getting ready for bed. When I get back, I want to see both of you in your pajamas with your teeth brushed." I looked from one young smooth face to the other, excitement on both, and resorted to bribery. "Brownies with ice cream and hot fudge for dessert tomorrow if you're both in bed when I get home."

Oliver leapt out of his chair and ran upstairs on all fours. Jenna rolled her eyes.

I kept my smile inside and kissed the top of her head. "I'll call Mrs. Neff right now and tell her what's going on. You know what to do, right?"

"Yes, Mom." Another eye roll. "Pajamas, teeth, bed."

That hadn't been what I meant, and I suspected that she knew it. "Keep my cell phone with you. If you have any questions about anything, call Mrs. Neff. If you get scared at all, about anything, call 911."

"Shouldn't you be leaving?"

My daughter was twelve going on thirty. I called Marina, asked her to keep an ear open for the phone for the next half hour, and left.

Chapter 19

It was odd, coming to the store in the evening. The traffic was different, the lights in the houses and buildings were different. Even the air didn't feel the same at night.

And it was night. Full dark, actually, back here in the alley. All summer long, I'd come to work in daytime and left in daytime and so hadn't paid any attention to the single streetlight that was burned out. I'd noticed it on the Wednesdays I worked late, but I never remembered to call anyone at the city about it the next morning.

Maybe this time I'd think to write it down. All I had to do was keep the thought in my head until I got in the store and found a piece of paper. "Streetlight," I muttered as I got out of the car. "Streetlight," I told myself as I walked up the steps. "Streetlight," I said as I unlocked the door and reached for the switch.

But when I turned it off, nothing happened. Because surprise, surprise, I hadn't been smart enough to get the broken switch replaced.

As I walked across the room, I thought about who might have left the lights turned on. Since everyone occasionally either opened or closed the store, we all had keys, but who would it have been tonight? This late?

I considered the three possibilities. Yvonne hadn't even been in today. Lois or Paoze, then. Maybe Lois had forgotten her purse, but since she always kept her keys stowed inside her purse, she couldn't have driven away without it.

Paoze, then. All afternoon he'd been preoccupied with finishing the first draft of his novel. With that kind of pressure—self-instigated though it was—he could easily have forgotten something. But what would have been worth his bicycling back the ten miles from his Madison apartment? And I couldn't see him leaving lights on, anyway. He was far too conscientious for that. They all were.

Well, it had to be one of them. I'd figure it out in the morning.

I flicked the switch, turning the lights off and the darkness on. I stood for a moment. If I waited long enough, my eyes would adjust to what little light there was. Slowly but surely, the outlines of shelves and books and spinning racks came into view, courtesy of the light spilling in the front windows. I concentrated on making my way to the back door without knocking anything over, and except for an elbow bumping a rack of coloring books, I made it intact.

I was out the door and turning around to lock the dead bolt, when I remembered. Streetlight. Yet again, I hadn't written it down. I flung my head back, opening my mouth to ask the sky, "Why *why* am I so stupid?" when three things happened simultaneously.

A loud *BANG!* echoed through the alley.

There was a loud *thwack!* noise on the wooden door.

Something dropped onto my shoulder.

I brushed at it, my ears ringing. Wood. It was a small chunk of wood. What was it doing on my shoulder?

Then the three things connected in my head.

Someone had fired a gun at me.

A gun. At . . . me? Not possible.

My brain refused to process the information. Tried to reject the conclusion.

Surely not a gun. It must have been something else. Two or three something elses, perhaps. A car backfiring, assuming cars still did that. A piece of the old wooden door reacting to the waves of sound pressure created by the backfire and so falling off the building. Sure, that could have been it.

I was satisfied with the rationalizations, both of which I worked through in a tiny fraction of a second. But then I remember thing three. The *thwack* noise? What could that have been?

It was too dark to see much of anything. I reached out and felt the door with the palms of my hands. If it really had been a gun—which was ridiculous; why would any-one in Rynwood be shooting a gun in this alley—and it had been a bullet that hit the door, well, the bullet would be in the door somewhere, wouldn't it?

My purse slipped off my shoulder and hung in the crook of my elbow as I searched. Door, door, nothing but plain old door in need of painting. No bullet. *What a silly conclusion to have reached. Beth, you are clearly in need of—*

Then I found it. Just above head height, high and to the right. A splintered hole. A new splintered hole that hadn't been there before tonight. Before ten seconds ago. Before someone had fired a gun at me.

The extreme danger of my position sank into my skin. I had to get out of there, and fast. Someone had tried to shoot me and had nearly hit me. What would keep him from firing again?

I whirled on the small stoop, thinking fast, trying to come up with a safe place to run, trying to come up with a plan, and failing at both things, because the gun fired a second time. This time the bullet zinged past my ear.

Clapping a hand to my head, I made myself flat against the brick wall, doing my best to hide in plain sight. After a few panting breaths, I started peering into the darkness. Someone was out there. But where? I squinted and looked, and just when I was sure there was nothing to see, I saw.

There, where the building ended and the alley began. Even in the dim light, her bright blond hair was visible as it curled around the building's corner.

Melody Kreutzer was trying to kill me.

As soon as I realized what my current and fairly unpleasant situation was, a thousand thoughts flooded into my head, most of them stupid.

I hardly even knew Melody. I told the kids I'd be back in half an hour. How will killing me change anything? There's nowhere for me to hide. The recycling Dumpster is too far away. How long does it take to recover from being shot? I don't have time to get hurt, there's too much to do. This can't be happening. Not in Rynwood. We're nice people.

All that and more rushed in and out of me in half a breath. Then all thought was wiped away. The blond hair moved forward. And even though the poor light should have kept me from seeing almost anything, I saw the barrel of the gun come around the building.

Pointed straight at me.

There was no time to run, no time to shout, no time to do anything except stare at the gun. Was this how Dennis had felt? Had he felt this frozen fear? Had he seen his death coming to him from that tiny dark circle?

No. I had to do something. I wasn't going to stand here and wait to die. Better to try and fail then not to try at all.

I held still, concentrating on gathering all my muscles together, willing myself to go. Ready, set . . .

"Hey!" a female voice shouted. "You with the gun!"

The dark circle wavered and dropped an inch.

No thought, only action.

I exploded, pushing myself off the wall with all my strength and all my might. I bounded across the back stoop, ran with giant strides across the stretch of open pavement in front of my car, and threw myself into a tumbling heap behind the Dumpster as the gun fired a third time, its reverberating report echoing in my ears.

"Gotcha," said the voice, whispering now. Her hand gripped my upper arm. "You all right?"

No, I wasn't all right. How could I be?

Over here on the back side of the Dumpster, the lighting was a little better, thanks to the fixture that Lou had installed at the entrance to his upstairs apartment. I panted, trying to recover, and looked at my savior. Fifty-ish, thick, black curly hair, and a body that didn't look as if it had ever seen the inside of a gym.

"Um, I think so. Thanks." I kept my voice to a whisper. "I'm sure the police will be here soon. Someone will call in about those gunshots. If we stay here, we should be okay." I hoped.

"So who's your friend?" My rescuer tipped her head in Melody's direction.

I stared at her. Laughter burbled up inside me. Hysteria, no doubt. I slapped my hands over my mouth and tried my best to keep it inside.

"Sorry," she said. "Lou always says I have a bad habit of saying the exact wrong thing at the right time. Whatever that means."

We were crouching face-to-face behind the Dumpster, whispering our conversation in low tones. "Lou?" I asked.

"Lou Spezza. My husband." She held out her hand. "Mary Margaret Spezza. And you're Beth Kennedy."

The battened-down laughter threatened again, but I twisted the screws on it and shook Mary Margaret's hand. Her grip was strong and reassuring. A lot like Lou's, come to think of it. "Nice to meet you."

"Back at you."

"Um, I didn't know Lou had a wife. Of course," I added hastily, "I don't know him very well. He keeps himself to himself, pretty much."

"I'm going to kill him," she said. "Just as soon as we get out of this, I'm going to kill him."

That sounded a little extreme. "He seems like a very nice man."

"Yeah, but he's an idiot. And I mean that in a very deep and profound way. We've been married for thirty-five years. He's the freaking love of my life, you know?"

"But you're going to kill him."

"First chance I get."

There was something very puzzling about all this. Maybe if there hadn't been a woman with homicidal intent roughly twenty feet away, I would have figured it out on my own. As it was, I was having a hard time. Visual aids would have been helpful.

"See," Mary Margaret said, "he ran out on me. Did he think I wouldn't understand? Did he think I was so wrapped up in my own life that I wouldn't see?"

Maybe he'd cheated on her. That made a little bit of sense. I'd wondered the same thing about Dennis, thinking that could have been the reason he was killed. I'd been completely wrong, of course, as I'd been wrong about Elsa and Kyle and that entire line of thinking. I'd been wrong about so much. If I hadn't been so wrong, if I'd seen through to the truth sooner, I wouldn't be crouched behind this Dumpster, shivering with fright and listening to a stranger talk while I tried to figure out how to save our lives.

"I mean, sure, I was making more money than he was, but so what?" Mary Margaret asked. "It's just money, for crying out loud."

Was, she'd said. Past tense. A clue, Watson, a clue!

"And then he loses his job." Her chin dropped to her chest. "He doesn't even tell me, can you believe it? He doesn't tell me. Weeks go by, and he goes off every day, just like he was still working. I had no idea. He took over paying the bills when the kids grew up, so I just ... didn't see."

For the first time, I looked at her closely. Sheer terror had precluded such an examination until this point. This wasn't what I'd call a perfect time to get to know someone, but now that an entire minute had gone by without a shot being fired, I was taking in more than my second-to-second future.

A tear was dripping off her nose and onto the gravelly pavement.

"You love him very much," I said.

"The stupid lump," she whispered fiercely. "The stupid, stupid lump."

I wanted to pat her hand, give her a hug even, but if I did, I was sure I'd fall over. Instead, I said, "And I'm sure he loves you very much."

"Then why is he being so stupid?" she asked.

In my experience, love and stupidity were a common combination, but I kept quiet.

"How could he think of running away from me?"

And this was what Lou had been hiding. He hadn't wanted anyone to contact his wife.

"Didn't he know how much that would hurt me? Didn't he care?"

Her anguish tugged at me. Unfortunately, I couldn't concentrate on easing her pain since I was trying to listen for approaching footsteps.

"I'm sure he cares," I murmured.

"Then why did he take off without me?" she whispered fiercely. "And why didn't he tell me where he was going? I've been looking for him for months! No one knew where he was, not even the guys down at the bowling alley."

Pride, that's why, but I kept still and just listened.

"All he left me was this stupid note. 'I'll be back,' it said." She snorted. "Like some stupid movie. He signed it 'Love, Lou,' and drew some X's and O's, but heavens to Betsy, did he really think that was going to stop me from finding him?"

Now that I'd known Mary Margaret for almost three minutes, I'd have thought it would take handcuffs and iron chains to keep her from looking.

"Finally I started using my noggin." She whacked the side of her head with her knuckles. "Lou had talked for years about a Made in the Midwest store. A little bit of search engine, and there it was on the front page of the Rynwood *Gazette*." Her head drooped. "The article was written by a Jean McKenna. I got the idea she likes Lou quite a lot. Do you think . . . ?"

I tried to imagine the possibility of caustic, driven Jean and laid-back Lou in the same room for more than ten consecutive minutes without the world imploding. "No," I said. "Not a chance."

Mary Margaret gave a sigh so small that I barely heard it. "I didn't want to think so, but if he's moved on, well, I don't want to stand in his way." She punched me in the shoulder. "Heck, I even thought he might have a thing for you."

I blinked. "Me?"

"Sure. You're pretty, young, smart. Why wouldn't he go for you?"

There wasn't enough time to even think about answering her. "What made you realize he wasn't? Isn't?"

She looked over her shoulder, over mine, then dropped her voice even lower. "Been watching you. Sorry about that, but I had to know."

"Watching me?" I asked loudly.

"Shhh!" Mary Margaret beat at the air. "Do you want her to hear?"

It wasn't as if Melody didn't know where we were, but Mary Margaret went on before I could point out that fact.

"Yeah, I kind of been watching you. Following you, a little, after this one time I saw you and Lou back here, talking like you were good friends. Couple of times I even called you, but I didn't have the guts to see it through."

So there it was. Stalker number two who wasn't a stalker at all. Number one was Staci, working up the courage to apologize. Number two was a confused wife who wanted her husband back. And yet . . .

"Did you have anything to do with the dogs? Do you know Flossie?"

"Whoa, hang on there. Dogs? What are you talking about? And who's Flossie? Sounds like the name of a cow."

I shifted, trying to lessen the screaming of my out-of-shape thigh muscles. Déjà vu all over again. "Your husband bought two dogs."

She made a *humph*ing noise, making me think that Castor and Pollux wouldn't be permanent fixtures in the Spezza household. "If they'd been decent guard dogs, they'd be barking, wouldn't they? Instead, here we are behind a Dumpster, waiting for the cops to show up. And where are they, anyway?" She looked around.

"Do you think Lou heard the shots?"

"That man?" She snorted and jerked a thumb in the direction of Lou's apartment entrance. "Just now I was at his door, trying to work up the guts to knock. He wouldn't have heard me if I'd banged with my fist for half an hour. He's got those ESPN commentators turned up so loud, he wouldn't know if a bomb went off unless the ceiling fell on his head. He probably thought those gunshots were part of Monday Night Football."

I thought of my cell phone, which was right where I'd wanted it, in Jenna's pocket. "My cell phone's at home."

"And I've never gotten around to getting one."

We looked at each other.

"Someone's going to come, right?" Mary Margaret asked. Her voice, which had been devil-may-care up to this point, was tight with strain. The mask was off, and the real Mary Margaret was talking to me. "You do have cops in this town, right?"

"Of course someone's going to come." When, though, was the question. Lou's was the only upstairs apartment on this side of the street, and the buildings on the rest of the block were retail and professional businesses whose employees and owners had gone home long ago. "Anytime now," I said. Now would be good. A couple of minutes ago would have been even better.

"Who are you trying to convince?" Mary Margaret whispered. "Me, or you? Because if it's me, I have to say you're not doing such a great job."

I took her hands and put them between mine. Four cold hands full of fear. And it was my fault that Mary Margaret was in this mess with me. "Someone will come," I said. "We have a great police department, they're just stretched a little thin right now. I'm sure someone will come soon."

And, without a doubt, someone would come. But would they get here in time?

Hard footsteps clicked toward us. "Beth?" Melody called. "I know you're back there. Come out here right now or I'm coming to get you."

Chapter 20

My hands grasped Mary Margaret's. "Don't worry," I whispered. "I won't let anything happen to you."

She half smiled. We both knew there was nothing that I could do. "I know," she whispered back. She crab walked a little closer. Our knees touched. "If you have a plan, I'd kind of like to hear it. So I can be ready if you need help."

Help would be good right now. Especially help in the form of multiple police cars, lights flashing and sirens blaring, zooming in to block the ends of the alley. I held my breath, listening as hard as I could. But I heard nothing save the thumping of my own heart and Mary Margaret's short, sharp breaths.

"Beth?" Melody called. "There's no reason for your friend to get hurt. All I want is you out here. All I want is to talk."

Right. Like you wanted to talk to Dennis just before you shot him.

"Tell you what," Mary Margaret said. "I'll make a move on this end of the Dumpster and you make a move on that end. That'll distract her long enough that we can run away. All she's got is some kind of handgun, and I bet she's a lousy shot. Most people can't hit the broad side of a billboard from more than twenty yards."

Melody was a lot closer than twenty yards. Of course, Mary Margaret and I weren't anywhere near the size of a billboard, so where did that leave us? Crouched behind a Dumpster with a gun-waving killer on the other side. "You're not going anywhere," I whispered. "Promise that you'll stay here out of sight."

She shook her head. "I'm not promising that."

"But it's me she's after. She doesn't even know who you are." *And, please,* I said to the dark sky, *let it stay that way. Don't let this innocent bystander get sucked into something that's none of her business.*

Mary Margaret bumped my knee. "Say, why is she after you, anyway?"

An excellent question.

"Beth!" Melody called.

She sounded closer. I whispered up a silent prayer to please keep my children safe, gave Mary Margaret's hands a squeeze, then released them and started moving away.

"What are you doing?" she asked in a fierce whisper. "You get back here right now."

"It'll be all right," I said calmly. For a great peace was flowing through me, in me, and around me. There was no doubt in my mind that this was the right thing to do.

Still in a hard crouch, I shuffled to the corner of the Dumpster. "I'm right here, Melody."

"Come on out," she said.

Talking to her might be the right thing to do, but I wasn't stupid. "I'm pretty happy over here."

"Well, I'm not happy. Not happy at all."

I closed my eyes for a moment. *Please, let me find the words. Please, let there be a way out of this.* "Bruce and I had a nice talk today."

"He doesn't know anything," she said quickly. "Not a thing. Don't you go telling Chief Eiseley anything about my Bruce. I know what you're thinking, but you're wrong."

Please . . . "What am I thinking?"

She blew out a breath. "You're thinking that you know what happened. You're thinking that Bruce killed Dennis Halpern because he got such bad advice from him. You're thinking that Bruce was so angry about Halpern ruining his business that he killed him."

"Did he?"

"No!" she shouted, then in a more normal tone, "Don't be ridiculous. Bruce wouldn't do a thing like that."

My thighs weren't going to last much longer in this forced crouch. Better to sit on the ground than to fall over in a screaming heap a few minutes from now. I brushed aside the worst of the gravel and sat. "What would Bruce do?" I asked.

"He's a good man," she said. "A very good man and an even better business owner. All he needed was to be pointed in the right direction. That Dennis"—the end of his name came out in a horrible hiss—"told him all wrong. And you can believe I called and told him so, more than once."

So the stalker Staci mentioned had been Melody. Of course it was. I'd been an idiot not to realize it. "Wrong?"

"If he'd told him right, the business would still be afloat. All he needed was some"—her voice caught—"some good advice. Was that too much to ask, that a financial consultant be able to tell people how to fix their finances?"

"No," I said slowly. "But what if the advice was given? And then not followed?"

"What? What are you saying?"

There were two clear paths here. One was to keep Melody talking long enough for the police to arrive. The other was to do what I could. I glanced over at Mary Margaret. She, too, had dropped to the pavement. Her head was resting back against the metal, her eyes closed. I watched her for a moment, thinking, then not thinking. Sometimes decisions aren't made so much as felt. "I'm saying that maybe Bruce did get good advice."

"That's ridiculous," Melody snapped.

"I'm saying he got advice that would have saved the business, but that following through was too difficult."

"What are you talking about?"

Less anger in her voice, more fear. I moistened my lips and went on. "The advice Dennis gave Bruce was to fire thirty percent of the work force. To fire fifteen employees to save the other thirty-five."

Melody drew in a short breath, but didn't say anything.

"Your Bruce couldn't see his way to firing people who didn't deserve it. He couldn't see how he could lay off hardworking employees who needed their paychecks to feed and house their families. He thought he'd find another way." All so sad, so very sad. "Your Bruce," I said quietly, "wanted more than anything to save all his employees. But it just wasn't possible."

Melody made a small animal noise.

"Dennis did his job," I said. "He told Bruce what the business needed. It wasn't his fault that Bruce was too kindhearted to make those awful layoffs. It wasn't his fault that Bruce thought he'd find new financing. It wasn't Denny's fault at all."

There a small mewing sound, then a hiccupping sob.

Then finally, finally, the metallic scrape of a gun sliding across asphalt.

I pushed myself closer, trying to hear. Couldn't. I leaned out from behind my hiding place. There was Melody, slumped against the brick wall, her blond hair bright even in the dim light. Her knees were drawn up tight to her chest and her arms were wrapped around her legs. Somewhere lay the gun, but I couldn't see it.

"I didn't know," she said, tears clogging her words. "I . . . I didn't know."

"Of course you didn't," I said soothingly, and got to my feet.

Mary Margaret grabbed at my arm. "What are you doing?" she whispered. "Are you nuts?"

Probably. I patted her hand, then pulled out of her reach. "It'll be okay." At least I hoped it would.

"It'll never be okay," Melody said into her knees. "I've ruined everything. Bruce was so depressed about the business. Nothing I did or said helped him. But how could I sit there and do nothing? I had to keep trying."

"Of course you did," I said, inching closer.

"He's my husband," she said simply. "I love him. I always have and I always will. I had to try and help."

"That's what wives do."

She wiped at her face with the heels of her hands, but her movement didn't stop the flow of tears down her face. The wetness reflected in the faint light, multiple paths of grief all down her cheeks. "I was so sure getting rid of Dennis would help Bruce feel better. It's like it was meant to happen, with him coming to talk to your PTA. Natalie Barnes, right before she copped out of being PTA secretary, was telling me all about it. But Bruce didn't get better, and then everything got worse."

I hesitated, but then moved a step closer. "What happened?"

"So stupid," she said. "How could I be so stupid?"

And here I was, trying to sneak up on a woman with a gun. Who was the stupid one?

"What happened?" I asked again, softly, using my Understanding Mom voice.

"It all went wrong so fast," Melody said, bumping her forehead against her knees. "You watch TV and think, geez, I wouldn't be that stupid if I committed a crime. Next thing you know, there you are, being stupid."

"It's hard to be smart all the time." Another inch closer.

"I'd be happy being smart even half the time. I mean, if I'd known Dennis didn't keep any of his files about Bruce in the office here in Rynwood, I wouldn't have broken in and I wouldn't have had to burn it down."

So simple, once you knew. "To hide evidence."

"And then I was stupid again when I got rid of the disguise I'd used both times. I tossed it into Flossie's bin, but she always takes the garbage out first thing in the morning, I knew that. She's done it for years. But I was so glad I'd found a place to get rid of my disguise without changing my routine that I forgot all about her routine. Stupid," she muttered.

"You put the disguise in Flossie's garbage."

"Yeah. I had one of those baseball hats with dark hair attached and a black sweatshirt and dark gray sweatpants. With clothes like that, I figured people would think I was a guy."

Which was exactly what we had thought. I moved closer and strained my eyes, looking for the gun. "So you thought Flossie might have seen you put something in her Dumpster." So, not a feint, after all.

"Right." She breathed in and out, in and out. "And so I had to do something, right? That's when I came up with the idea of using those dogs."

"Lou's dogs."

"Is that his name? Short, hairy, Italian-looking guy with the big arms?"

Behind me, I heard Mary Margaret stir. "Yes," I said quickly. "That's Lou. He's a very nice man."

"Well, he may be nice, but he doesn't know anything about dogs. Talk about stupid."

I risked a quick look over my shoulder. There was Mary Margaret, on her hands and knees, crawling out from behind the Dumpster. I made frantic "stay put" gestures at her, but on she came.

"He just got the dogs," I said. "I'm sure he'll learn fast."

"Doubt it," Melody said. "He reminds me of a guy I knew in school. Dumb as a bag of hammers."

Mary Margaret had reached the halfway point and was moving forward fast. But she wasn't looking at me or at the huddled Melody. She had her gaze trained on something just out of my reach. The gun.

Slowly, soundlessly, I repositioned myself, moving between Melody and the gun. I wouldn't block much of Melody's view of the oncoming Mary Margaret, but it was all I could do.

Melody giggled, sounding much like I had a few minutes ago. "Maybe they're brothers. I tell you, this guy was so stupid that in geography class he asked where Old Zealand was? Think Lou knows?"

Mary Margaret stood and stalked toward the gun. Even in the dark, her fury was made clear by the set of her arms and her stiff-legged walk. She scooped up the handgun.

Melody, still talking to her knees, was oblivious to the danger.

"Don't," I whispered, but Mary Margaret didn't hear. Or didn't care to hear. The gun slid into her hands as if she'd practiced for months. She raised her arms and pointed the gun directly at Melody.

I was between them, hands out toward Mary Margaret. *Don't do this. You know you don't want to. It's not worth it, nowhere near worth it. Please . . .*

"Then tonight," Melody said. "I wasn't so bright then, either. The light back here is horrible. I can't believe I didn't check that out beforehand. If I'd been smart, this would all have been over by now."

And I'd be dead, but I wasn't going to think about that.

Melody rested the heels of her hands against her eyes. "When I saw you talking to Bruce today, I was sure you were thinking that he did it. I was scared that you'd go to the police right away. But they didn't come and they didn't come, so I figured you hadn't told them yet. I thought maybe I had time to stop you."

"It almost worked," I murmured.

"What I should have done," she went on, "was test that key first. Check things out, you know? Do a dry run. Then I would have gotten it right for sure the second time."

"Key?" I asked, turning around and looking at her. What key?

"The hidden one." She nodded in the direction of the back door. "You know, up on top of the doorjamb. Marcia told me about it."

Her friend, my former employee Marcia, who had never once mentioned the hidden key to me.

"Should have done it all differently," Melody muttered, rubbing her forehead against her knees. "There's so much I'd do different, if I could do it over again."

"What's the first thing you'd change?" I asked.

She brushed at her face again and shook her head. "I'm going to jail, aren't I?" she asked.

"Yes, I'm afraid so."

"What about Bruce? What's he going to do? Who's going to take care of him?" Her words wobbled and broke down. "Why . . . did I . . . ? Oh, Bruce . . . Oh, I'm . . . so sorry . . ." Sobs racked her shoulders, her arms;

then her entire body gave over to the horror of what she'd done, of how she'd ruined her life and the life of her husband. All over, all gone, gone forever.

I sat down next to her and gathered her into my arms, rocking her back and forth, back and forth.

Mary Margaret crouched down next to us. "I wasn't going to shoot her," she whispered. "I was just making sure she didn't make a break for it."

Back and forth, back and forth. I put my hand on top of Melody's head and held her tight. "Go find Lou," I said quietly. "Call 911. We'll be here."

Mary Margaret started to stand.

"And call my daughter, too, please. It's going to be a while before I get home."

Chapter 21

The first thing I did Tuesday morning was find the hidden key. I held it in the palm of my hand and looked at it, feeling gray and old and tired. "It's done," I said to myself. "All you can do is move forward." I made a fist over the key and hoped Bruce would find his way through the dark months that were sure to come.

The second thing I did was call a locksmith to get the locks changed, and the third thing I did was sit through follow-up interviews with the sheriff's office. There was no fourth thing because half of Rynwood stopped by to hear what had happened the night before and there was no time to do anything else.

Except for one small item.

I talked to Lois and Yvonne and called Paoze, telling all of them whom I'd like to hire as our new part-time staff member. After I got two wide smiles and one solid, "That is an excellent choice, Mrs. Kennedy," I walked out of the store with the utmost confidence. The candidate was surprised, but soon saw the benefits of working for me and agreed to start work—trial basis only, mind you—on Thursday morning.

Wednesday, full of rain and wind, had only a dribble of calls from reporters. By afternoon, things were settling back to normal, with one addition. Jenna. She'd asked that she be allowed to walk to the bookstore after school instead of having to go to Marina's house.

"Please, Mom?" she asked. "It's barely half a mile. That's, like, not even a ten-minute walk. I'm tired of having to play with the little kids. I can come here and get my homework done."

I said I'd think about it, then called her father to hear what he thought. Predictably, he thought I was worrying unnecessarily. "She's twelve years old," he said. "A young woman. How long are you going to try and baby them?"

Forever, if he wanted the absolute truth. But I gave Jenna permission to walk downtown with the condition that there be a two-week tryout period. "If I think it's not working out," I told her, "it ends. And I don't want to hear any whining if you have to go back to Mrs. Neff's."

The slamming hug she gave me took my breath away. "Thanks, Mom! It'll be fine. I promise."

Wednesday afternoon she came in exactly fifteen minutes after school let out, just as she'd said she would. She shook the rain off her raincoat, said hello to Lois and Yvonne and myself, poured herself a glass of milk from the carton I'd purchased for the occasion, took a cookie from the bag I'd purchased for the occasion, and sat down at the workroom table with her homework.

Lois raised her eyebrows at the sight. I shrugged, but I was sure the glow of my inside smile was shining through my skin. My daughter, my heart, my joy. She was growing up. She was going to be all right. Sure, there were fights and battles and sulks and tears in our future, but in the end, it would be all right.

By Thursday morning the rain had moved east to Michigan. So the sun was shining and the birds were singing when my new employee walked through the front door. A good omen, surely.

"Good morning, Flossie," I said, smiling. "Would you like a cup of tea?"

"Thank you, dear, but I'm a coffee drinker."

"That's right. Um, there might be a coffeepot somewhere back there." I looked over my shoulder to the kitchenette. Although where, exactly, I wasn't sure. When Lois and Yvonne came in, maybe one of them would know.

"Goodness, don't worry about that. If this works out, I'll bring one in." She looked around at the shelves and shelves of stock. "I've been in this store a thousand times, but I never quite realized how many books you had until this minute."

I laughed. "When I started working here, I felt exactly the same way. I think everyone does. You'll learn fast. A grocery store is a lot bigger than this little place."

"Yes, but . . ." She picked up a copy of *Owl Moon* and started turning pages. "What a lovely book."

Smug, that's what I was feeling. Downright smug. This would all work out. Flossie needed to retire from the backbreaking grocery business, but she also needed to be doing something. All she needed was a little time to learn the books. And if her great-nephew needed some advice on how to run the store, well, she wasn't far away.

She looked up at me. "How are you feeling? You've had a difficult time these last few days."

"Yes." I wrapped my hands tight around my tea mug. Although my difficulties were nothing compared to Melody's or Bruce's.

Poor Bruce. She'd done it all for him. I spent a moment wondering if I could ever inspire that kind of deep love in anyone. Not that I'd want to incite anyone to murder, of course, but it might be nice if—

"Beth?" Flossie was frowning at me. "Are you all right?"

"Fine, thanks."

"I would like to tell you something," she said. "About Dennis Halpern."

No. Whatever it was, I didn't want to hear it.

"Well, not so much about Dennis as about what I thought I saw."

Still didn't want to hear it.

"You know how the grocery store is always open until eight? How most times we're the only business open at night? The grocery's front door isn't far from Halpern and Company's front door. Twice I saw Dennis leaving his office late with a woman who wasn't his wife. The second time, she saw me quite clearly."

No, don't tell me this now. It's all done, all over with. I want to forget.

Flossie smiled faintly. "But it's not what you think, or what I thought at the time. I assumed he was having an affair, so I assumed she'd sent those dogs to me. I was . . . scared, so I didn't say anything."

I frowned. "Do you know who you saw?"

"Tuesday night I found out. She was interviewed on a television station as one of Dennis's coworkers. Elsa Stinson. Apparently, she and Dennis were writing a book together. Nonfiction, combining the elements of . . . Beth, are you sure you're feeling well?"

There are times when you truly don't know whether to laugh or cry.

This time, I managed to do both.

That afternoon, after giving Flossie some quick lessons on our point-of-sale software, I guided her through a purchase. "You get a gold star for the day," I said, watching her beep the books one by one. "I'll be in my office if—"

I broke off. Through the front window I could see two

people walking past the store. A common enough occurrence, but one of the two people was my son. The other was Pete. Oliver's head was down, and Pete's hand was on his shoulder.

Why on earth was Oliver with Pete and not at Marina's? Why was he so downcast, and what was Pete saying so earnestly?

I charged out from behind the counter and ran smack into Lois. "Excuse me," I said, trying to sidle around her. "I need to—"

"No, you don't," she said calmly. "Marina called a little bit ago, but you were working with our newbie here and I didn't want to bug you. She said Pete Peterson and Oliver were going to do something important."

"Okay, but—"

"And she said to make sure to tell you that Oliver finally talked to Pete."

"He . . . ?" Light dawned. "Oh. He talked to Pete, you mean."

Lois squinted at me. "That's what I said, so I'm pretty sure that's what I meant."

My smile was deep and wide. "He talked to Pete."

"Yeah, I . . . oh." The rising sun made it over to Lois's side of the conversation. "He finally talked about what's been bothering him." She danced a little jig. "This calls for a celebration!"

"Not until I find out what this was all about."

Her dance ended with a foot stomp. "Ah, it'll be nothing. The kid's barely nine years old. How bad a thing could he possibly have done?"

I looked at her. "Auntie May told me that you and one of your siblings played tic-tac-toe on the side of your neighbor's house with spray paint when you were seven."

"Well, yeah, but that was me. Oliver's a good kid. I'm sure it's nothing."

Somehow that didn't set my mind to rest, because even good kids could do bad things. But I nodded and tried to act as if I was reassured. Maybe if I acted that way, I'd start to believe it.

"Either way," she said, "you'll know before long, right?"

Unfortunately, that only raised my anxiety level. And that went up another two painful notches when I saw Pete and Oliver walking back the way they'd come. This time my son's head was hanging even lower and Pete's arm was around Oliver's shoulders.

Pete turned his head just before they moved out of sight. As we made eye contact, he nodded and smiled.

I stared out the window long after they'd passed by. Had that been a reassuring smile? A don't-worry-it'll-be-fine smile? Or had it been a smile manufactured to mask Pete's worried concern? What on earth had Oliver done? I shouldn't have let him walk away. I was his mother. I should be with him. I should—

"Shouldn't you be doing something?" Lois asked. "Or are you going to stand there and mope away the rest of the afternoon?"

I didn't move from the window. "When did the employees start telling the boss what to do?"

"When the boss started staring off into space like a zombie. Say, you know what might fix your zombie-osity? New shoes. You never did get a pair."

I glanced at her shoes. Plain and brown and very un-Lois-like. "Where did you dig those up? They look like something out of your great-aunt's closet." Actually, her entire clothing ensemble was unusual. Dark brown pants, ivory sweater, simple gold studs at her ears. She looked nice, but she didn't look like Lois.

"Don't you recognize them? They're just like the pair you always used to wear. And this outfit?" She held out her arms and spun in a circle. "I decided to try wearing what you do. Just to feel what it was like."

"And?"

She shrugged. "I feel old and boring. No offense."

"And if I wore what you do, I'd feel that I'd never be taken seriously by anyone over the age of ten." I smiled. "No offense."

"None taken. Say, do you want this?" She plucked at the sweater. "It's an old one I dragged out of the attic."

"Thanks," I said, "but I already have one almost exactly like that."

The front door bells jingled and Gus walked in. "Beth. Lois. How are you ladies this afternoon? And, Yvonne, I see you back there with Flossie. Hello to you both."

I crossed my eyes at him. "Please don't tell me I have to talk to more police officers. Haven't I fulfilled my quota for the decade?"

He smiled. "Just me. I spent some time at the sheriff's office yesterday, going over the details of Mrs. Kreutzer's case, and there are a couple of things I think you'd like to know."

"Doubt it."

"It's about Dennis Halpern's will."

Something popped up out of the deep recesses of my memory. "He'd planned to change it," I said. "Marina and I overheard his attorney at the visitation."

Gus nodded. "Halpern's wife was cleaning out some of his papers and she found a note. Remember that book he wrote? What he wanted to do was donate all royalties the book earned to the Tarver Foundation. Mrs. Halpern, who is financially very healthy thanks to Halpern's investments and life insurance, has decided to go ahead with the donation."

Suddenly and desperately, I wanted to sit down, put my arms on my desk, lay my head down, and bawl like a baby. Mrs. Halpern could have ignored the note and no one would have known the difference. Instead, she was honoring her husband's wishes. Instead, she was the living definition of loyalty.

"That's nice," Lois said as Yvonne and Flossie came forward to join us, "but there are royalties and there are royalties. What kind of sales does the book have? Does it have any kind of legs?"

I blinked away the threatening tears. "It's doing well. Dennis told me about it when we were setting the date of his talk. He said he had hopes of it becoming a standard reference for personal finances. He said . . ." I stopped.

What he'd said was that he wanted to write more books, that the next one would be written with young adults in mind. After he finished that, he was considering a children's book on personal finances, and did I think that would be a good idea?

"He sounds as if he was a very nice man," Yvonne said.

"Yes."

We stood there for a quiet moment, the five of us each thinking our own thoughts. Then, like a blue bolt, what Gus had said penetrated my tiny brain. "All the royalties will be donated to the Tarver Foundation?" I asked.

Gus nodded. "That's what she said. She's going to make the call this week."

A brilliant idea popped into my brain. The administrators of the foundation followed a strict set of rules that no one except the administrators had ever seen, but I'd tried as best I could to track the projects they were willing to fund and the projects that got turned down.

If the two competing PTA committees got over their fear of the nonexistent curse and came up with solid proposals for approximately the same amount of money, and if I got the support of the PTA board, we could go to the Tarver Foundation and ask for matching funds.

We'd present our case that both fine arts and sports are equally important for a child's development. Explain that we'd raised a significant amount of money from our own book sales, but the funding of both important projects would require more capital than we had, and wouldn't the Tarver Foundation like to support this two-pronged approach to growing children to well-rounded adults, especially considering the upcoming donations from the widow of Dennis Halpern?

My thoughts ran ahead. Maybe I should call Mrs. Halpern and see if she liked the idea. Maybe she'd come with me to meet with the foundation, and maybe, just maybe, this would all work out.

And if it did, we'd have money to buy new playground equipment, the high-quality kind designed to absorb years of abuse without fading into brittleness. We could buy new soccer goals. We could pay for a music teacher and buy instruments that the children could rent. Maybe hire an art teacher. We could have concerts and—

"Hey, Mom." Jenna waved as she walked to the back of the store.

"Hi, honey," I said. Or at least that's what I intended to say. My mind was exploding with ideas and projects and possibilities, and for all I know, I told her that dinner was in my pants pocket and we'd be eating after the PTA meeting next week.

The door bells jingled and Lou and Mary Margaret Spezza walked in, hand in hand, wide smiles on their faces.

"We want to thank you," Lou said.

"You're welcome," I said. "For what?"

"For getting us back together." Mary Margaret snuggled up to Lou and put her head on his shoulder. "If it hadn't been for you, I would have left town the other night."

I frowned. "But you said you were about to knock on his door."

"Yeah, well, that was a lie. I was too scared. I'd decided it was up to him to come back to me."

Lou slung his arm around her. "And I'd decided I wouldn't go back for her until the store turns a profit. That'll be Thanksgiving, at the earliest."

Mary Margaret rolled her eyes. "Like I care about that."

"It's not about you, sweetheart," he said. "A man's got his pride, you know? If I can't keep you in furs and sports cars, I'm not doing my job."

"And where would I wear a fur coat?"

He kissed the top of her head. "Anywhere you want, my sweet, anywhere you want."

Most of me listened as they talked about the plans they had for Lou's store, about how they hoped to become part of the fabric of downtown Rynwood, and how did I think a haunted house would go over?

Part of me, though, watched their obvious delight in each other's company and was . . . well, not jealous. No, the emotion tugging at me was more a wistfulness, a yearning for that rare relationship that made two separate people one happy whole. Early on in our marriage, my former husband and I had been like that, but it had withered under the daily pressures of life.

Not these two. I smiled as they started arguing about what to order for the Christmas season. Even in full-tilt argument, they were still hand in hand.

Loyalty. It was everywhere, once you started to look for it.

The bells jingled and Summer and Brett Lang walked in. They, too, were holding hands.

"Can we talk to you a second?" Summer asked. "Or is this not a good time? I mean, you look kind of busy."

"Nah, we're just here taking up space," Lou said. "C'mon, honey, I want to show you that catalog of maple syrup candies."

But Mary Margaret was ignoring him and introducing herself to Summer and Brett.

"Lou's wife?" Summer asked. "Really? I didn't . . ." She turned a prickly shade of red.

"Didn't know he was married, did you?" Mary Margaret jabbed her husband in the ribs. "See what happens when you tell lies? You get caught and look like an idiot."

"I didn't lie to anyone," he protested. "I maybe didn't tell the whole truth, is all."

Brett grinned. "Big difference," he said. "Both ways can get you into trouble, though."

Lou, Mary Margaret, and Brett launched into a vaguely philosophical discussion about lies and truth, complete with anecdotes and hand gestures. Summer detached herself from her husband and pulled me away.

"I wanted to apologize," she said. "For the way I've been the last few weeks. No, let me finish, okay? I've been a wreck, and it's all because of that stupid money I won. It was messing me up six ways from Wednesday, and you were right. There's no way I should have kept any of it a secret from Brett." She grimaced. "I don't know what I was thinking. I really don't."

I did. What she'd been thinking was that her husband had no right to tell her what to do. Which was both right and wrong at the same time.

"So, anyway," she said, sighing, "after we heard on the news about Melody—speaking of which, you getting her arrested must mean that stupid PTA curse is lifted, right?—anyway, that's when I told him about Destiny and the casino. About everything."

I glanced at her husband. "He doesn't seem too upset."

She laughed, an easy run of happiness. "Oh, he was mad. All red-faced and feet stomping at first, but then he got sad." Her face went quiet. "That was worse, really. I started crying, and he started crying, and oh, geez, don't tell him I told you that, okay? That's when I saw what all that lying had done." She pressed her lips together. "How could I have been so stupid? No weekend with a girlfriend is worth a single lie to my husband. How could I not have known that?"

"But you do now." And their marriage would be the stronger for it. Plus I was getting the sense that Destiny wasn't on Summer's A-list of friends any longer, and that could only be a good thing.

"What about the money?" I asked.

"I gave it to him," she said simply. "Every penny. I handed it over and told him he could do anything he wanted with it."

I stared at her. "Summer, that's . . . that's . . ." I hunted for the right thing to say.

"Brilliant?" she asked, laughing. "The best idea ever?"

Since I'd been thinking more along the lines of "worst idea ever," I smiled and didn't say anything.

"Know what he's going to buy?" she asked. "A motorcycle."

I took in a quick breath. Two wheels on pavement were not nearly as stable as four wheels. And gravel, rain, bugs—nothing to a car, but all hazards to a motorcycle. "You're okay with that?"

"It sounds great to me," she said, grinning. "As long as I get to ride along."

I shook my head. "You're a braver woman than I am."

Summer looked at me, a curious expression on her face. "You really think that?"

"Well, sure. There's not enough money in Wisconsin to convince me that getting on a motorcycle would be a good idea."

This time it was Summer who laughed. She laughed so hard that I didn't hear Marina come in the door. She looked at Summer, who was wiping tears from her eyes, then looked at me. "What's so funny?"

I shrugged. "No kids this afternoon?"

Marina dusted off her hands. "Got rid of the last one ten minutes ago. Ran over here right off the bat because I want to commend your genius master plan to hire Flossie. Smartest thing you've ever done."

"Last week you said teaching Jenna how to launder her hockey uniform was the smartest thing I've ever done."

"And now you've topped that. Excellent work." She clapped me on the shoulder. "Guessing what you're going to do next is what gets me out of bed in the morning."

"And you think I believe that?"

"Nope." She gave me a crooked smile. "But maybe you should."

I rolled my eyes.

"Say," she said, "you do realize the PTA curse vanished like the mist when Melody was arrested, right?"

"I'm not overly familiar with the behaviors of curses."

"Well, neither am I, but since I started that one, accidentally of course, I decided I can finish it. Soon as I heard about Melody, I started blabbing about the end of the curse on Facebook and Twitter. And you know what Claudia said? She said there's no such thing as a curse, just runs of bad luck, and that the Tarver PTA will be stronger than ever."

Truly, wonders never did cease.

I introduced Marina to Mary Margaret and saw the instant spark of friendship. Peas in a pod, those two. The only question was, would the similarities bond or repel them from each other? I was smiling, listening to their discussion of the best roller coasters in the country, when the bells on the front door jingled once again.

"Hi, Mom!" Oliver bounded to my side and wrapped his arms around my middle.

"Goodness! Hello to you, too." I held him close and looked through the crowd for Pete. "I hear Mr. Peterson picked you up at Mrs. Neff's this afternoon."

"Yeah. When we were cleaning his garage last Saturday, remember I went over there? Well, he said I could call him anytime. He even gave me his card and wrote his cell phone number on it." Oliver's voice was full of awe. "No one ever gave me a business card before."

Bless Pete. "So you called him this afternoon?"

"Uh-huh. At school, Mrs. Jefferson said it's important to talk about stuff that bothers us, and that a . . . a trusted family friend can sometimes be the best person of all."

And bless Millie. Tomorrow morning I'd send her a thank-you note. And chocolate. Lots of chocolate. "That sounds like very good advice," I said.

"Yeah." He gave me one last squeeze. "So I called Mr. Peterson and told him about . . . about . . ." He swallowed.

Gus appeared at Oliver's side as Pete came out of the crowd and stood at Oliver's other side. Both men put a hand on one of my son's shoulders, giving him strength, rooting him in honesty and goodwill.

"It's okay, Oliver," Gus said. "You can tell her."

"I'll help you start, if you want." Pete said. "It'll be easy once you get going. Ready? One Saturday, a little after school started, I rode my bike downtown. . . ."

Oliver's thin shoulders curved forward. "Do I have to?" he asked.

"The sooner you tell it," Gus said, "the sooner it's over."

"Yeah. Okay." He took a deep breath and let it out. "Okay. I rode my bike downtown. I know I wasn't supposed to without permission, but, I don't know, I was just out riding around the block and then, like, I was downtown all of a sudden."

I bit back the words I wanted to say so badly. "And then what?"

He kicked at the carpet. "And then I went into the gas station, you know, the one Mr. Jarvis owns? And I . . ." His voice dropped low. "And I took a candy bar."

"Took? You mean you didn't pay for it?"

His head hung low. "I . . . stole it."

I stared at my son. Where was the mother manual when you needed it? I supposed at some point I'd be grateful that the theft of a simple candy bar could have caused him such mental trauma, but that point wasn't even visible from the current point, which was me being appalled.

"Well," I said, then didn't know what to say next.

Gus stirred. "Oliver, why don't you go in the back with your sister while I talk to your mom a minute?"

I nodded, and Oliver scampered off.

"When I was ten," Pete said, "I stole a soda and a bag of potato chips."

Gus chuckled. "I took a pack of gum."

I looked from Rynwood's police chief to the forensic cleaner and back again. "He shoplifted! Don't tell me you're condoning this."

"Of course we're not," Gus said, unperturbed by my outburst. "But before you decide on a punishment, hear us out."

Pete put his hands in his pockets. "When Oliver called, he was crying. Said he didn't want to be a thief anymore, that he wouldn't ever eat candy again. Took me a while to get the whole story out of him. When he finally did, I said we'd have to go to the police." He smiled. "Thought I'd lost him for a minute there, but he bucked up and said okay."

Gus picked up the story. "They came into the station a little while ago, and I've never seen such a long face on a youngster. Oliver told me what he'd done, and I told him he'd have to confess to Mr. Jarvis." He laughed. "His face went even longer. I wouldn't have thought it possible."

The poor boy. "What did Randy say?"

Gus smiled. "I called Randy when these two were walking over. Told him what was going on and asked him to take it seriously, to give the boy a little lesson."

"So when we showed up," Pete said, "Randy played like he was sad and angry at the same time. Oliver was shaking so hard, I thought he was going to fall down, but he stepped up and said he'd pay him back as soon as he got his allowance. Then he asked if he'd go to jail. Randy told him no, not if he came in and swept the floor on Saturday. Then you know what Oliver did? He pulled a crumpled, beat-up Snickers bar out of his coat pocket and put it on the counter."

"He never even ate it," I whispered.

Pete shook his head. "Too guilty. You've got a good kid there, Beth."

His smile warmed my heart. "He's not bad," I said. "Thanks, Pete. You're the best. I'm not sure what I would have done without you." As he made a mild protest, I peered at him. Was he blushing? No, why would he? It must be the heat in the room, that's all, gone up from so many people in the store.

"Hey, Mom, look at what I drew!" Oliver ran up and thrust a piece of paper at me.

On it was a picture of what I assumed was our house. Next to it, standing approximately fifteen feet tall if the house was drawn to scale, was an assortment of people and animals. There was George, looking like a black meat loaf. There was Spot, floppy ears and all. There was Oliver, there was Jenna in her hockey gear, there was me with books in my arms, and standing next to me was . . .

I pointed. "Who's that? Your dad?"

Oliver smiled. His real smile, the one that had been hidden for weeks, the one I'd longed to see, the great big contagious smile that lit the world. "It's Mr. Peterson. It's okay that I drew him in with us, isn't it?"

I looked at Pete. His gaze met mine, and the intensity in his eyes went deep down inside me, down into a quiet space I'd never even known was there. Then I blinked, he turned away, and the connection was gone.

"Mom?" Oliver tugged at my elbow. "It's okay, right?"

"Of course it is," I said vaguely.

And wondered how I could have been so blind.

Also available from

Laura Alden
Plotting at the PTA

Beth Kennedy likes to multi-task—and that's a good
thing. As a PTA secretary, children's bookstore owner, and
single mom, Beth has to work hard to schedule time for
sleuthing. But when murder strikes close to home and one
of her regular customers dies from bee stings, Beth is
determined to get the buzz on who used bees to send the
victim to her eternal rest.

"Excellent." —Fresh Fiction

"Well-crafted." —*Publishers Weekly*

Available wherever books are sold or
at penguin.com

facebook.com/TheCrimeSceneBooks

OM0101